BUILDING RUIN

WRITTEN BY

MICHAEL LOEFFLER

COVER ART BY

J.T. LINDROOS

Part 1

Desperate Times &

Desperate Measures

1

Vance Fisher and Trevor Jones were about to embark on the biggest mistake of their lives, only they didn't realize it yet. And to think, it all started because of a chance comment made by an eavesdropping stranger. Maybe if they hadn't decided to leave the Twin Cities for the weekend to score some dope at the behest of Jacob Black, the chain of deaths that followed could have been easily avoided. But that's the crux of life. It's filled with a million questioning scenarios that hinge on seemingly innocuous little moments that have a terrible habit of blowing up like a badly timed hand grenade when you least expect it. Old Man Jones chalked it all down to Murphy's Law. As he was known to say after swimming down the wrong end of a few bottles: "Life is like one big obstacle course that constantly tries knocking you down and getting in your way. If things *can* go wrong, *they will*. Why else would I have lost half of my goddamn hand down at Burning Man? Murphy's Law... she's the real twat that keeps everything in check. She's like a raging goddamn river that separates you from the things you want. If you could just fight your way across her wicked currents, if you could just keep her tributaries from overflowing and washing you under, you could finally be happy. But of course you're always stuck on the wrong goddamn shore wanting what's on the other side."

Who knows? Maybe Old Man Jones was onto something, but whatever the reason, whether Murphy's Law or not, neither Vance nor Trevor could've predicted the web of chaos that would ensue due to their lust for money and drugs.

2

It was in a booth at the Ding Cafe that Vance Fisher would hear the ill-fated comment that would spin everything into motion.

He'd been driving steadily down highway 94 with Trevor nodding out in the passenger seat for nearly two hours and felt horribly cramped. The dull kernel of hunger he'd been feeling in the pit of his stomach had grown into a full fledged monster and his legs had turned to pins and needles. He could no longer avoid stopping, despite only being a handful of miles from Jacob's place. He pulled over at the chinese restaurant knowing that if they didn't stop to eat now, they likely wouldn't be eating again anytime soon over the next few days. After all, food is like kryptonite when on an epic weekend of binge tweaking.

They are sitting in the corner of a red vinyl booth, Vance finally regaining some of the feeling in his legs, when a skinny twink of a waiter checks in to see what they'd like. Vance orders some General Tso chicken with a side of fried rice and an eggroll. Trevor keeps staring at the menu like it's the cockpit control panel of the Millennium Falcon. The only thing missing was a line of spittle dangling from his lips to complete the picture of him being a complete and utter imbecile. He is clearly still lost in the tunnel vision daze of a mind that had been operating at warp speed for far too many days without reprieve, but what else was new? When he finally comes back from his mental hiatus he opts for an order of chicken lo mein. It doesn't take long for the food to arrive, and they quickly realize why Ding was an appropriate name for the cafe. The food tasted like leftovers that had been reheated and taken straight from a microwave.

"Christ, this is terrible," Vance complains after choking down his first mouthful. "I'd just as soon eat Ramen noodles from a hooker's bearded clam trench."

Trevor shakes his head in agreement. He is noncommittal as usual. His mother used to always say that if he was a country he'd be Switzerland, because he avoided conflict at all costs, and had the terrible habit of always going with the flow to not upset the boat.

"Hooker's bearded clam trench," he mumbles in agreement. "Definitely preferable."

"If Viet was still cooking in the back everything would be right as rain," a voice chimes in from the neighboring booth. Vance turns to find an old man with a receding hairline staring at him from above a battered copy of *The Crookston Herald*. "Viet was an expert with the wok. I'll promise you one thing, the egg fu yung never had the consistency of snot when he was on the clock. You'd best believe that."

"Why did he leave?" Trevor asks, not realizing the Pandora's box of consequences this seemingly harmless little question would bring.

"They had to let him go," the portly gentleman replies, itching at the collar of his maroon sweatshirt featuring Goldy the Gopher. "Just like everything else in this town, the owners were tight on funds and couldn't afford to offer him enough incentive to stick around. I swear, ever since they elected that orange baboon of an asshole to the Presidency. pardon my French, everything has gone to hell in a handbasket. Unions getting dismantled. Collective bargaining rights going right out the window. Reproductive rights taking the back seat. Hell, everybody's rights are getting infringed on, aside from the rich. Even our local police force has been cut down to half of what it was. But what did we expect? We knew healthcare was going to get decimated. We knew the only ones prospering would be the elite. We got what we asked for."

If there was one thing Vance detested above all others it was discussing politics with strangers, especially when the stranger in question was clearly a sympathizer with the crooked Muslim ape that was really responsible for everything terrible about the country, so he just politely nods his head and turns back to his shitty noodles.

He figures that his lack of interest is apparent, but, as was usual when dealing with the general dipshits of the population, this old fart can't take a hint. He just continues prattling on endlessly about the economy and perceived social injustices until Vance can't hold it in any longer.

"You just like to hear the sound of your own voice, don't you?" he asks, with a shit eating grin. "Ever since retirement you've had nothing to do with your time, and your wife has heard all of your same old boring ramblings a hundred times over, and your friends are either dead or have moved away, so you come here to find some sort of purpose. But I've got a newsflash for you, buddy. You're horribly uninteresting, and your opinions don't amount to the drops of sweat trickling down my balls. So could you please bugger off?"

The old man is finally, mercifully, at a loss for words. His mouth just momentarily opens in a dumbfounded O of shock, as he pauses like a deer in the headlights. Vance figures he might try fighting fire with fire by launching off into a tirade of his own, but the old man just sheepishly shrinks back into his booth, burying himself behind the latest copy of *The Crookston Herald*. Apparently he realized he would be outmatched and outwitted. Or, who knows, maybe he just feared the potential for destruction he saw behind Vance's unhinged grin and desperate eyes. Whatever the reason, he just hides behind the newspaper like it's a cloak of invisibility, and finally minds his goddamn business. **Another Child Goes Missing in Stearns County**, the main headline screams in stark bold font. **Authorities Fear it May Be Connected with the Work of The Chameleon.**

"What the fuck?" Trevor asks, shoveling down another mouthful of gruel. "Where did that come from?"

Vance just shrugs his shoulders and smirks. He doesn't need to explain his actions. He's a grown ass man. He just finishes his meal in awkward silence and walks back out to his car after scrawling a brief note to the twink waiter letting him know that more focus on the quality of food and less focus on flamboyant dialogue and mannerisms would be required if he intends on ever getting a real tip. Trevor joins him in the car a few minutes later, and they continue their awkward silence for the remainder of the trip to Jacob's.

It isn't until nearly an hour later, after he's just finished testing Jacob's purported superior goods, that Vance is struck with the inspiration that would doom them all.

3

Jacob Black has serious mental health issues. This much is certain. He also happens to be a great childhood friend of Trevor's. Vance can't trust the guy as far as he can throw him, but desperate times call for desperate measures, and now that their main source of meth had turned belly up, after being found shot dead in his Crown Vic on the corner of Gerard and Dupont amid allegations involving snitching to the police in precinct 4, he was unfortunately the only source Vance could turn to.

It was in juvenile hall during the summer of 96 that Trevor first met Jacob. They were roommates. Or, perhaps, cellmates would be a more accurate description of events. Trevor had been busted selling a bag of weed to a fellow classmate. Jacob had plead the fifth on why he'd been brought in, only deepening the mystery, so rumors had begun to fill in the dots and shade in all the possibilities. Diamond Pete said that he'd heard Jacob was in trouble for spray painting anti-semitic epitaphs on the town hall amphitheater. Johnny Cox claimed he'd been busted fooling around with underage pussy, and not just any dime a dozen underage pussy, but Doctor Wainwright's daughter, and Doctor Wainwright had a huge reach when it came to law because his sister was none other than Gwen Palomino, and Gwen's best friend was married to Sheriff Tarkenton. And then, of course, there were all the stories about animal cruelty. The rumors spread faster than wildfire, but whatever the reason for his stint, one thing was universally agreed upon: Jacob Black had serious mental health issues.

Where these mental health issues stemmed from was a source of much contention, because Jacob's childhood years, much as his reasons for entering juvenile hall, were likewise shrouded in much mystery. It was known that he'd been adopted by a kindly woman from the Dominican Republic in the late 80's, and Keliani was notoriously tight-lipped about her surrogate son. When he initially moved into the neighborhood and the local animals started disappearing, Keliani didn't think twice about the strange correlation. She just chalked it up to coincidence. I mean, sure, Jacob was awkward and painfully silent, but that was to be expected after being uprooted from his original family and shuffled around from foster home to foster home like some uselessly trapped pawn on a chessboard. Sure, once in awhile he was prone to emotional over exaggeration, but what self-respecting teenager didn't go through a phase of the theatrics? Surely he wouldn't hurt a fly.

Needless to say, Miss Black continued turning a deliberate blind eye to Jacob's misdeeds until they could no longer be avoided.

It was in the latter part of May in 1994, the month between Kurt Cobain's suicide and O.J. Simpson's ill-fated Bronco escapade with the L.A.P.D., when Principal Curtis Talbot visited Jacob in the lunchroom after hearing some disturbing allegations. It turns out a fellow classmate of Jacob's confided in her guidance counselor that she overheard Jacob telling a friend of his about experiments he'd been performing on animals in his shed back at home. Now, had it been any other girl beside Maddie Steinbergen, Principal Talbot might have just taken the news with a grain of salt, or fuck it, maybe even a bucket of salt, and moved on about his business. The kids at his school were notorious for their outlandish tales, but Maddie happened to be the daughter of Maxwell Steinbergen, the most prominent lawyer in all of Crookston, and let us also not forget he was one of the leading philanthropists of the school district. God forbid she ended up going home that night and discussing what she heard around the dinner table and he hadn't done something to act on the information. So, off he went to the cafeteria with his proverbial tail tucked firmly between his legs like a good little obedient dog.

Principal Talbot found Jacob sitting alone at a table beneath a Crookston Crows Rule the Roost mural. He was immersed in his Biology book. When Principal Talbot inquired about Maddie's accusations he expected staunch denial, but Jacob just smirked and turned back to his book with zero regard. Talbot was more than a little flustered. He reiterated the allegations, emphasizing the seriousness of the situation, noting to his extreme chagrin that he couldn't mask the annoyance in his tone. Normally he was cool and collected, but something about this boy's complete indifference to his position of authority got under his skin and rubbed him the wrong way. Unfortunately for Talbot, indifference would have been the best possible scenario, because there was something much deeper and darker and primal that was at play going on behind Jacob's piercing blue eyes, as was evidenced when he suddenly struck out with his fork as thoughtlessly and instinctively as a man attempting to rid himself of a pesky mosquito, and stabbed Talbot in the back of the hand. Talbot grimaced and pulled his hand away, leaving a web of sticky blood trailing across Jacob's tray.

The rest of the afternoon was a blur, from the pandemonium of the school liaison officer tackling Jacob to the ground and trying to subdue him after hearing Talbot's screams, to the manic ride in the ambulance. At about the same time as Talbot was getting his tetanus shots, Jacob was being escorted off the school grounds in the back of a police car, and subsequently his shed was searched. What the authorities ended up unearthing inside the shed was demented beyond even the outlandish rumors Maddie had hinted at. Jacob had transformed his shed into an experimental laboratory that would've made Hitler proud.

The responding officer that searched the shed, Jeremiah Pavlov, had heard the wild tales about the Nazis controversial human trials in a *Philosophy of Ethics* course at Saint Cloud State, but to witness such a similar level of human cruelty first hand was soul numbing.

The first animal Pavlov noticed was a chihuahua. It was cowering in the shadows beside a pug that had had its eyes removed. The chihuahua, likewise, was missing pieces of itself, as were all the other whimpering animals that had been locked away in the darkness. He found a Welsh terrier with shaggy hair the color of rust that had a long white tail that ended in the unmistakable cottony fluff of a poodle. The tail had been sloppily secured with a staple gun, and the skin around the stapled wound looked irritated and inflamed. The previous owner of the white tail was found a few minutes later hiding in the corner of the shed behind a faded red snow shovel. The poodle had had all of its needly little teeth removed. It was so gaunt and skeletal that every one of its ribs was protruding in a pitiful cage. The poodle's teeth were later found on a necklace that Jacob wore around his neck for good luck.

Pavlov later ascertained that the animals had been surviving on the carcasses of road kill Jacob had been collecting, as well as squirrels that he'd caught in little makeshift traps he'd learned how to make in a survival book he'd checked out from the Crookston Middle School library. The level of sadism exhibited in these attacks was something Officer Pavlov had never experienced before. And to think, these tortures had been conceived and perpetuated by somebody who was practically still a child. One could only imagine how twisted and sick the possibilities of such a mind, one that was already so clearly warped and damaged, could become with time. It was frightening.

That night, when Pavlov went home to his wife and she asked him how his day had gone, he couldn't bring himself to talk about it. He just stared through his wife like she wasn't there, and chewed on the hunk of steak in his mouth with growing repulsion at the saltiness of blood that stung at his gums. The unease stayed with him all night, and indeed would continue to haunt him until the next winter when he died of heart failure on a cold lonely dawn in February, leaving in his wake nothing for his newly pregnant wife but a mountain of debt. Some cruelties were too harsh to be erased with time...

By the time Trevor met Jacob in juvenile hall, a lot of the rumors surrounding him were murky at best. Trevor had heard the tales of animal cruelty, including about how, allegedly, the huge sandpit in Jacob's backyard was a haunted animal boneyard, but he refused to accept them as reality. He knew how the kids in town liked to talk shit, and even though he was only fifteen, he was already well aware of how shit had a habit of rolling downhill and snowballing with a life of its own, until it became something completely alien to the truth. Jacob was no demon, and his backyard wasn't the fucking Micmac burial grounds. Small town kids just clearly had too much time on their hands, and not nearly enough excitement, so they had to work with what they could create.

Jacob took Trevor under his wing while he did his brief stint in juvie. Because of Jacob vouching for him, Trevor's experience went extremely well. People didn't want to fuck with Jacob, because they weren't sure what he was capable of. Therefore, by default, people also didn't fuck with Trevor, even though he knew a few of the guys were itching to make his days a living hell. Trevor just kept his head down and waited as the clock methodically ticked along as slow as molasses.

On the eve of his release, Jacob exchanged numbers with Trevor and told him that he'd call him as soon as he was free, implying that they should hangout. Trevor agreed that they should hang out at the soonest available convenience, not really expecting to receive a phone call. He knew that, just like before summer began, kids made promises to hangout and keep in touch, but rarely did once their obligations of the school year were finished. This was just a variation on an obligation of a different sort.

Therefore, when the 4th of July weekend crept up, and Trevor came back home after a long day of hitting the trails with Vance on their dirt bikes, it came as a surprise when his mom told him he'd received a phone call from some strange kid who insisted on referring to himself as Diamond Pete. Trevor recognized the nickname, but was at a loss as to why Diamond Pete would be trying to get ahold of him. He'd barely said two words to the kid the entire time he was in juvie. All he knew about the douchebag was that he got his nickname for trying to hawk stolen jewelry which turned out to be cubic zirconia. So, in a way, his nickname was really misleading. Realistically, he should've been called Zirconia Pete.

When Trevor called the number back he recognized the laughter on the other end of the line instantly. It wasn't Diamond Pete, after all. It was just Jacob being a smartass, but what else was new? Trevor asked how it felt to have his newfound freedom, and Jacob said it was nothing short of amazing, but would be even better if they could meet up at Lake Winterfell on Friday night. Apparently there was a huge bonfire going down, and his friend Clint was going to be bringing a guitar and some beers. Who knew, there might even be some skinny dipping involved. Tammy Nicholson had shown up last weekend and walked around most of the night with her tits hanging out. She even let Travis and Randy run a train on her out in the Smoke Shack. If Trevor could hook them up with some good weed and not that gutter shit, there'd be no telling what this podunk slut might be good for. Everyone could probably take turns using her as the town pump. Would Trevor be willing to make an offering to the party gods for a night of mischief and merriment? Was he *willing*? Did the Incredible Hulk have a giant green cock when he turned angry? You bet your sweet ass he was interested.

5

The night of the party was unseasonably cool for July, but that didn't deter teenagers from flocking out in droves to drink and be merry. There had to be at least thirty kids milling about the bonfire, most of which Trevor didn't recognize. Just as Jacob promised, his friend Clint had brought his guitar and an arsenal of beer. Trevor, on the other hand, arrived with a baggie of his primo hydroponics. He also arrived with Vance in tow, and Vance in turn brought along a girl he was infatuated with named Sasha. As was to be expected of a teenage gathering in a small town where not much usually took place, the guestlist was multiplying at a rapid rate that Christ with his loaves of bread and fish would've had a hard time keeping up with.

Trevor walked down near the beach shore and sat in the shade of a giant maple tree as Clint casually started strumming the opening chords of *Mr. Self Destruct* from the bonfire. Dressed in ripped jeans and a white cowboy hat, with a wad of snuff tucked neatly inside his upper lip, he looked entirely too old to be hanging out with this crowd. But, hey, as long as he was old enough to purchase alcohol, there was little doubt that he'd be allowed, hell, even enthusiastically encouraged, to show up at whatever functions he so saw fit. As long as the booze kept flowing at his expense, there'd be no limit to his access of underage friends.

Vance wandered off with Sasha after taking a quick toke from Trevor's pipe. Trevor stayed back at the beach, marvelling at the beauty of the lake shimmering in the glow of dusk. Once the sun finally went fully down, he joined Clint at the bonfire. He attempted flirting with a girl in a black halter top and mini skirt. She had rad fishnets and neon pink hair that reminded Trevor of post-apocalyptic sunsets in the aftermath of atomic warfare. Unfortunately, his interest in her wasn't initially reciprocated. It wasn't until he broke out his pipe stacked with a mound of Grade-A crystallized weed that she sheepishly sauntered back over and attempted to gain his esteem. She even topped his weed off with a sprinkling of maroonish hash, which she lovingly referred to as space rocks, that made the fire appear brighter and more colorful and made the energy around the bonfire gain clarity and ripple with electricity.

Trevor was just starting to learn some titillating details about his beautiful new punk rock friend, (she'd recently gotten her nipples pierced and they were still sensitive. She was thinking about getting her clitoris pierced, but she had a friend who'd gotten it done and now suffered from nerve damage that made it harder for her to orgasm,) when the drama started. A guy that he'd previously seen swimming by the shore when they first arrived, no skinny dipping involved, came running out of the Smoke Shack, his trunks still sopping wet, raving about how a fist fight had just broken out between Jacob and some new guy he didn't know. All the teens that were within listening distance were drawn to the shack like moths to a flame. It didn't take a degree in logic to deduce who the new guy might be.

    The first thing Trevor noticed when sprinting through the entryway of the shack was the card table. It had been flipped helter skelter on its side, and poker chips were scattered everywhere. Then, sure enough, he saw Vance caught up in a chokehold, desperately attempting to elbow Jacob in the ribcage in an attempt to break free, but Jacob wasn't fazed in the slightest. The shack was clouded over with enough smoke to put a Native American tribal ceremony to shame, and Trevor felt like he was drifting through some strange sort of Leonard Cohen afterworld. He knew that Vance would never be able to break free on his own. Jacob was stacked like a brick house, and Vance was just a puny little twig. He didn't stand a snowball's chance in hell. Trevor knew he'd have to intercede. He yelled for Jacob to stop. Thankfully, mercifully, Jacob was kind enough to oblige. He released Vance, and, predictably, Vance spun around to start swinging on Jacob again, but Trevor was more than prepared for Vance's shenanigans, and jumped in between the both of them. He was able to drag Vance out of the shack with the help of a few other party goers, but for what Vance lacked in physical voracity he compensated for with a verbal tirade that would've made Richard Pryor blush. *Limp dick mother fucker,* he screamed, as they escorted him away from the newly deserted bonfire. *Think you can just make out with my girl right under my nose without any consequences? This isn't over yet, mother fucker! I'm gonna haunt you!* And, true to his word, Vance kept his grudge alive and well throughout the intervening years. Even after he was dragged along down south to live with his dad in the Twin Cities, the animosity hadn't cooled in the slightest. Trevor continued maintaining his friendship with Jacob and Vance, but he knew better than to expect much more than an icy reception when fate dictated that they were all forced to hang out together. Vance couldn't forgive Jacob for making moves on Sasha. She continued haunting him even after the incident at the shack. So, obviously, having to come to Jacob now after all these years grated on Vance's nerves greatly. He couldn't trust the weasel as far as he could throw him, but pride had its limitations, and there was nothing more powerful to bring about a reunion and mend damaged egos quite like the need for drugs. Vance was down and out, and he would've sucked off the pope if that's what it took to gain access to some quality dope.

6

When they arrive at Jacob's house, he is waiting for them in the driveway. A black cat is at his feet, lazily threading its way between his legs in a figure eight, its ears flattening in annoyance as they approach.

"What's up, man?" Jacob asks, leading them around to the back. He gestures absently to the cat trailing at his heels. "Don't mind Jasper. He has a bad habit of getting in the way. He's a lot like my old lady, come to think of it. Thankfully, she's out for the day. Harvey has a ballet lesson, which should buy us a couple hours."

They gain entry to the house through a sliding glass door that keeps jamming in its track and does a terrible job of living up to its name. "You're gonna love what I have in store for you today. There are few things you can count on in this world, but I can promise you that. This shit is gonna make your head spin like that chick from *The Exorcist*. So, without further adieu..." Jacob spreads his arms out before him as if presenting an elaborate buffet. He gestures for Vance and Trevor to sit down and scrambles around in a kitchen drawer until he finds what he's looking for. He joins them at the dining room table a moment later with his glass pipe and a baggie filled with glistening crystals. It only takes one deep drag for Vance to realize that Jacob isn't exaggerating the potency of his stash. He feels his bowels twist inside him like an agitated snake, and runs to the bathroom like his ass is on fire and the rest of him is catching. He is barely able to pull his pants down around his ankles and fall into position on the toilet seat before his body starts rejecting every bit of sustenance he'd devoured at the chinese restaurant in a clumpy tannish spray of barely digested waste that makes his stomach turn from the pungency.

"Fucking chinese food," he mumbles under his breath. His head suddenly feels lighter. The stress of the previous few days is no longer weighing down on him quite so drastically. He can hear Jacob and Trevor chattering away in the kitchen incessantly, but their voices feel like they are coming from a distance, crackling in and out of clarity as if through a loudspeaker with bad reception. He is still sitting in silence, enjoying the feeling of lightness and flight from his mind, when a cold reality pierces through his veil of contentment without any warning. These feelings only come to him when he blitzed out of his mind, and once he flutters back down from this perch, they will flee him as surely as night follows day. And he'd be down to scraping for nickels and dimes at the bottom of his pockets and only coming up with lint. And lint wouldn't bring this bliss back. He'd have to get caught up in risky business again, and he was tired of committing small scale crimes that carried big pen consequences. If they intended on maintaining their lifestyle, and if he wanted the bliss of these highs to continue, they needed to make a move that would set them up for a longer term vacation from reality. Because, whether he'd like to admit it or not, he'd rather be dead than live a life without dope. But what would be the best way to come into a large sum of money with minimal risk? It was then, as if by some strange sort of divine intervention, that Vance happens to notice what Jacob uses for reading material on the vanity to his left. It's a current issue of *The Crookston Herald*, and it only takes a brief glance at the dire headline- ***Another Child Goes Missing in Stearns County. Authorities Fear it May Be Connected with the Work of The Chameleon***- for Vance to make the mental connection back to that douche canoe at the Ding Cafe, and the comment he made about budget cuts resulting in a lack of police presence. Just like that, all of the pieces start falling into place, and by the time he leaves the bathroom, the seeds of his idea have already taken shadowy form.

7

Trevor is standing next to the table when Vance re-enters the dining room. A collection of discarded vinyl records is spread out before him and he holds a copy of *Dark Side of the Moon* in his hands. He places the album in a record player that sits atop an old Pioneer speaker, and lowers the arm from its perch. The comforting scratch of the needle fills the room, and like audio heroin, they are transported from the dusty confines of suburbia to a time and space that melts with depth and overdoses with meaning.

Vance glances at a clock hanging over the doorway in impatience. He is not in the mood to tune in and drop out. Now that inspiration has grabbed him by the balls, he is ready to set his plans into action. But, he'll be damned if he speaks so much as a word of his inspiration in front of Jacob. He'd rather cut off his nose to spite his face before he'd let that happen.

"Why are you being so quiet?" Trevor asks.

As if the answer wasn't fucking blatantly obvious.

"I'm just not in the mood for this theatrical space shit," Vance grumbles back.

"Do you mean the music or the dope?"

Vance glances back at the clock and then down at his jittering leg. His heart has started jack hammering and he can feel pins and needles collecting and gathering in his arms and chest. "I'm just frustrated," he replies. "I'm crawling out of my skin. I need to do something productive before I lose my mind."

Trevor laughs. "I'm pretty sure your mind took a one-way trip to a faraway land a long time ago. Last time you tried doing something productive on this shit you ended up taking Old Man Jones' transistor radio apart and couldn't put the pieces back together again, and anyway…"

"I'm serious," Vance gripes. "I'm not in the mood to just hang out and shoot the shit. Let's just pay what we need to pay and hit the road. We've got a long drive ahead of us and I could use a change of scenery." He makes a distinct point to stare at Jacob as he uttered this last statement.

"No problem," Trevor says. He wasn't in the mood for arguing. He knew how pissy

Vance could get after his high gained momentum. An argument with him when he was in this frame of mind wasn't worth pursuing. He reaches into his pocket and pays Jacob with a handful of faded twenties that had probably been in commission back when Eisenhower was still in office. God could only imagine the levels of fecal matter and cocaine dust that had accompanied it on its journey.

"Sorry my friend has to be such a pamp," he tells Jacob. "Guess we'll just have to continue our tribute to Syd Barrett some other time."

"It's all good," Jacob says as he leads them back to the car. "My record player shouldn't be growing feet and walking off anytime soon. Just hit me up whenever you're available. I'm always down for some company."

"Sounds good."

It wasn't until they were pulling back onto 94 that Vance reveals what was really eating at his thoughts. "Don't you ever get tired of struggling through every day just to scrape by?"

Trevor seems taken aback by the question. "Of course I do, but that's just how things go. Everybody treads water. It's the American way. Eat, pray, struggle, pay taxes, die, and if there's reincarnation; rinse and repeat."

"Oh, there better not be fuckin reincarnation, One life is more than enough," Vance signals and shifts over into the fast lane. "You know we're running out of money again, right?"

Trevor chuckles. "What else is new? We didn't get shit from that 7-11 we hit up."

"That's why we need to think big," Vance says. "We need to take our game to a higher level and land a score that will set us up for the future. I'm tired of all the risks we keep taking by committing all these small time crimes." Vance pauses, glancing at the rear view mirror as if in paranoia before continuing: "I was thinking about what that fucktard at the Ding Cafe was saying earlier today about Crookston's police force."

Trevor raises his eyebrows in perplexity. "What are you suggesting?"

"Crookston is a sitting duck trapped in a barrel. They have no lines of defense. We could just swipe in like a wolf in the night and take our next heist to a higher level and not have to worry about shit."

"How much of a higher level are you thinking? Like a pharmacy or somethin?"

Vance pauses, continuing to stare at the threat in the rearview, which, as far as Trevor can tell, is still nonexistent. "I was thinking more along the lines of First National."

Trevor is floored. *"You wanna rob a fucking bank!?"*

Vance is unperturbed. "I mean, yeah, sure, why not? If we could cause a diversion I don't see any reason why we shouldn't be able to score big without the risk. The cops are spread out thin. All we need to do is cause a huge distraction on the opposite end of town, and it would be a cakewalk."

"What kind of distraction? Fake a domestic assault? How is that gonna help?"

Vance is exasperated. "Haven't you been listening to a goddamn thing I've been saying? We've got to think bigger. We need to cause a diversion that is so fucking big it can't be ignored. Something that will make the whole fucking town shake. And you and I both know the perfect guy to help us out in that department."

Trevor nervously starts fiddling with his hands in his lap. "Are you fucking kidding me? We're not getting my dad involved in this. Besides, he's on house arrest. If he steps so much as a foot off his property his ankle bracelet will scream holy hell. How's he gonna help us when he's quarantined in North Minneapolis?"

Vance isn't deterred. "We don't need him to be at the heist in order to help our plan. We just need him in spirit. Maybe he could give us some good pointers that will set us in the right direction. We could just pick his brain a bit. No harm done. I'm sure he'd be more than happy to help us out. After all, he hates the establishment more than you and I combined. He's always talking about how it's a broken world filled with broken people. Why do you think he likes fire and explosions so much? He wants to watch everything burn. I mean, can you really blame him?"

The look of concern in Trevor's eyes makes it brutally clear that he still has some reservations. "How are we ever going to be able to pull all this off with only the two of us? It seems like too much to handle on our own. I mean, first we'd have to stake out the place and figure out a good time to make the score. One of us would have to get the money from the teller while the other kept a lookout to make sure nobody gets any bright ideas and tries to play hero. What if danger approaches from the outside? What if somebody from the community recognizes us?"

"Well, we'd obviously have to go in disguises of some sort. I mean, I may have been born at night, but it wasn't last night. What kind of numb nuts do you take me for? There's no reason to worry about not being able to pull this off on our own. We're resourceful. And just think. We'd set ourselves up for the long haul. We could leave this shitty state if we want and go somewhere that isn't complete misery in the winter. We could check out Colorado like you've always wanted and smoke some of that good medicinal herb. We could hit up the Florida Keys or fly out to San Fran and get a free tour of Alcatraz."

Trevor glances at Vance like an entomologist trying to make sense of some new form of unidentifiable specimen. "It seems to me that this plan of yours might end up getting us a lot more than a free tour of Alcatraz. If we don't play our cards right, we might just end up finding permanent residence."

"C'mon, man," Vance implores. "You know this is a good idea. Old Man Jones would be the first to tell us how reasonable casing First National is. We wouldn't have to worry about getting a score for a long time to come. We could be living on easy street for a change."

Trevor feigns reluctance, as is his customary habit. He sits with his head in his palms in the passenger seat, appearing to give the proposition grave deliberation. As is expected, he ends up relenting, but only after hesitating long enough to convince himself that it's on his own terms.

Now that he is officially onboard, Vance realizes it's time for the real work to kick into high gear. The devil is in the details, as the saying goes.

8

Vance starts plotting these said details of their new endeavor in the back of a battered diary that had belonged to his mother once upon a time, but was now so dog-eared and faded that it resembled a relic taken straight from the Smithsonian. It doesn't take long for the pages to start accumulating as their objectives gain clarity. In fact, the scheme begins unravelling at such a rapid pace that he almost feels like an ancient soothsayer dictating preordained messages plucked down from the stars.

The first detail he'd written down in his frantic chicken scrawl was the location of the heist- First National Bank in Crookston.

The location was appealing for a multitude of reasons. First, it wasn't near their primary stomping grounds where people were prone to be familiar with their antics. It was a good hundred miles northwest of the Twin Cities near a small woodsy town they'd lived in back when they were knee-high to grasshoppers. Although they'd moved away back in high school, they still visited sporadically, particularly on years when the hunting opener weekend had weather that was conducive with scavenging, and the environment was as intimate and familiar to them as the curves of a lover's body.

Crookston also made sense because it was relatively obscure and forgettable. It was the sort of town that you only passed through because it happened to have the bad geographical luck of being along your path as you continued through to somewhere more desirable. Most of the people who lived in town had complacently stuck around since their days of learning to stack blocks and sucking on mom's teat, and were perfectly satisfied with spending their endless nights rambunctiously wasting away at the same dive corner bars with the same regulars drunkenly slurring their way through the same drunken karaoke songs ad infinitum. The youth that harbored any ambition, or happened to be blessed with the increasingly rare ability of having any common good sense, tended to move elsewhere shortly after reaching puberty. Even the town's claim to fame, poet and artist Sheldon Lawson, hadn't bothered sticking around past his eighteenth birthday. By the time he'd won his Pulitzer for *Cruel Contradictions* he'd already holed himself away in a cabin in Lake Tahoe at the ripe old age of twenty seven without so much as a wasted glance in the rearview.

Another reason why Crookston was appealing had to do with its isolation. A swath of forest encircled it from all borders aside from its northern boundary, which was primarily a rock quarry that was now defunct, and former marshland that had been rezoned for development. Long story short, not only was it a safe navigational hike from their old stomping grounds, but it was also a community swallowed in wilderness with an immense cop shortage. Almost all of the loose threads that could tear this heist apart were nearly accounted for. *Nearly* and *almost* being the operative words. But it never hurt to have an insurance policy in place, and what better way to prepare for the unknown than to burn away the uncertainties with righteous flame?

9

Old Man Jones lives in North Minneapolis across the street from the Crystal Lake Cemetery on Dowling, and to say his reputation precedes him would be an understatement to say the least. He was notorious in his corner of the world, and rumors had a bad habit of following him wherever he went. Like last summer, when the liquor store off Penn burnt to the ground. The smoke hadn't even dissipated from the source of the crime before the police had shown up and started sniffing around his place. They claimed that one of the neighbors had reported seeing a man fleeing the scene wearing a Matrix-style Columbine jacket, and boy if it wasn't coincidental that that happened to match the same description as the trenchcoat Old Man Jones happened to wear around town. Thankfully, he had an airtight alibi at his disposal. He'd been verified by multiple sources as spending most of the night off West Broadway, bickering with his on-again off-again side action Latitia down at Fire 'N' Ice: Home of the Famous Philly Cheesesteak and Ice Cold Lemonade.

In the police department's defense, however, Old Man Jones had a litany of prior offenses, most of which involved arson in some way shape or form, so their suspicions weren't completely uncalled for.

It was due to this infamous pastime of his that Sunday morning found Trevor and Vance arriving at his doorstep with a laundry list of questions. Vance had brought his journal along, and like any decent reporter worth his weight in gold, he left no stones unturned in his line of inquiry.

"I know you told me this before, but how did you lose your fingers again?" Vance asks. "My brain doesn't work for shit anymore, though I guess I've got nobody to blame for that but myself."

They are hanging out in the kitchen. Trevor and Vance have just finished smoking some dope. Old Man Jones has politely declined his offer at the pipe. Random drug testing doesn't allow for him to have too much of a good time. Instead, he has to settle for his alternate drug of choice: pizza. And if his belly is any indication, it has cast just as powerful a spell over him as dope, although now his body mass is swinging on the opposite end of the spectrum than it's used to. Moderation has never been much of a friend regardless the source of inspiration.

"Life is like one big obstacle course constantly trying to knock you down," he begins, a string of cheese dangling from his mouth as he finishes tearing through a slice of pizza with ravenousness that borders on lust. "That's why I lost so many goddamn fingers down at Burning Man. Because of Murphy's Law."

"Oh, here we go again," Trevor laughs. "If you've told it once, you've told it a million times. Another famous sermon about Murphy's Law and how the whole world is stacked against you."

Old Man Jones is as indignant as ever. He wipes his face clean with a napkin and shakes his head in annoyance. "You can make fun of my views all you want, but that doesn't make them any less true. Every time I start to make a break, shit blows up in my face!"

Trevor smirks. "That's an appropriate metaphor, although I'd say most of the time you bring the chaos on yourself. There's no luck in this world. Play stupid games and get stupid prizes. Nothing more, nothing less."

Old Man Jones narrows his eyes like a bird of prey going in for the kill. "Oh, that's rich coming from you. Seems to me my stupid games are the reason you came by. Seems to me the only reason we're talking right now is so you can avoid your stupid prizes. Do you want my fucking advice or not?"

Trevor relents. "Oh, come on pops. You know I'm just fucking with you."

Old Man Jones relaxes. Despite his annoyance, he is a creature of habit, after all, and if there is one thing he loves more than fire in this world it's an endless stream of idle chit chat, and once he gets started up, getting him to slow down again or relent is an act in futility. "So you're dead set on following your old man's instincts, eh? No bull shitting?"

Vance takes a drag from his crack pipe, nodding his head emphatically. "We're serious as a heart attack. Crookston isn't gonna know what hit em. We're gonna tear through that town like a goddamn tornado."

Old Man Jones shrugs noncommittally. He throws his arms out from his side like a conductor about to orchestrate a grand symphony. "Well," he says. "In that case, the *Big Book of Mischief* is always a great starting point for having a little fun. It's the holy grail of arson, and all you need to know about the art of the big bang."

"I'm not looking for anything way too complicated," Vance clarifies. "We just need something quick and simple that will catch the town by surprise."

"Well, if you're looking for a simple way to fuck things up, you can't go wrong with loading up on hydrogen peroxide. That's as simple as it gets. But you have to be careful. Most hydrogen peroxide is diluted to only three percent in most products. Hair bleach from the salon has thirty percent. Much more bang for your buck, no pun intended." Old Man Jones grabs his formidable gut and his cackle explodes through the silence like a verbal hand grenade. "You can also start a good fire with acetone, but this time you're gonna want to avoid the salon altogether and avoid items like nail polish remover because it isn't very strong. Just go down to the local hardware store and buy acetone by the tin can. The golden rule is to always avoid dilution. Pro Liquid Drain Opener is a powerful example for fucking shit up. It's loaded with a purity rate of over ninety percent sulfuric acid."

"Now we're talking," Vance chimes in. "But I'm worried about leaving a paper trail. To start a huge fire we're going to need an incredible amount of chemicals. It's gonna raise a lot of red flags driving all over town getting this shit. All the authorities would have to do is canvas the area about suspicious purchases and run surveillance camera footage, and the pigs would be on our trail in no time. I was hoping more along the lines of seeing if you'd be able to give us some pointers on how to get our hands on some chemicals in bulk. Trevor mentioned that you used to work at Paradise Pool Supply. Surely you weren't there for the pay or benefits."

Old Man Jones pauses to process the sudden directional shift in conversation. "Ummm… This probably isn't the right time for me to be supplying you with information about my former employer, what with being on house arrest and all, but, after what that bastard did to me, he can go fuck himself."

Trevor instantly starts shaking his head no at Vance. He doesn't want to get Old Man Jones all worked up, but Vance can't resist. He has to go for the bait. "What happened to get you kicked out of Paradise?"

"You mean, how did I end up *Paradise Lost*?" Old Man Jones laughs once again. His parade of bad dad jokes knew no bounds. "It's simple really. Tom Dillinger is a twat. That's why. That, and Murphy's Law, of course! I was busy closing shop one night, because Darren called in and Dillinger wouldn't let me off. I was just minding my own goddamn business when Latitia stopped by. She was annoyed because I told her I'd pick her up from the Havenshire, but wasn't able to. I tried leaving a message for her at the wet house with Marissa. But Marissa must have been overwhelmed or something from all her volunteer hours at the soup kitchen and needle exchange, because do you think the message ever ended up reaching Latitia? Of course not! She ended up having to scrounge together enough loose change to take the Metro out to meet me, and boy was she something else. She came clamoring in through the door of Paradise and starts bickering with me about Jared. She swears she checked in a bottle of Karkov at the Havenshire yesterday, and when she came back to retrieve it, Jared claimed it wasn't there. He said he'd already given it to her the night before and she must've forgotten!"

Vance interjects. "What do you mean she checked in a bottle of Karkov at the Havenshire?"

Trevor takes a drag from the glass pipe and exhales a trio of smoke rings. "The Havenshire is a wet house," he explains. "It takes in people that treatment doesn't work for and provides them with a place to stay so they don't have to die out in the streets. Those mother fuckers at Alcoholics Anonymous can't stand it. They think the Havenshire is just giving up on people too easily, that it's never too late for a person to turn around in treatment, but the Havenshire pretty much considers some people beyond hope, and if you need a place to check out, they provide you with a room so you can at least opt out on your own terms with some human dignity. It's not like a halfway house at all. They let you drink whenever you feel the urge, and you can come and go as you please. They only have one rule, and it's pretty straight forward. You just have to check your liquor in with the staff at the front desk so they can keep tabs on how much everyone is consuming. They'd rather not have people dropping dead like flies from alcohol poisoning if it can be at all avoided."

"They prefer their death in moderation," Old Man Jones agrees. "It's a lot easier to digest in small doses."

"So what does Latitia have to do with Paradise letting you go?" Vance asks, trying to reign his scatterbrained style of storytelling back to the topic on hand.

"Welllllll…" Old Man Jones begins, lingering his L to give him time to get his thoughts in order. "If it weren't for that cocksucker Dillinger making me stay late I would've never had a problem meeting up with Latitia on time in the first place. If I would've never had a problem picking Latitia up on time, she would've never came swaggering in through the doors of Paradise all in a tizzy. If she would've never came swaggering in through the doors all in a tizzy, I would've never felt the need to placate her by playing her favorite Stone's song *Brown Sugar* on the boombox and sharing a joint. If I would've…"

Trevor jumps in, his patience for meandering thoughts having melted away like ice cream on a hot summer day: "Dillinger was driving back to Paradise because he misplaced his debit card and he heard the loud music blasting inside. He walked into the horrific sight of Latitia giving my dad dome, and his vision has never been the same since. Some attribute his eventual vision loss to staring into the eclipse earlier that summer, but those who are in the loop know what really brought the damage on."

Old Man Jones throws his hands out from his side in a dramatic show of exasperation. "We were making up," he says, by sheepish way of dismissal. "Would you have turned down the opportunity had you been in my shoes? Of course not. Only a dirty commie-loving Puritan would've denied a peace offering of sex, drugs, and rock 'n roll."

"Apparently Dillenger must have been a commie," Trevor interjects. "Because he canned him on the spot."

"The insensitive fucker wouldn't even let her finish slobbing my knob," Old Man Jones laments. "He forced me out of the store still naked from the waist down and told me if I ever came back he'd be pressing charges. Can you believe the nerve of the prick? Just because he wasn't getting any at home didn't mean he had to take it out on me."

Vance laughs in agreeance. "I hear ya, man. That's some hard knocks alright."

"So fuck him!" Old Man Jones chimes in.

"Fuck him!" Trevor and Vance echo in unison.

"I'll drink to that," Old Man Jones says, grabbing a Leinenkugel from the fridge. "Do either of you boys care for a cold one?"

"Don't mind if I do," Vance replies.

"Pops, you know you're not supposed to be drinking," Trevor complains. "They could test you anytime."

"Oh, hogwash," Old Man Jones chuckles. "They just tested me yesterday. They also tested me on Thursday. I should be good to go for awhile. Besides, this isn't like heavy drugs. It'll be out of my system come morning. Quit getting your panties all in a bunch."

"Whatever," Trevor mumbles. "It's your life."

"So it is," Old Man Jones agrees.

Vance twists open his bottle of beer and takes a swig. He has no interest in getting involved in their little spat. "Help us get back at Paradise," he says. "We'll be forever in your debt and pay you back tenfold, I swear. Just give us some advice"

Old Man Jones glances from Vance to Trevor, and then back to Vance again. A part of him wants to escalate into an argument with his know-it-all son, but if there was one thing he loved on the same level as idle chit chat it was servitude and favors owed.

Old Man Jones sits down at his dining room table. As he leans forward and tilts back his bottle of Leinenkugel, the chair he sits in wheezes in protest. "If it's an explosion you're looking for, I think I've got just the trick. Have you ever heard of pool shock?" He pauses to belch loudly, then proceeds explaining without waiting for a response. "Well, basically pool shock is chlorine. There are two types of chlorine that are used for shocking a pool: organic chlorinating agents and inorganic. Calcium hypochlorite is a very strong oxidizer that is inorganic in nature. When you mix it with the chlorine tablets that have trichlor a strong chemical reaction occurs. But it only occurs if the chemicals are introduced to a liquid. They need to dissolve and merge to ignite. If you want to see the most chaotic unstable explosion you could dream of, mix the chlorinating agents with brake fluid. It will rock your fucking world!"

Trevor glances up from the notebook he'd been scribbling furiously in, his pen hovering between muriatic and acid. He gazes blankly into the distance, clearly overloaded and perplexed by the tsunami of technical names Old Man Jones is tossing out with the casual disregard of Rain Man reciting algorithms. Two words are underlined at the bottom of the page for emphasis: <u>Brake Fluid</u>. Beside them he's scrawled the name Jacob with a looping question mark after it. An idea is forming.

10

Vance Fisher is livid. "I can't believe you included that jackass in our plans without asking me first.

Trevor sits in unrepentant silence. As someone who is used to playing second fiddle when dealing with Vance due to his natural predisposition of passivity, having to defend himself is out of his comfort zone. But in this situation he absolutely has to put his foot down and stand firm. Vance is simply too stubborn and obstinate for his own good to realize what a perfect match Jacob will be for ensuring everything goes off without a hitch.

"I tried telling you we can't pull this heist off on our own, Trevor begins. "But you wouldn't listen. It's too risky having you go into the bank all alone. If somebody tries to go all Batman on your ass with vigilante justice, what good will I be if I'm just sitting out in the getaway car with my thumb up my rear end? You need me to go in with you to keep tabs on what's happening."

Vance brushes his hand back through his close-cropped blonde hair as he contemplates. "Maybe you're right about us needing help," he finally relents. "But *Jacob*, of all people? You know how much I can't stand that guy. He's shady as a mother fucker."

"You've gotta let what happened with Sasha go, man," Trevor says. "That's water waaay under the bridge."

Vance is annoyed. "It's not just about Sasha. It's a lot more than that. You would know this if your head wasn't so far up Jacob's ass you could give him a proctology exam with your tongue. He can't be trusted. He's a fucking psycho! You've heard the weird rumors about what he does with animals and how unstable he can be!"

"And if I could get a dollar for everytime I heard a rumor that has no basis with reality I could buy an island in the Fiji's and wake up to Pamela Anderson motorboating me every morning before breakfast," Trevor quips. "Besides, that was a lifetime ago. People change. When you were in the bathroom having a butt miscarriage before we started playing *Dark Side of the Moon*, I had a conversation with him that would make your head spin. He's been going through a rough patch no different than us. Ever since his mom passed away he's been struggling to make ends meet. He's trying to take care of Tori and Harvey, but working in a toll booth and at Valvoline isn't paying nearly enough for him to keep up on his mortgage, and his place is sliding into foreclosure. He needs this money more than both of us combined. We can trust him. Believe me. I wouldn't vouch for him if I thought he'd jeopardize our plans in any way. He's been through the prison system already, and I can guarantee you, after the sentence he finished serving, he has no intentions of ever going back."

"Well, he better not complicate things," Vance grumbles.

"Not only will he not complicate things, but I can promise you one better. He will help make sure that things go much smoother," Trevor reassures. "Right when my old man mentioned brake fluid as a possible catalyst, I knew it was meant to be. He told me he can hook us up with enough brake fluid to make an explosion large enough to blind the eyes of God."

"That's a pretty lofty statement," Vance says.

"Well, the point I'm trying to make is that he'll deliver. He's a manager at Valvoline. He can get us an endless supply of brake fluid. So we can quit fixating on him, and instead focus on something more productive like the diversion itself. I've been putting a lot of thought into where we should set it off, and I think it would make sense for the location to be a bit off the beaten path."

"How about Lucky Strikes?" Vance asks. "Ever since they finished construction on that new bypass almost nobody heads out that way."

"You're in the right constellation of where I was thinking, but you've chosen the wrong star," Trevor says. "Remember where Betty got busted for shoplifting? Her dad was bragging about it all over town, saying that while you could say what you want about the arrest, it was at least proof that he must've done something right with the way he raised her."

"Hmmm…" Vance stares blankly through the window. "Are you talking about that book store up off Avon?"

"Bingo. That's the one. It's called The Hungry Mind. It also went under when the city approved the bypass that connects with Main."

The skepticism on Vance's face has melted away and been replaced with reluctant optimism. He is looking at Trevor with an expression bordering on awe.

"Goddamn," he says. "Who *are* you? Has there been an invasion of the body snatchers and I'm the last to know? You really have thought this through, and damned if I'm not impressed. The Hungry Mind actually makes perfect sense. But don't think you're completely off the hook for bringing Jacob into this. You're still on my shit list for that."

Trevor shrugs, but the glow of approval in his eyes and the slight upturn of his lips betrays his ambivalence. It has been a long time since he's heard any sort of positive affirmation from Vance for his actions, and even longer since he's taken the reigns and led with initiative. Although he'd be loathe to admit it, even if held at gunpoint, he is tickled pink.

"If you think the location I came up with was impressive, just wait until you hear the idea Jacob has," Trevor says. "It's genius."

As much as Vance hates Jacob, he can't resist the bait. "What did he come up with?"

"Well, we know *how* we're going to cause the diversion. Old Man Jones and Paradise Pool Supply are gonna help us in spades in that department. We know *where* we're going to do the heist and what positions we need to take up, but we still haven't settled on *when*."

"So, when does your Almighty Jacob think would be best to hit up First National, and why should I give a rat's ass anyway?"

Trevor repeats everything Jacob had suggested to Vance, and Vance is at a total loss of words, which is rare.

"Pretty good idea, huh?" Trevor asks, and even though Vance has known logically that all this talk wasn't just pie in the sky philosophizing or idle chit chat meant to waste time, the reality of the moment brings Vance to his knees.

"My God," he says. "We're really going to do it. We're really going to pull this fucker off…"

"That we are," Trevor agrees. And then, as if to emphasize the moment, he repeats: "That we fucking are…"

11

The next few weeks sped past in a drug-fueled blur. As the warmth of summer faded away and the chill of fall continued its invasion, Vance and Trevor finalized their plans with the help of Jacob. They hit up Paradise Pool Supply with ease. Old Man Jones was correct in his assumption that Frank was too lazy to bother changing the access code, so gaining entry is a cakewalk.

It's shortly after three in the morning when they enter the pool supply store. Clad in black masks they easily blend in with the darkness that surrounds them. It only takes fifteen minutes to load up the back of Jacob's truck with all the chlorinating agents. If a silent alarm was triggered they are none the wiser. They lock the door behind them on their way out and then circle around to the front of the store to shatter the windows. Obviously they don't want anyone on the outside to know how they really gained access.

The next day, after the grand pillage of Paradise, they visit a manufacturing plant on the outskirts of Melrose. A group of Mexicans are out smoking in the back parking lot and enjoying their lunch break when they arrive.

"Jesus," Vance mutters. "What is it about polka music that gives beaners such a boner?"

"The hell if I know," Jacob replies. "But the accordion must have something to do with it."

"Yeah," Trevor agrees. "It must be like an aphrodisiac or something. Who needs oysters or Viagra when you have shitty beaner music?"

Vance walks up to a Mexican who is using a pile of skids to rest on. "Hey, essay," he says. "Do you mind if we grab some of these pallets? We have a rager of a party coming up this weekend, and we need some wood for a bonfire."

The Mexican looks at Vance with his eyebrows knit together in confusion. "Lo siento," he says, in a well rehearsed drone.. "No hablar Ingles."

Vance points at the stack of pallets the man in the orange windbreaker is lounging on. "Can I have these skids, por favor?"

The man climbs off the pile of skids, pointing back at them. He smiles, revealing a set of teeth that haven't been acquainted with a toothbrush in quite some time.

"Skeds?" he repeats. "Skeds, for you?"

"Si," Vance nods emphatically. "El woodo, Senor. El woodo for our bonfire-ito."

"You get wood?" the man questions.

"Si," Vance agrees. "I get wood every morning when I think of your hermana."

Jacob walks over to the pile of skids. As he bends down to gather them, his shirt hitches up. Trevor grabs a quarter out of his pocket and takes the opportunity to use Jacob's ass crack as a coin slot. Jacob jumps to his feet like a man stung by a bee.

"Knock it off, prick," he says indignantly. "We don't have time for these childish games. I've gotta be back home by three. I told Harvey I'd take her to the corn maze today, because I cut out last week, and if I don't follow through this time Tori is gonna shit a brick."

Trevor chuckles. "That woman has got you pussy whipped. I'm glad I don't have to deal with all that domesticated bullshit. It would drive me…"

The look Jacob shoots Trevor stops him in mid-sentence. Of course, like everybody else in town, he's well versed in all the rumors that have hovered around Jacob like flies drawn to shit, but his rational mind has never been willing to accept them as fact. Sure, Jacob could be hard headed and was prone to the occasional emotional outburst, but that wasn't proof of animal torture. And that rumor about what happened to shoplifter Betty in the backseat of her Mercedes Benz was clearly hogwash. Betty had been ridden by more men than a mechanical bull. That wasn't fabrication. Why else would her nickname around town be Sweaty Betty Mattress Back? But, the look of sudden gravity in Jacob's eyes, eerie as a sky gone green without warning, hinting of devastation lurking just below the surface just waiting to slash out, makes him have to pause and reevaluate everything he'd previously accepted as fact.

"Sorry, man," he says, glancing away. He can't bear to look into the eclipse that has suddenly surfaced.

"Let's just get what we came for and move on," Jacob says, suddenly returning to normal, as if at the flip of a switch..

Vance and Trevor follow his advice. They load up the back of Jacob's truck with all the available pallets and bid adieu to the group of Mexicans as they finish up their cigarette break.

They arrive at The Hungry Mind half an hour later. The place is a complete ghost town. Jacob parks near the rock quarry. It's surrounded by a chain link fence that's covered with signs warning to keep out.

The Hungry Mind looks a lot different than Vance remembered. It's old and dilapidated and covered in unremarkable wooden planks that were weather faded and loose. If you didn't know any better you would think you were entering a saloon from Deadwood, and if the building hadn't been closed from lack of sales after the re-routing of the bypass, it undoubtedly would've been shuttered regardless for being a safety hazard.

A side window that leads into an office off the back has been shattered, and broken shards of glass glisten on the pavement like jagged tears. They do a thorough search of the building to see if anyone is still squatting within. They come across a couple red sleeping bags and a ration of old Chef Boyardee cans hidden in the shadowy confines near the rear of the bookstore, but otherwise, there no signs of life. Whoever once squatted here is long gone, and the empty aisles are downright eerie. Although nobody says it aloud, a sense of uneasiness lingers with everyone. After discovering the building vacant, they retrace their steps to the back office and are about to climb through the broken window when Vance pulls out his glass pipe and suggests they smoke a quick bowl before they get started. Of course, smoking a quick bowl ends up becoming an act in futility, as is usually the case when dealing with a fiend. Throwing three fiends into the mix, needless to say, only complicates the situation. They are well into their fourth bowl when a blaring alarm pierces the silence.

"Holy shit!" Jacob gasps, nearly tipping over the chair he'd been reclining in. A few seconds later the blare of the alarm is followed by an angry hiss as a sprinkler system they hadn't even noticed wildly sprays water down all around them like rice being thrown by an overeager crowd in the aftermath of a wedding.

Trevor opens the door of the office and glances in the bookstore. The sprinklers are going off in there as well. He starts giggling like a madman.

"We better get the hell out of Dodge," he says.

They vault through the broken window and sprint to Jacob's truck like Olympians. They peel out of the parking lot, a few skids tumbling from the truck bed as they whip out from the gravel drive. Taking a road that runs parallel with the rock quarry, they end up parking on the shoulder amid the wild brush.

A fire truck comes careening past them a couple minutes later. Due to the open terrain they can hear the firemen and firewomen surprisingly well as they finish checking out the bookstore.

"Just those kids messing around again," one fireman says to another. "That's all they ever do. Just sleep all day and beg for handouts all night."

A fire woman interjects. "You can't really blame them for the way they act. It's not their fault they were discarded. If their parents had a little more tolerance and were a little less dogmatic, they wouldn't be in such a bind. I'll never understand how some people can bring a life into this world only to turn their back when shit gets real."

The idle chit chat between the firefighters is muted as they climb back into the firetruck.

"Just another false alarm," Vance says. "I guess we better keep our smoke sessions confined to the outdoors. The sensors are way too sensitive."

"Tell us something we don't know," Trevor chimes in.

It only takes ten minutes for them to unload the back of Jacob's truck, once their progress is no longer impeded by the stagnation that goes along with getting baked. They make a few more trips as the afternoon bleeds into nightfall, until Vance is satisfied that they are thoroughly equipped with enough kindling for the diversion.

During their final trip of the evening Jacob mentions that he's going to stop by Valvoline and load up on all the brake fluid that the store has to offer.

"We've only got a week left until the heist," he says. "It's best to get this out of the way right now."

"No better time than the present," Trevor agrees.

"Actually, more like, no other time *but* the present," Jacob quips. "But I catch your drift."

He gathers all the brake fluid and brings it back to The Hungry Mind shortly after midnight. He's about to enter the building through the broken side window when a shadow from inside the office comes to life and he hears a voice: "Who the fuck are you?"

Jacob is dumbfounded. Then he remembers the red sleeping bags and the empty cans of Chef Boyardee, and his unease lessens.

Jacob doesn't reply, and the voice rings out once again: "Are you the guy that filled this place up with pallets and made it look like shit? You barely left us with anywhere to crash."

A young male steps out from the shadows. He is joined by a girl that is roughly his age. They are dirty and dressed in clothing that clearly came from a Goodwill.

"I'm with Mill Tech Security," he quickly improvs. "I'm here because of all the recent activity the neighbors have been complaining about."

The girl looks at Jacob with her eyebrows scrunched together. It's obvious that she's dubious. "Security?" she says. "You don't look like security."

"And what neighbors are you talking about?" the boy chimes in. "This area is a dead zone. Nobody lives out here."

Luckily for Jacob, his memory is sharper than he gave himself credit for, as a memory from his past resurfaces without any indication like a reanimated corpse from a George Romero zombie flick. "Are you trying to tell me that the Millers don't still live up around the bend? Because that would be a blatant lie, and you and I both know better."

The look of doubt on the girl's face changes to one of concern. "Where are we going to stay?"

Jacob pauses as he considers her question. "I'm sure your boyfriend can come up with somewhere for you to stay awhile."

The girl scowls. "Jonathan isn't my boyfriend. As much as I love him, we're not compatible with each other. That's kinda the crux of our dilemma."

Exactly," Jonathan agrees. "Marianne was kicked out of her house for the same reason I was. We can't go back."

Jacob shrugs. "That's not my problem. There are plenty of other places in this podunk town you can squat at. Check out Lucky Strikes or hitch a ride down to the Twin Cities. Do whatever it takes, just as long as I don't see you here again. Because if I do, there will be serious consequences. Just grab your shit and move on."

He expects the teens to argue back, but they just go into the bookstore and gather their possessions without debate. Being uprooted and displaced without notice was clearly the rule and not the exception for their lives on the run. But everyone had a sob story to tell, and he didn't feel any guilt for making them leave. He had Tori and Harvey to think of. If he didn't pull this off they'd be in the exact same predicament as these wayward teens, and would anybody take any mercy on them? Un-fucking-likely. So fuck guilt.

Jacob goes back to his truck and finishes unloading the brake fluid, this time, thankfully, without further interruption. As he walks through the office after finishing the final load and sinks back in the office chair to take a breather sleep is the furthest thought from his mind, but, as unexpectedly as the water that soaked him earlier when their weed smoke triggered the sprinklers, it rains down upon him anyway and washes him away from The Hungry Mind and his duel burdens of money and dope...

12

Jacob is sprawled out on his cot reading a book, and his cellmate, Diamond Pete, is sitting across the cell on the shitter, his powder blue prison-issued pants billowed down around his ankles. Diamond Pete is chattering a mile a minute like he always does, seemingly oblivious to the fact that Jacob is preoccupied by the Cormac McCarthy novel held before his face.

"I'm the king of this bitch," Diamond Pete boasts loudly. "If any nigga needs anything they gotta go through me. I've got the best hook ups. Commissary ain't got nothin on my ass. Warden Childress might think he's got all the power, constantly trippin and flexin to make up for his small cock, but once I get outta here he's gonna realize his power don't amount to shit, cause I know where that nigga rests his head. Jaquan has his place on lockdown. All I gotta do is give the word and that nigga will get got. You best believe that."

Diamond Pete stands up from the toilet and wipes his ass. Jacob continues trying his best to ignore him. He's just getting done reading a passage where fate is being dictated by the flip of a coin toss and a cattle prod is about to be utilized, when a surprise guest enters the cell.

"Jasper, what are you doing here?" he asks in bewilderment, as his slim black cat saunters through the bars of the cell to curl up at his feet. He reaches down to pet his furry beast, but instead of his fingers running over the familiar sleekness of Jasper's fur, his hand makes contact with something that's stiff and damp and twitching. He jerks away, and the book he was reading drops from his lap to land on the ground beside two black birds, and, contrary to one of The Beatles greatest hits, they are most definitely not singing in the dead of night. The first bird is lying flat on its back, wings outspread in twin crescents. Where its face should be, only a gaping hole exists. The other bird, face still intact, is temporarily alive, but its spasming indicates it probably won't be for long.

"Jesus Christ," Jacob says. "You've really outdone yourself this time, haven't you?"

Jasper looks up at Jacob expectantly, as if impatient to get a reward for the bounty he's so gracefully provided.

"He sure is a hell of a slick killer," A voice agrees, with what can only be interpreted as admiration.

Jacob assumes it's Diamond Pete speaking, but he's wrong. It would make sense for it to be Diamond Pete, considering he was the only other person in the cell, after all, and nobody else has neither came nor left, but nonetheless it isn't him.

"Here we meet again," Trevor says with a smirk. "Back like a bad habit!"

"Some things never change," Jacob agrees. "Aside from getting older and fatter and uglier with time."

Trevor looks down at the peace offerings that were left for them. "Oh man, that's a bad omen," he says. "A harbinger of death, some would say."

"So is sitting in a cell and having someone materialize out of thin air, yet here you stand," Jacob says. "If I didn't know any better I'd think we were in a dream."

"Life is but a dream," Trevor chips in. "But there's nothing merry about it."

"So, what brings you here?" Jacob asks.

Trevor smirks. "Just think of me as the ghost of Christmas past. Remember when we fell out of touch all those years ago?"

"Of course. How could I forget?" Jacob asks. "It was after you moved away. Hell, it seemed like everyone I knew was beating the track to get down to the Twin Cities back then. Looking for a fresh start and a new life, or some such happy horseshit. But who am I to judge? Hell, I was no different. After Tori cheated on me and I put her man in his place and ended up in prison, there was no reason left for me to stay. I knew you'd moved down to North Minneapolis, so I figured I'd come down and give it a go. The only problem was I didn't know how to reach you after your number was disconnected, and I had no idea where you were staying. So I got a shit hole apartment and set up shop down in North Minneapolis myself. I looked everywhere for you and Vance, but I had shit for luck. It wasn't until I got pulled over by a pig for driving erratically, and he got me on meth charges that we met again. I ended up in a cell just like this. Go figure."

Trevor walks over and sits down on the cot beside Jacob. He glances dismissively at the novel by their feet, before putting his hand on Jacob's shoulder like a funeral director about to lead a fresh widower to a casket for the final viewing. Jacob continues: "But at least I wasn't alone. You know how surprised I was to find you as my roommate? I felt like I must be dreaming. Like I'd hit the fucking lottery. Here we were, childhood buddies reunited again. From the cradle to the cage. And you know what made my day the most? It was like we never missed a beat. When I told you about that studio apartment down on Dupont, and how my slumlord of a landlord kept raising the rent even though he refused to ever fix shit, you offered me a place to stay when we got back on the outside. I caught you up on Tori, and how she'd been playing games behind my back, and you were there for me when I found out she was pregnant."

"Do you remember the advice I gave you?" Trevor asks.

Jacob grins deviantly. "I remember your advice like it was only yesterday! You told me to watch out for girls that like to spend all their time on their back with their dresses pulled up and panties pulled down."

"But did you listen?"

"Of course not. Tori ended up pleading her case and talked me into going back home."

Trevor shrugs. "I wish I could take credit for those pearls of wisdom, but Vance was actually the one who came up with that little ditty about dresses up and panties down."

Jacobs face darkens in annoyance. "Of course Vance is the one leading you by the leash. It's always been that way. He's such a fucking pansey! He still can't get over what happened with Sasha and move on, and for some reason he still has a magnetic hold over you. If you don't start thinking for yourself he's going to drag you down to the fuckin sewer with him, cause guys who roll around in shit hate nothing more than when someone else breaks clean. They need company to wallow with."

"Oh, you're one to talk," Trevor complains. "You're no better than us. You're no fucking saint."

Jacob interrupts: "But at least I'm doing this heist for the right reasons."

"Heist?" Trevor questions. "Who said anything about a heist?"

"I'm assuming that's why you're here," Jacob says. "You materialized in this cell for some reason. I'm assuming it's for the heist on the other side of this dream."

Trevor looks at Jacob with a perplexed expression. "If you're aware this is just a dream then why are you wasting so much time asking me anything at all? Clearly I'm nothing but an aspect of yourself. You'd do just as well to get advice from the cell wall as to why I'm here."

Jacob stares at Trevor in annoyance. "You're hiding something from me. I can feel it."

Trevor laughs. "Like I just said, I've got nothing to hide. If anything, you're hiding something from yourself. I couldn't be any more transparent if I were a window."

Jacob gets up from the cot and starts pacing the cell. As he paces, being ever careful to give the dead black birds a wide berth, Jasper follows at his heels. Trevor stands off to the side with a knowing smirk. He takes a joint out from his back pocket and lights up. "We reunited in this cell," he says. "You were here on drug charges, as was I."

Jacob pauses to ponder. "I told you about how the cop pulled me over for driving erratically. He wanted to know if I was on something. I told him I'd been swerving because I was tired after pulling an all-nighter at work, but the cop wasn't satisfied. He asked if he could check my vehicle since I had nothing to hide, and like a big dummy I allowed it."

Trevor laughs. "Remember how much shit I gave you for letting that pig search your vehicle?"

"How could I forget? You also gave me shit for putting the baggie in the glove box. You said it was a rookie move. You said if I had any brains in my thick skull I would've used one of those hidden compartment units to hide my dope, like the Mountain Dew bottle that you use. The one that looks unopened and full, but has a hollowed nook hidden behind the label."

"Yes, I did," Trevor agrees. "I told you you have to be creative and not predictable if you wanted to get away from all the bullshit."

"So how does *then* tie in with *now*?" Jacob asks.

"You already know," Trevor responds.

"You're hiding something from me," Jacob insists. "You're not being transparent like you say you are."

To that, Trevor simply replies: "It's your dream, not mine," with a snide grin on his face that Jacob can't stand. It reminds him of every jock he knew in high school when it came time to pick teams and he was one of the last guys left standing to be chosen. He thinks about how he'd like to wipe that smug shit eating grin from Trevor's face, and no sooner has the thought crossed his mind before the grin does disappear. In fact, his mouth fades away entirely.

Jacob stumbles away in shock, overcome by a strange sense of vertigo. Without warning, the room suddenly begins spinning rapidly, like a carnival carousel on steroids, and everytime the room spins past Trevor he seems to lose more substance. At first, Jacob thinks it's just a trick of his imagination. Surely he can't be seeing the outlines of the cell's white bricks through Trevor's shirt. But when the whiteness starts bleeding through Trevor's jeans as well, he knows it to be true. With each crazy tilt and whirl of the room Trevor is disappearing before his very eyes. Just when it seems he can take it no longer, and he can feel the bile rising in the back of his throat, the room quits its crazy trajectory and comes to a jarring halt. Trevor has fully faded away, and behind where he'd been standing, carved into the brick wall like a testament to his prior existence, are two simple points of advice: ***BE CREATIVE. NOT PREDICTABLE.***

13

Jacob wakes up in the office swivel chair with the lethargy of a grizzly bear awakening from a long hibernation. Surprisingly, the memories of his dream are still fresh and at the forefront of his mind, and he doesn't have to strain at all to recollect his experience back in the cell.

BE CREATIVE. NOT PREDICTABLE.

The words start repeating in his mind like a mantra, as if summoning something lurking just below the surface. As the loop repeats itself, (*BE CREATIVE*) he visualizes the Trevor in his dream, (*NOT PREDICTABLE*) joint in hand, a cloud of smoke billowing around him in a veil. He still has that same silly smirk on his face, (*BE CREATIVE*) taunting Jacob to see through the veil and reveal to himself what he already knows. As Jacob leans back in his chair to ease his aching back, (*NOT PREDICTABLE*) he glances up above his head and the meaning behind what his dream was trying to tell him crystallizes. He breaks out in a smile that looks as ludicrous and out of place as a Hell's Angel sitting in a church pew praying for repentance. This diversion is going to go smoother than he could have ever dreamed possible.

Inspiration never felt so good…

14

And now the day of reckoning is finally upon them. The final piece of the puzzle has aligned, and all their preparations have blossomed into the reality of this moment. There is nothing left to do but act.

The former bookstore is absolutely desolate when they arrive. The homeless kids Jacob encountered the other night have thankfully kept their promise to remain scarce. While occasionally there are people jogging along the main path near the marshlands, or horny couples parked at the turn-about on the edge of the Miller's property necking, today they are nowhere to be found. All is calm and at peace. It's the same deceptive tranquility that commonly precedes storm clouds or tornadoes before they materialize on the horizon.

Trevor kneels before The Hungry Mind with his back firmly against the wall and a small glass pipe pressed tightly between his lips. His face is virtually unrecognizable as he inhales a deep drag of silken white smoke with the same fervency an overzealous sinner utilizes upon the beads of a rosary in the vain hope it may guide like a northern star along a path toward something better. The cloud of smoke he exhales surrounds his head like the ethereal halo of an angel. Only, the angelic resemblance of the halo stands in stark contrast with his facial features, which have been transformed to deflect prying eyes. Jagged bloody scars crisscross Trevor's jawline amid a sea of blistery craters. Molten furrows resembling the burnt aftermath of a nuclear fallout trail down his cheeks and throat. His face more closely resembles the topographic map of a scorched mountain region than that of flesh. If Freddy Krueger had been torched during the final stages of AIDS ravishment then perhaps Trevor would have an equal counterpart in encapsulating the grotesque.

Vance stares at Trevor as he smokes, with obvious growing impatience. His eyes keep glancing nervously at his watch as if he half expects it to transform into a viper and strike for his jugular. "Jesus, you look like something that crawled out of the wet dream of a nightmare," he says. "Give me a puff of that shit for good luck, Trev. Don't Bogart it. We're running low."

Trevor obliges. A few minutes later, after both are as satisfied as they are capable of getting, Jacob steps out of his car and joins them on the sidewalk. His expression is one of grim determination. "Are we about ready to get moving? I don't feel comfortable wasting too much time here. We need to get this show on the road, pronto."

Vance adjusts his wig and tries to remain serious, but they all look so ludicrous he can't help but chuckle. "Our getup just might be the best idea I've ever come up with," he says.

"And that's not saying much," Trevor chimes in.

Jacob remains neutral. He has no time for humor in the situation. There are other worries eating away at him that take precedence over comic relief. "Alright, time to let the chemical bath begin."

They have piled most of the crates near the back of the bookstore where the dusty bookshelves still stand like abandoned sentinels. The neglected thoughts from each orphaned book that never managed to find a home silently scream at Vance in protest from the dusty shelves of ages long forgotten. The pages seem to resent the fact that they are destined to be consumed by flame. They'd rather continue living, by planting seeds, and resurrecting in thoughts anew.

"It's crazy how quickly something can be destroyed and torn down," Vance marvels, as they maneuver through the empty aisles. He pauses for a moment as they stop to ponder his words. The silence stretches on for nearly a minute before he continues: "To think that a group of people put their hearts and souls into everything we see around us. They slaved over creating the foundation, and spent countless days laying the brick and mortar. They worked together to measure and place every plank in just the perfect spot. They sweat and bled endless effort to bring something into the world that can add a brief moment of color and meaning to the world, when all it takes is any random person to blindly spark a flame and take it all away. Anyone can come along with the power of mindless destruction and wash it all away..."

Trevor opens the door to the back office. Jacob glances up at his handiwork as they enter. All he can do is hope that his inspiration wasn't misguided.

"A little late for us to start thinking about regrets," Trevor says. "This was mainly your idea, after all."

Vance looks him directly in the eye. "Don't misunderstand me. My words have nothing to do with backpedaling. I was just making an observation. I have no regrets. Regrets are for the weak, and I'm not about to start wasting thoughts on them. These flames are going to be our salvation, make no doubt about it. We've been pushed to the edges by society our whole lives, and now it's our chance to push back. We're done playing subservient faggots and niggers."

Trevor fumbles a lighter out of his pocket with his free hand. He flicks the flame to life and takes a deep drag, igniting the Lucky Strike cigarette that is jauntily perched from his lips. He applies the cherry of the cigarette to a collection of old newspaper scraps that are overflowing from a wastebasket he's placed beneath the office chair. The scraps hesitantly start sputtering smoke and a flickering flame reveals itself from within and starts spreading like cancer. Once the scraps have adequately taken flame, they rush out through the broken side window and enter Jacob's car.

They peel out of the deserted parking lot like the four horsemen of the apocalypse are scratching at their heels as the huge *woosh* of an explosion, the type high schoolers in chemistry class would undoubtedly have wet dreams over, shatters the silence. Bricks and metal and random wooden debris erupt and rain down from the faultless blue sky, blotting out all thought with the immenseness of their fury.

"It actually worked," Jacob marvels as they curve along Main Street. He does his best to maintain a look of nonchalance as Trevor and Vance stay crouched down in the backseat. "When I tapped into the water main and swapped out the sprinkler system with all the brake fluid, I was worried it wouldn't go off. But when we triggered the smoke alarm and it actually worked, goddamn was that vindication!"

Trevor chuckles from the backseat. "That's probably the first time in history that a sprinkler system was used to *start* a fire instead of put one out. Gotta love the irony!"

They are halfway across town when they hear the blare of sirens coming around the bend. Three cop cars careen past in a cacophony of squealing tires and flashing lights. The sonic madness builds to a crescendo as a fire truck joins them in hot pursuit. The procession of chaos tears off in the direction of the quarry as Jacob closes in on the bank. He parks his car in the shadows of a cluster of pine trees in a parking lot that adjoins the bank near the rear of a Rainbow Foods.

"Do you have your walkies on the right channel?" Jacob asks, gesturing to one of the walkies he procured while visiting Old Man Jones. "We can't afford to have a simple mistake end up biting us in the ass. Tori needs me around. She can't take care of Harvey on her own."

Vance and Trevor reassure Jacob that everything is on the up and up. They give him one last reminder that he needs to stay on guard, not that their warnings are really warranted. Everyone is clearly electrified and tweaking to the gills. They couldn't possibly be any more alert were they defusing an explosive in the middle of Times Square on New Years Eve.

They give Jacob a pat on the back and bid him farewell. Jacob has a hard time making eye contact as they leave. Perhaps he's distracted thinking about the handgun Trevor is carrying and the legal penalties that go along with armed robbery. Perhaps he's contemplating the stubborn habit criminals have of getting released from confinement only to recycle their way back into the prison system, like human excrement passed through queasy bowels given the chance to fertilize soil and grow life anew, only to have the new life become digested and turned to shit yet again. Whatever his thoughts may be, he is left alone with them temporarily as Vance strides across the parking lot of First National with Trevor in tow.

As he approaches the bank, with two empty canvas zipper bags crotched safely down the front of his pants, Vance finds it hard to resist itching the brown face paint he'd applied only a few hours earlier. It's smeared across his neck and face and arms and looks almost natural in the fading sunlight. Even the afro he's wearing doesn't look too suspect by the light of the encroaching dusk. It certainly doesn't draw as much attention as the gruesome scars and burns canvassing Trevor's face. He has little worries of being identified. But even if someone were to instantly recognize his disguise for what it was, it wouldn't draw too much unwarranted attention. Not on this night of all nights. After all, Halloween is meant for strange sights.

"Are you ready?" Trevor inquires as the bank's menacing hulk grows in proportion with each step of their approach, his facial scars and burned flesh looking foreboding and ghastly, like a harbinger of death, as the doors open before them like a maw. The casual tone of his question seems wildly out of proportion with the moment. As if they could possibly turn back now that they were finally almost in the belly of the beast. They'd set out on a quest, and Vance was damned if he was going to turn back now. For better or for worse, he was going to finish this pursuit no matter the cost. Just call him Captain Ahab…

15

Vance enters the bank paying careful attention to detail. Upon a quick scan of the room he determines that there are only three tellers on duty and four patrons waiting to make transactions. Thankfully none of these patrons are children. He wastes no time cutting ahead of everyone in line, to the complete chagrin of an aging woman who blends in with her vivid orange petticoat like a chameleon due to the desperate shade of her tan. She sighs in indignation as her eyes roll toward the ceiling. She dramatically flings her arms upward in the same generalized direction of her disgusted gaze as if to say *can you believe the nerve of this asshole?*, and as a result her petticoat inadvertently flaps open revealing a low-cut floral gown that more closely resembles lingerie than the evening wear it's supposed to be. Little does she realize how low on the totem pole budging in line is about to seem in the grand scheme of things.

"Don't anybody fucking move or I will cut you down into pieces, so help me God!" Vance screams upon reaching the partition at the front of the line separating him and the teller. "Your lives hold no fucking value with me! Unless you have a death wish or a strange desire to become an amputee for fetish porn I'd advise all of you to think of me as Medusa and consider yourself stone."

The lady who looks like she just climbed fresh from a Mary Poppins-themed whorehouse phonily makes an over the top gasp and clings to the portly man beside her who is undoubtedly her husband. She shrinks within her petticoat like rose petals exposed to frost, pulling the parasol she is carrying in her right hand tight against her bosom as if it's a talisman that can protect her from what's about to transpire. Her husband seems to be experiencing the reality of the situation slightly slower than everyone else around him. His dazed expression holds about as much vibrancy as a reflection on a surface that has nothing stirring beneath.

Trevor stands guard near the exit of the bank with his gun aimed nervously at the congregation of people as Vance jumps over the partition and proceeds to grab the nearest teller by a clump of her hair. She shrieks in surprise, her reaction decidedly more genuine than that of Whorey Poppins in the floral nightie. "Open all the drawers and empty them quickly. Don't even think about triggering a silent alarm. I'm watching you like a hawk, and if you try pulling any funny shit, trust me, there will be consequences. Keep your hands where I can clearly see them!"

As the teller grabs a key from her pocket with jittering hands, and motions for another teller to join her, Miss Poppins decides now is the best time to ask the ever-important question involving her self-preservation: "Are you going to hurt us?"

Vance wheels around on her, all the while mindful of keeping an eye on the teller's as they apply their keys together to start unlocking a main drawer: "Didn't I make myself clear? Stone doesn't speak or make activity! It waits patiently unless it wants to get chiseled! I can tell you've already had your nose hacked by a half-assed surgeon who probably got his credentials from a cereal box, so would you really like me to make any other permanent changes you'll later regret?"

She glances over at her husband, her mouth open in an expression that is comically aghast. He sheepishly looks down at his shoes, his gaze trailing like a vague beam of light thrown off from a dead star, leaving illusions that something is still carrying onward with vibrancy despite the evidence of emptiness that trails in its wake. He clearly has limited interest in standing up for his precious belle who's obviously unaccustomed to being treated with such nerve. She's probably thinking about asking him why he's looking down at his shoes when he should clearly be searching for proof of his balls instead. She scowls at him with the trout lips he likely paid for. God only knew how much money he spent to make her look so cheap.

The teller starts shoveling fistfuls of banded-money into a bag, ignoring the microcosm of drama transpiring between the lady who is deathly afraid of aging and her kiss-ass husband who is deathly afraid of growing a spine and walking tall like the rest of his fellow vertebrates. She wisely chooses to focus on the larger threat hovering before her instead. Vance feels sorry for the terror he can see radiating from her every spastic movement. Her shifting eyes drive a spike into his heart. God only knew she likely made next to minimum wage working this shit job just to keep her mortgage afloat and the repo man at bay, the last thing she needed was this emotionally-numbing bullshit. But, oh well, it was a little late to start growing a conscience now. She finishes filling up the first bag and hands it over, as the other teller opens a second drawer. As they begin fumbling money into the second bag, Trevor's walkie talkie suddenly crackles to life: "Jesus Christ, guys. We have company."

Trevor stands dumbfounded. He is still at attention near the rear of the room although his gun has lost its trajectory and instead of focusing on the line of frozen people has now strayed in the general direction of the ceiling tiles above them. He clearly isn't anticipating this bit of interruption. He takes the walkie from his belt band and raises it to his lips, which have unexpectedly begun quivering: "Could you come again? What do you mean by company?"

There is a brief hesitation, and then Jacob's voice is heard angrily drifting up through a sea of static distortion in a blind panic: "You know, *company*, as in misery loves company! As in what Paul Sheldon is to Annie Wilkes! As in that stupid fucking show with Suzanne Somers before she started peddling exercise equipment! Company! A fucking Dunbar armored vehicle is rolling up! I'm not shitting you! An armored *fucking* vehicle! You need to take whatever money you've managed to grab and GET THE FUCK OUT *NOW*!"

"Jesus Christ," Trevor mutters.

"Hey Vance!" he yells across the room which seems to have suddenly grown in leagues and is starting to waver in and out of focus along the edges with every trip-hammer of his heart. "Jesus Christ, Vance! Grab the last of the money! We need to get the fuck out of here! Hurry! There's a fucking armored vehicle outside!"

Vance yanks the second bag of cash from the teller and vaults over the partition in response. He grabs the lady with the Oompa Loompa tan before even fully realizing what his intentions are. He drags her forward with him in the vain hope that her plastic will sufficiently double as kevlar. He jerkily shuffles toward the lobby with his arm thrown around the woman as he struggles to maintain his grasp on the gun and duffle bags. The people in line part before him like the Red Sea succumbing to the presence of Moses. Instead of looking concerned for her welfare, the rotund husband of Whorey Poppins seems almost relieved as she's whisked away.

"Hey, can I get a hand!?" Vance shouts to Trevor as he barrels forward, feeling like the proverbial bull in a china shop.

Trevor obliges Vance by taking a duffle bag. He throws open the doors to the lobby just as two men from the Dunbar truck enter pushing a dolly. Dressed in plain brown uniforms from head to toe, they resemble UPS drivers more than armed security, and seem completely unprepared for the freak show unravelling before them. They hesitate for a split second, their expressions short-circuiting at the sight of the blistering burn victim alongside the black male whose skin is losing pigmentation with every trickle of sweat; but their momentary pause is all Trevor needs to gain leverage. He reflexively chops forward with the precision of a grandmaster black belt and pistol-whips the guard standing nearest him. As the guard collapses to his knees in a daze, a geyser of blood already bubbling at his temple, Trevor staggers forward and jams his gun deep into the fleshy jowl of his partner. "Put your hands up to the sides where I can see them!" he instructs. "No sudden movements!"

The guard who is still standing cautiously raises his hands before him, his palms facing blankly forward as his fingers hesitantly splay in a gesture of submission. Trevor is randomly jolted from the gravity of the situation as he is besieged by the ludicrous thought of a down on his luck mime trying to earn coins for an empty coffer by performing a half hearted attempt at jazz hands. He has to bite down on his tongue to refrain from laughing maniacally as a wave of delirium washes over him.

Luckily for him, Vance is still fiercely grounded in reality and displaying his grit. "Lower yourself down to the ground!" he bellows at the guard standing before him. He waves his gun in the general direction of the other guard who is hunched over a puddle of crimson and gazing into the reflection like Narcissus, as the blood gathers and spreads. "You too, asshole!"

They both obediently flatten themselves to the cold tiles.

"Follow me!" Vance intones as he pushes past Trevor with his hostage held before him like an offering for Pele. "I'll lead the way!"

He exits the confines of the inner lobby and is briefly blinded by the glaring sunlight as he makes his way onto the concrete sidewalk outside. His vision swims in the honeyed glow of sunshine, and as he regains his orientation and vision, he half expects to find a SWAT team strategically assembled before him, waiting with amber shafts of light shining forth from sniper rifles, anchoring his every movement. Luckily for him, his imagination is somehow more outlandish than the reality of the moment. All that awaits him is a mostly vacant parking lot being commandeered by a large armored Dunbar vehicle parked arrogantly aslant.

"C'mon Trev," he calls back over his shoulder. "What's taking you so long? Get your ass out here! The coast is clear!"

A few seconds pass, although they could be minutes or years for all the difference Vance can make of it. Time has melted like a psychedelic clock in a Dalí painting and no longer holds any meaning. After what seems a brief lifetime Trevor comes backing through the door slowly. He's pulling the dolly with him as he maintains his aim on both guards in the lobby. "Stay down on the ground!" he barks as he creakily wheels his way toward Vance and the hostage.

"What the fuck are you doing?" Vance inquires.

"There's nothing wrong with having your cake and eating it too," Trevor says in way of explanation, his lips curling up in the vaguest hint of a smile. "Those assholes came to fill up the ATM. I'm just making a bonus withdrawal. This is just the extra bit of icing on top we deserve."

His smile is a smile reserved for well-earned victory. The type of smile one makes when reclining by the hearth and resting feet that have grown weary after completing a marathon and taking home the gold. They've made it out of the bank without a hitch. They've gotten all the money they'd hoped for, and then some. The end is in sight and things have gone as well as could humanly be expected. It's as if a veil of perfection hovers over everything.

16

And then, suddenly, out of nowhere, the momentary perfection is destroyed…

17

What happens next will repeat itself in Vance's mind again and again, like a skipping record, leaving indelible imprints as surely as fingers on wax. Looking back, he'll often ponder how things spiralled out of control with such rapidity despite all their careful deliberation. Old Man Jones, of course, would be quick to remind him of the cruel bitch responsible for everything.

18

Trevor is wheeling the dolly toward Vance, the shadow of a smirk still lingering on his lips, when suddenly everything explodes around him as the bag he's carrying ruptures from within, spraying forth a jet of crimson ink that spatters him from head to foot. He jerks in response to the dye-pack explosion, his emotions scattering like the ripples on a pond in the aftermath of a flung stone, and inadvertently pulls the trigger on his gun as a result. As the saying goes, when it rains it pours. The shot rings out, fracturing the tranquility of the afternoon, and a second later a return shot thunders back in competition. The veil of perfection that's been clinging over their every action reveals itself to be a funeral shroud as Trevor glances across the parking lot in shell-shock.

The third guard from the Dunbar vehicle, the one who'd been left waiting at the wheel while his partners went inside to restock the ATM, stands with his legs spread-eagle and his eyebrows furrowed together in a tightly woven knot of concentration. He'd heard the desperate shouts coming from within the lobby, and had been walking around the vehicle to see what was causing the dilemma when out of nowhere the freakshow that occasionally whispered to him from the shadow's of his psyche on those lonely nights when sleep was evasive suddenly came materializing its way into reality with a single blast. It only took a split second for him to puzzle out the details, and the training he'd received just a few weeks earlier on his hire date panned-out as his trigger finger sprang to action. Never does one come to life so strongly as when caressed by death, and this was no exception to the norm. His three shots go off in a rapid succession that prove to be deadly. The first bullet tears straight through Trevor's jugular, and before Trevor even stumbles backward or has a chance to splay his fingers across the gaping wound that a fan of blood is starting to spray from in an arc, the second bullet misses its target completely and strikes the hostage that Vance is dragging in the breast. It splatters open like an overripe watermelon in a grotesque trifecta of blood, fleshy pulp, and silicone gel. She is just beginning to scream as the final bullet tears a strip of scalp from Trevor's skull as cleanly as cleats tearing up turf, and he hits the pavement at the awkward angle of someone flung from a great height. Vance pushes his hostage toward the guard and scurries over to Trevor who is gurgling and choking on his blood. She clutches at what remains of her chest as the ghastly orchestra of death continues to play its lush symphony of destruction around them. There is at least a liter of blood pooling along the pavement and surrounding Trevor's head in a halo. It's blatantly obvious that there will be no saving him. His attempt at stemming the crimson flood erupting from his throat had been an act in futility. A steady stream of liquid ruby continues to spurt forth from between his fingers. His face, what's noticeable beyond the burn-tissue gore, that is, is becoming a mask devoid of color. It's transforming into milky porcelain, all pale and glass-like. His eyes, likewise, are already losing vitality, becoming as inanimate and unseeing as the marbles they used to play with near the train tracks down by the old rock quarry. His death is swift.

Vance grabs the gun that has fallen beside his lifeless compadre. He swings it up in reckless disregard, pulling the trigger repeatedly in a blind panic. One of the bullets clips the guard in his leg, and he drops to one knee as if in proposal. Vance grabs the zipper bag from Trevor, and is just starting to reach for the dolly when his walkie crackles back to life once again: "There's movement behind you!"

Vance instinctively collapses to the ground as a deafening blast shatters the glass door separating him and the lobby. Vance twists on his side like a python, barely having time to react as Mr. Narcissus crosses the shattered threshold like Lazarus crossing the plane between one world and the next. Blood is still trickling down from his head wound, blinding his vision, and his hand is twitching spasmodically, as if attached to invisible electrodes. Even still, his proximity still guarantees him success as he pulls the trigger once again. Vance manages to pull off a quick blast as well, despite his awkward angle, that knocks Narcissus back through the entryway and beside the bloody pool where he belongs, but not before taking a hit himself. He feels a sharp and jagged sting, but is still so hopped-up on adrenaline and the remnants of meth that he barely registers a thing. He swings back toward the guard who has regained his footing and is positioning himself for retaliation. He pulls Trevor up against his chest in a last desperate attempt at survival as a barrage of bullets hail down around them like a storm summoned by a wrathful God.

He knows that his life is over.

All the years of scavenging and searching for a temporary roof have led to this.

His nights of wandering the streets and improvising ways to get a fix have come to a close.

Yet, strangely enough, now that he is arriving at the place everyone warned him he would reach if he didn't change his path, he realizes in a strange flash of revelation that he really doesn't feel any regret. All his years of conning have been worth every moment, and he wouldn't alter a thing. Some people wasted their lives adhering to rules and regulations, taking status and social-rank seriously. They grew old lying around on couches at night watching television to take their minds off the taxes and bills that have them in a stranglehold, working jobs that bring little satisfaction to buy things that didn't matter to impress neighbors they could barely tolerate. He wouldn't trade his nights of partying until the sun came up with Tobias and Gerald and Clint off Chesapeake Way for a thing. All those nights of easy laughter and even easier pussy from the fixer-upper girls that followed him around like a dog on a leash, eager for excitement and the next Almighty orgasms their boyfriends couldn't provide at home. While the people he'd grown up with went to bed early, putting in overtime to save money for a retirement that wasn't guaranteed, Vance had been taking full advantage of every moment that arrived, milking it for all its worth. They could keep their 401K's and investment packages, and enjoy their empty conversations and bragging rights. He'd pick losing over winning any day of the week, if winning meant having to deal with insincere people that only had self-serving intentions. At least he'd led a life laden with conviction, and could die with the ease that comes from knowing he'd said what was on his mind without sugar-coating or sitting in moral judgement of others. He'd never allowed himself to remain tethered to location or commitments. He'd never wasted time praying to false idols and worshipping at the altar of wealth and greed. He'd avoided getting trapped in the snare of temptation material possessions provide that so many of his old friends had fallen victim to. While most everyone around him had lived a life of servitude, he'd experienced moments of freedom that no amount of money could compare with. As he'd figured out at an early age, money makes the world go round, but it was also the root of all evil. He could die with the freedom that comes from not living for this world, which was flawed in so many ways. He may die a shunned down-trodden junkie in the eyes of society, but regardless of whether he gained approval in the awareness of the masses, he could die knowing he still held a strength that most could only dream of attaining. If others thought he was a worthless piece of shit, so be it…

19

And yet, despite making amends and coming to terms with his inevitable demise, fate has other plans for Vance that don't involve dancing with death, at least not at the moment. While every day can be a potential curse, it can also be a miracle.

20

The hail of bullets continues raging down around Vance as he cowers behind Trevor. He doesn't dare lift his head. He lets Trevor take the brunt of the impact like a sacrificial lamb. Something lumpy and moist spatters against the side of his cheek, and despite all his years of joking to the contrary, he's pretty sure it's likely a chunk of Trevor's brain. Mrs. Poppins is still shrieking somewhere in his periphery, mangled chest and all, and suddenly her shriek is joined by the hellish squeal of tires on pavement, as Jacob, crouched down behind the wheel like a hunchback, comes darting across the parking lot in a chaotic blur of steel and glass. He swerves around Vance and Trevor, tires momentarily lifting off the pavement in response to his jerky yank of the wheel. The guard manages to pull off one last shot which shatters the windshield into thousands of shimmering diamonds before the the tires make contact with the ground as the car veers toward him. He attempts to leap out of the way, but is clipped and spins like a top into the bushes alongside the sidewalk. Jacob then shifts into reverse and squeals back to Vance and Trevor. The car shudders to a stop and Vance flings the passenger door open. He throws both zipper bags into the car. By now, the guard in the shattered lobby is no longer lying in a pool of his own blood has regained enough of his senses and manhood to join in the fray. Vance is about to go for the dolly when he notices the guard climbing to his feet.

"Fuck it!" Jacob yells. "It's not worth it!"

Luckily for Vance, he heeds Jacobs advice. He leaps into the car, and Jacob starts accelerating before he even has a chance to slam the door shut behind him. Jacob swerves around the armored truck as more gunshots shatter the tranquility. Vance notices the clock on the dashboard as they peel out of the bank's parking lot leaving a lengthy trail of skid marks in their wake. As incredible as it seems, only five minutes have transpired since they first entered the bank, although it feels more like five years.

"Jesus Christ!" Jacob shouts, repeatedly bashing his fist into the steering wheel as he turns onto a side road named after a local author who moved away as a child but is still the town's main claim to fame. "Jesus fuck! Jesus fuck! How did this happen? Fucking Trevor? I just can't, can't… This is just too bad to be real!"

Vance crouches down in the seat next to Jacob as he continues driving. He glances at the rearview mirror. The road is practically empty. As they exit onto 94 there is only one beatdown pickup truck behind them. Their diversion has worked perfectly.

"Try to take a deep breath man. We've come too far now to fuck everything up over something simple like forgetting to signal or getting a speeding ticket."

Jacob is incredulous. "Are you kidding me!? We're already fucked! Fucked beyond belief! Trevor is dead! I was forced to pull into the parking lot to save your sorry ass! It's only a matter of time before they ID Trevor and link him back to you! After that they'll trace you guys and the vehicle straight back to me! Jesus Christ! What is going to happen to Tori and Harvey? I can't go back to prison again. I'd rather die than go back!"

"No need to be overly dramatic. We can figure something out."

"No need to be dramatic!? Are you so cracked out that you've lost all touch with reality!? We were fucking idiots to even get involved in all this bullshit! We never stood a fucking chance! What were we thinking? A fucking *bank*!? They had the advantage from the get-go! How could we not think they'd have every possible defense already figured out!? We were fucking idiots! And what do we get for it!? Two zipper bags full of money? No! Of course not! Not even that. We can't spend currency covered in ink. No one will accept it. We'll be tossed in jail so quickly our heads will fucking merry-go-round. They fucked us. Now we only have one bag of money left to split, and even that… even that could be… *Oh shit*!" A look of realization lights up his face as clearly as dawn on the horizon. His mouth drops agape and his eyes widen to the point where he resembles an anime caricature. Had the situation been different it would've been quite comical. As things are, Vance is suddenly alarmed. "What is it, man?" he intones.

"Oh fuck!" Jacob yells. "We *were* fucking idiots? No, *we still are* fucking idiots! Fuck! Fuck! Fuck! They knew exactly what they were doing! Those bags! They didn't just tamper with one…"

"Wait. What are you saying?" Vance asks, as Jacob pushes the buttons that make the front windows slide down.

Jacob slows the car slightly and without the slightest hesitation chucks the bag of money that didn't suffer from the dye pack explosion out the passenger window, where it rolls down an embankment and slides down into a thicket of yellow wild plants and primrose bushes surrounded by birch trees. Vance tries struggling with Jacob as he grabs the second duffle bag, but it is to no avail. Jacob forces it out the window and it tumbles into a dark thicket of tangled greenery.

"Well that's fucking fantastic," Vance replies, leaning forward and putting his head in the palms of his hands. He grimaces and takes a deep breath. His hands start trembling as if he's trying to hold back a force he can't contain. He reminds Jacob of a livewire skittering across pavement toward water, or a hand grenade lacking a pin and nearing explosion.

"Everything we've worked for," he snarls through gritted teeth. "Everything we've sacrificed. All gone to rust."

Jacob shakes his head vehemently. "It's not all a waste. We're down the rabbit hole now, man, sure; but that doesn't mean we have to be easy prey. There's still a chance the bag wasn't tampered with, but I'll be damned if I'll allow leading the pigs right to my doorstep without at least taking a precaution. We can't afford to act impulsively. We can stop back in when night falls after having a chance to soak this all in. Then we can scout out the woods on foot and see if there's anything suspicious going on in the area. If everything seems on the up and up we can do a thorough search of the cash to make sure it's legit and we aren't being tracked."

Vance turns toward Jacob with the intense focus a coiled rattler has when waiting for the slightest misstep. "I knew I should've trusted my instincts and told Trevor to never let you get involved, but he swore up and down that you could be trusted. He vouched for you and said you were like Midas with the golden touch."

"Oh, don't go there. You're a big boy. You knew what you were signing up for. Don't try to twist this shit around on me now just because things went south. This didn't implode because of me. In fact, you wouldn't even be alive if I hadn't put my neck out on the chopping block for your ass. A little gratitude wouldn't kill you."

"*Gratitude?*" The smile on Vance's face is all teeth. It's the type of smile that unmistakably warns of entering dangerous territory. "Gratitude for what? You said it yourself! We have nothing to show for all we've done. Trevor is dead! It's only a matter of time before the cops start sniffing out our trail forcing us to live life on the fucking run! It probably would've been for the best if you just left me behind to die…"

Jacob pauses to consider Vance's words. He slows the car to a crawl as he exits onto Redemption Boulevard. He shields his eyes from the sun glare as 94 becomes a faint ribbon in the rearview. By now they are far enough away that the chaos of sirens has faded to a minimal background buzz, like a mosquito hovering on the periphery and tempting fate with the persistence of its annoying pitch, only in this scenario they are the ones in danger should the buzz get closer. And the consequences are a hell of a lot worse than the swift approach of a flyswatter.

"I'm in the same boat you are," Jacob replies. "You think I'm not aware of what's at stake? I know the stakes. You better believe it, because my stakes are on a higher level. I've got Tori and Harvey to worry about. We've slid behind on the mortgage and our house is going down quicker than a whore on a cock dusted with cocaine. Harvey is going to be starting kindergarten next year, but until then her preschool is raping us a new asshole. Not to mention the payments for volleyball classes Tori insists on having Harvey take. Have you ever had to think of anyone beside yourself?"

Vance doesn't respond. He's tempted to punch Jacob, but forces himself to restrain. He realizes that what Jacob has been saying is logical. It's entirely likely there could be a tracking device. The only advantage they have at the moment is that the cops likely have no idea that Jacob is involved. But tracking device or not, his time is numbered unless he can come up with a good strategy. Staying in Minnesota is just asking for trouble. He needs to wipe the slate clean and start fresh.

The silence stretches and becomes almost unbearable. Jacob turns on the radio and the silence is neatly severed as the bass from a rap song thumps to life. The song is only playing for a few seconds before Vance snaps the track off.

"I refuse to listen to that shitty jungle music," he mumbles as they pull onto Jacob's road. Two kids carrying smiling neon orange buck-tooth pumpkin pails half-filled with candy are walking along the dusty shoulder of the road caked in makeup and cloaks. The boy is dressed up in a long cape with a red satin lining and a bejeweled cane. The girl is in a spider webbed gothic dress with shiny red nail polish and lipstick. Jacob can't make up his mind if the boy is supposed to be Dracula or a pimp. He also can't decide whether the girl is maybe Wednesday from *The Addam's Family* or some random gothic call girl. They walk from one house to the next without a care in the world. They are still at that age where they can become anything they want. Much like the night that has brought them out, their future is a buffet filled with endless delights. They haven't had to deal with heartbreak or aching loneliness yet. They have adventure and treasures to look forward to. Life is all innocence and candy. Only adults have to worry about the reality of the razors that sometimes lurk beneath.

Just when he can take the silence no longer Jacob glances over at Vance. "Here's the deal. You can stay at my place tonight. Tori will be gone until Tuesday. She had to go to North Dakota for her uncle's funeral. Harvey is spending the night at her friend's house, but she's going to be coming back early tomorrow afternoon. You have to be out by then. I can't have her asking any questions. You're probably going to be on the news once everything is pieced together, so we need to pick up what we left behind and then part ways. Understood?"

The sun is starting to set as they pull into Jacob's driveway. The house is nothing special. It's just a random white bungalow drowning in a sea amid a thousand other random white bungalows. Vance climbs out of the car and walks up to the sliding glass door. "It looks like someone left you a little present," he says with a smirk. Lying at his feet are the desecrated remains of two dead black birds.

"That would be Jasper," Jacob replies. "I always tell the girls to keep the door closed, but would you think they listen? He's been out all weekend scavenging and kicking up dirt. Everytime he gets out he brings some new form of death to my doorstep. I'm getting real sick of it. I didn't even want the damn cat in the first place, but Harvey found it when she was out playing with the neighbor's daughter, and once she has her heart set on something she pesters until she gets her way, much like her mother."

Jacob unlocks the sliding glass door and steps inside. Vance follows him. It is much cooler inside. Vance is about to turn on the light when Jacob grabs his arm and stops him. "Don't turn that on. We don't want to advertise to all the kids in the neighborhood that we're here. It's already been a hectic enough day without having to deal with random snot-nosed brats ringing our doorbell every ten minutes looking for a handout."

Vance takes off his shoes and steps into the kitchen. "Where is your bathroom at? I need to wash up and get all this shit off my face. I'm all niggered out."

Jacob chuckles. "Yeah, your first day as a black man and look at all the shit you get into. The bathroom is the second door on the right. Make it snappy."

Vance comes out ten minutes later. His face is all red from being freshly scrubbed. "Do you have any clothes I can change into?"

Jacob gives him a pair of blue jeans and a plain white t-shirt that is ripped and two sizes too large. "Christ," Jacob exclaims when noticing how baggy the clothes are on him. "If I didn't know any better I would swear you just got out of a concentration camp."

Vance gives him the finger. He notices a pack of cigarettes lying on the kitchen table and proceeds to take a smoke from the pack.

"Just make yourself at home," Jacob replies as he lights up. "You haven't changed a bit since high school. You're still just as much of a mooch now as you ever were."

Vance exhales and is lost behind a thin veil of smoke. "At least I have plenty of company. Very few people change. What should I do with all my shit?" He gestures to the pile of dirty clothes on the table upon which lies the fake afro which is a snarled and frizzy rat's nest.

"I'm going to throw all that shit in the fire pit out back and light it up to kingdom come," Jacob responds. "The less evidence the better. Speaking of which, did you wash all that paint down the sink carefully, or did you just do a half-assed job and leave chocolate streaks all behind?"

"Don't worry. I took care of it. It doesn't look like someone had explosive diarrhea in there anymore. What time are we going to head back to get the money?"

Jacob looks up at the clock on the microwave. "I'm thinking around midnight should do the trick. Why? Do you have a hot date to get to?"

Vance takes another deep drag before replying. "I just have to pay my respects and leave an important message to an old friend of mine before I hit the road for good. You know who I'm talking about."

Jacob nods his head in affirmation. "Yeah, I know the old goat, and he's still kicking around on his mama's farm. Normally I would try to talk you out of seeing that old buzzard, but seeing as how he's only a few blocks away, I don't see how any harm could come of it. Just make sure not to mention one goddamn breath about me. That woman of his has got a mouth on her that opens and spreads rumors even quicker than she opens and spreads her legs, which is saying something."

"Oh, that won't be a problem. You can rest assured."

"It better not be. Just remember to stay to the trees, and if you see anyone approaching just keep to your own business. I'm sure it will take the authorities awhile to figure out who Trevor is, so you should have a little time before your face becomes a local phenomenon, but I wouldn't advise taking any unnecessary risks. Just make sure you get back here by sundown. We have a busy night ahead of us."

"Oh, I'll be back in plenty of time," Vance replies. "And no need to worry. Things can't possibly get any worse than they already are…"

Part 2

Life on the Fringe

21

Tobias Atwood came from a long lineage of trash, and those that knew him best were liable to say how the old adage about the apple not falling far from the tree applied to his plight as surely as midwestern days in the winter can be relied upon to cut to the bone with chill.

He came from an endless caravan of ancestors, a rank and motley lot of folk that had haunted virtually every nook and cranny of America—from the bootleggers of the Badlands, to the trailer-dwellers of Eastern Tennessee, to the brow and weather-beaten vagabonds that traipsed and circumscribed the land by train and boat and blistery foot from Tallahassee to Aberdeen and everyplace in between, living on moonshine and everclear and snuff with nary a pot to piss in nor window to throw it out. They lived and breathed and spat and bred, and when they slept it was never to dream.

As can probably be surmised, Tobias and low expectations were synonymous with one another in the minds of the townsfolk. Yet, even expectations can prove unpredictable and surprising once in awhile. The old adage about the apple not falling far from the tree was factual when it came to Tobias, only his apple was decidedly more poisonous than even the lowest of expectations could've anticipated, and unlike his predecessors, the sharp glint of awareness lay lurking buried within like a hidden razorblade—just yearning for the right moment to slash out and inflict…

22

Tobias sits beneath the limbs of a gnarled old oak with a bottle of Jack Daniels clutched in his right hand, his fingers turning fish-belly pale from the fierceness of his death grip. Leaves lazily zigzag down from their dense canopy above and collect in a pile about his feet as he periodically takes swigs from his bitter brew, yet he barely notices due to being immersed with annoyance at wondering what's taking Maggie so long to return back. She'd left to get money and drugs down in the city several hours earlier. She knew how crabby he could get when jonesing for a fix, and yet here she was, still taking her sweet everlasting cock-knocking time. Some things never change.

It's the end of October, the day before Halloween to be precise, and the winter that had only recently seemed illusionary and unworthy of wasting unwarranted thoughts upon is now waving from the horizon and starting to let its distinct presence be felt, with each casual gust of wind sending shivers of anticipation down his spine.

This is now his third or fourth winter staying at the farmhouse—he can't quite recollect with his thoughts always skipping and scattering along like a record that's rarely in sync with reality—and the winters always manage to creep in and catch him off guard. He has to remember to go to Casey's Hardware soon to get a portable propane heater. The one that he's been using for the last decade or so has gone on the fritz, and no amount of fuckery is ever going to bring that rusty old shitheap back from the mechanical graveyard.

His frustrations with Maggie continue amplifying as the sun commences washing away and dissolving the vibrant cotton-candy skyline and transforming it into a dusky honey-tinged pool of blood.

His bottle is three-quarters empty, and his patience even further depleted, by the time she finally pulls up in his squealing blue Ford that's held together by rust and hope and little else.

"Where the fuck have you been?" he inquires.

She stumbles out of the truck, mumbling under her breath. Her bleached hair glows in the fading light like a halo. Little else is discernible about her as she enters the shade cast by the maple tree. The only color that flashes out from the shadows are her smokey emerald eyes and the garish red lipstick she always wears that makes her mouth look like a knife gash or festering wound. Before she can even attempt a response, a bright scarlet outline starts blooming along her cheek and jawline. It takes Maggie a moment to realize that she's been hit. Drugs always have that delayed and numbing effect on her, and besides, she's used to it.

Tobias pulls Maggie up against him. Spittle flies from his lips as he begins to scream: "What's the deal? Are you that much of a stupid whore that you didn't figure I'd notice you leaving me high and dry all day? You better have some good shit for me, or all those cockrides you've given in the past are gonna seem like nothing compared with the soreness I'm gonna throw your way."

Maggie shrinks into herself, her eyes staring down at the tips of her patent leather Mary Janes. "I'm sorry, Tobi. I didn't know it was getting so late. I was down on Lyndale all afternoon, busy as a fox in a henhouse. You know I'd never leave you high and dry without a cause. I tried scoring from Lucky, but he was all dry. You ask me, he was just saving shards for that jiggly tit toothless tramp of his for later. I ended up havin to track down Gerald instead, and he was way up off Chesapeake Way out salvaging metal with Clint."

"Of course he was." There is no sense of irony in Tobias's voice, and certainly none to be found along the surface of his cold dead piranha eyes which are always lacking in depth. "Those boys have been stealing my ideas ever since we were in cradle school. I start slangin tires, they do the same. I start making money on metal, they take it right out from under my fuckin nose like a couple of cowardly weasels too piss-ass retarded to remember that I know where they roost. If they think they can just keep taking from my collection without any consequences, then they may somehow be even more inbreeding stupid then they cousin-fuckin look. You shouldn't've given em a bloody red cent, Magpie."

Maggie absentmindedly rubs at the handprint which is starting to purple and stands in sharp contrast with the rest of her skin, which looks anemic and as sickly as spoiled milk. "So, you want me to take it back then? Is that what you're saying? Cause we don't have to smoke it if you don't want to. It's not like I'm holding a gun to your head. It's only a goddamn crack pipe."

"Now don't go jumping to conclusions and putting words in my mouth where they don't belong," Tobias replies, looking slightly sheepish. "I never said any such thing as we should return the crystal. It's late and I'm fixing to lay low for the night. Not much in the mood to be out driving the truck after dark without a license or tabs. It's not smart to be taking extra risks and drawing attention to ourselves, as you should well know. The last thing we need is another vehicle in the impound. I say we just smoke what we got here and let bygones be bygones."

Tobias leads Maggie up onto the sagging porch of the derelict farm in a staggered shuffle. He bends over by the dooryard, and in the moonlight, with his gaunt frame and his shaggy silver beard crowned by a drift of snowy white spirals, he reminds Maggie of Old Saint Nick after an extended vacation at a methadone clinic.

When Tobias stands back up, his face is illuminated by the glow of a Coleman lantern he'd retrieved from the stoop. By the light of the Coleman they navigate their way through the entryway and into the sparsely furnished shadowy confines of the main living area.

No sooner have they crossed the threshold and sat down upon the mattress before a crack pipe materializes in the palm of Maggie's hand. She takes a deep hit, rotating the glass neck of the pipe back and forth with her thumb and pointer finger as the lighter hovers below the bulb, her brows furrowed as she gazes down into the depths of the flame, a plume of velvety smoke spiralling out from her lips and wafting about her hair all ghastly and spectral. After exhaling, she proceeds to pass the pipe to Tobias, and the rest of the night flashes past in a blur of confusion. They experience quasi-delusional peaks of heightened awareness followed by soul-numbing bouts of paranoia. They take faithless plummeting leaps into the darkest depths of depravity that can only be achieved when dancing with a void.

The following morning finds them still in a self-induced state of disrepair. Maggie is extremely wired and agitated. She's rearranged what meager relics and pieces of furniture they possess multiple times throughout the night, but realizes that she is still dissatisfied with the fruits of her labor.

"Nothing fits," she whispers—her hollow voice an eerie echo of the wind in the eaves.

"There's no balance. No matter how I try to rearrange, no matter how I take things apart and try to put them together again and build something better and new, it never fits right. Something is missing. But how can something be missing when everything still looks the same as it was?"

Tobias is lying on the mildew-stained mattress in the corner trying to tune her out. He's realized it is best to leave her alone when she is in a manic state. Yet, despite his intentions of ignoring her until she burns herself out, she still continues prattling on ceaselessly.

"How can something be missing when everything is still here? Where has it gone to? It should still be the same, but it's not. Why can't I bring back what's missing and make it fit?"

It's as if she uses her words as a form of verbal weight, each syllable keeping her tethered to the ground and reality, each consonant helping hold the darkness at bay. If she were to stop chattering momentarily perhaps the entire Earth would stop rotating on its axis and everyone would start spinning end over end out into the stratosphere. She could trigger the end of urban sprawl and herald the omega of all forms of ownership, and what would become of the material possessions left behind? Would they serve any purpose without someone to be dependent on them? Would they mourn the creators that left them behind in a world without meaning?

"I have to go back to the start again to discover what led me to where I am," she continues. "You have to help me put things back to the way they were. But, even if things look the same as they were, they won't be the same, because they've been changed by the move. They've been changed by the journey. So you can't help me go back to the start, because the path has already been walked. But there has to be a way to get past this dead end, there just *has* to…"

Tobias can't handle what she's saying. It's starting to make his thoughts spill out unbidden like blood from a fresh cut. "Stop it!" he snarls. "You're talking in circles that lead nowhere. What's done is done and can never be undone. It's just furniture from fucking dumpsters, for Christ's sake. It's just garbage that doesn't matter. You need to move on!"

"But it's not just garbage, Tobi," Maggie pleads. "It's everything we are and ever were. It's not just furniture made to be used and forgotten!"

"What are you *really* talking about? It all just sounds like gnats buzzing in my ear to me. Just white-noise nonsense."

"Maybe it's because you only listen with your ears, and only see with your eyes."

Maggie takes a stack of yellowed newspapers and tosses them into the corner, covering a shallow scattering of mouse dung. She pulls at her peroxide curls in distress. "Even the stains of shit still show through. I can cover the mess and dress it up to walk around town, but it's still only a corpse behind a veil. It still bleeds through and can't be avoided, and eventually everyone will see what's been hiding in the shadows."

Tobias shakes his head in disgust. "Whatever. I don't have time for this psychobabble! You don't need any more dope today. What you need is a good caseworker, you crazy bitch!"

Tobias leaves the farmhouse behind and gets in his truck. He can still hear Maggie rambling away to herself and whatever other farm critters happen to be hiding in the rafters and between the walls. He figures misery may love company, but even misery has its limits. Rats and snakes are the only kin that should have to suffer with the nonsense always spewing from her mouth. He has bigger fish to fry down in the city. If Maggie thought she could take the truck all day yesterday and leave him high and dry, it was only fitting that he return the favor. Tobias shifts his truck into reverse and leaves Maggie and her madness behind to wither in the dust…

23

    Minneapolis has never seemed more alive as Tobias navigates his way through the city. The sidewalks are flooded with people of every random imagining in an endless tide of hustle and bustle. He notices a little girl with golden hair crossing the road aside a bulky man in a tweed overcoat. In her left hand she's carrying a vanilla ice cream cone which she licks with a breezy disregard. Her eyes shine with a glow that has nothing to do with sunshine, but more to do with a halo of innocence and the beauty of a carefree existence that has been blessed with fortune and rarely exposed or tainted by shadows. And the little girl is hardly the only person tracking along with a spirited sense of purpose. In the distance he glimpses a couple of strapping young construction workers talking about last week's Vikings game.

    "Kirk Cousins has been killin it," one of the construction workers says to the other. "It's about time we had a quarterback that can throw for a shit."

    The other man agrees. "Ponder and Bridgewater were disasters, and Bradford was about as reliable as a canoe in a monsoon. Keenum was decent, but we let him go right when things were getting interesting. Today's game should be pretty epic, though."

    "It's a nooner, right?" asks the first man to the second.

    "You better believe it," the second man states. "If I'm lyin I'm dyin."

    Above them some window cleaners are having lunch on a scaffolding. One of the workers is casually dangling his legs from the ledge with the complete indifference and confidence of a man who thinks he must be made of titanium. They carelessly enjoy themselves from above in a way only men cloaked safely and comfortably in the armor of youth can afford.

    As a twinge of pain flares up his leg, Tobias can't help but resent them and everyone else he passes. It repulses him the way everyone appears so flawless and unquestionably at ease with the world around them and their places in it.

    Tobias suddenly feels so unexpectedly alienated from everyone around him that his vision swims blurry with tears. All the happy people, beaming with sunshine and purpose, start fading away from him as if in a fog. And in the fog they remain, a little sunshine tribe, a golden oasis of hope, marooned away behind his veil of tears. And his thoughts, the ones he guards so fervently, begin emerging from their isolated depths and haunting him with a sadistic glee. Thoughts about Emily and their brief whirlwind of an affair in the springtime of his youth; that night under the moon by Minnehaha Falls when he proposed, and how she glowed. They married, and for a time, everything was alright, until he got his first DUI after a night of heavy partying with Clint and was forced to waltz through the annoying mandated dance known as treatment sessions. But despite his misguided love for Emily, eventually he was introduced to a lover that held even more sway over him, and it didn't take long before the rot that began with alcoholism fully materialized and took hold--- that special crystal hell. He remembers the fights over his chemical abuse that led to their marriage dissolving; the final one in particular that took place on a moonlit night much like the night it all began, but with her glow now extinguished from time and experience. And like dominoes tumbling in a row, his thoughts start spilling in succession even further back to his other life before that, back to his childhood when the farm had yet to achieve dereliction--- when he'd lived with his real family by blood. He'd been taken away from them after showing up to school one too many times with half-hearted excuses to camouflage his bruises; but the emotional neglect and the strike of the belt had been a paradise compared to his years spent as a prisoner with his foster father. Layers upon layers of hell begin re-exposing themselves, defying the safety mechanism his mind has put in place to wash it all below the surface, and like the victim of a vampire having been bled white and left for dead only to regain vitality and life anew, the colors and blots begin blossoming and blooming forth in all their forlorn technicolor grandeur, and he is held captive and awash by the whim of his thoughts that flow and dash like a tide upon rocks that somehow manages to sustain despite the cesspool that tries to keep them down below.

    Tobias stops in his tracks, deterred by the undertow his reverie has wrought upon him. He takes a few deep breaths, his hands trembling slightly, as if from a subtle electrical current, and rests his head in his palms. He still feels jittery and out of sorts from the meth and the memories, and has to stop for a moment to calm his aching mind. He lights a cigarette and takes a deep drag.

Once he's sufficiently recovered, he starts walking again from the outskirts of the city toward the epicenter, his feet moving of a volition of their own, brought on not so much from a sense of determination and resolve but a fear of remaining stagnant and in place. The neighborhood starts changing from a state of neglected disrepair to moderately swanky and filled with a motivated perpetual vibrancy that only the heart of an urban metropolis can capture best.

It is after twenty minutes of thoughtless reprieve, the blankness of the walk creating a temporary false sense of security, that Tobias notices a crew of STS workers contentedly picking up debris from the trash-strewn gutter up ahead while debating, what else, but annoying politics, and once again he feels queerly cut off from reality--- like a limb that has grown infected and for the greater good of survival must be removed to avoid infecting and destroying the clockwork precision of the rest of the organism. There are four men and one woman all crouching and retrieving various pieces of discarded trash with the careful diligence reserved for matters of grave importance; as if they are archaeologists being tasked with the excavation of delicate rare treasures.

They stand beside a white stretch utility van with *At Work in Your Community* emblazoned along its side in their reflective vests, covered in dirt and filth, and somehow, like every other annoying ass motherfucker in the city, they have the tenacity to smile and laugh, content in the gutter with their trash, like children wallowing in a sandbox aware that they might not have any authority worth mentioning immersed in a world controlled by forces larger than themselves, but still have complacency with the knowledge that at least they still tower over ants.

One of the roadside workers is feverishly explaining the merits of the President's accomplishments, while the other is arguing in favor of the opponent in the upcoming election. They are both engaged in a battle of converting each other to switch allegiances, but of course neither one of them are making any headway.

"Entitlement?" The taller man with the hawkish beak-like nose looks incredulous, leaning in and pointing his finger towards the smaller rotund man with a faceful of stubble. "Is there a hidden camera somewhere and you're just trying to get a reaction out of me? I know nothing about entitlement. What I *do* know is that I spent seven years in the manufacturing industry and I'm no better off today than the day I was hired, despite dedicating myself to endless backbreaking work. What I *do* know is that our attempts at unionization are being stigmatized and thwarted by upper management and good men are losing their jobs fighting to get a basic living wage. I have child support that cuts into what little I've managed to earn, and all I'm asking for is a little bit of food to put on my plate to continue putting one foot in front of the other. Why is it looked down on and considered entitlement to get a little bit of help for a basic necessity for survival, but barely frowned upon when big business is taking advantage of every tax cut and loophole under the sun while arrogant bigwigs are sending money to offshore bank accounts to avoid paying taxes they can actually afford? It seems like politicians want nothing more than to pit us against each other because we're easier to hold down when divided poor against poor. They want us to worry about welfare and foodstamps and ignore the big elephant in the room that plays by its own set of rules. After all, it's easy to twist rules when also being the people creating and dictating them."

Their political banter spirals endlessly nowhere, and Tobias forces himself to pick up pace and tune them out because they are reminding him entirely too much of manic Maggie on a meth binge. He chuckles to himself as he turns onto Lowry. They are both clueless fools being led by wolves of the same cloth off a cliff. He knows better than to waste his time trusting people in power. It takes a certain kind of self-serving manipulative person with a special blend of moral detachment and delusions of grandeur to make it through the political arena, and only filth manages to slither its way through the corrupt system and into the limelight. Absolute power corrupts absolutely, as the saying goes, and the world was made for filth.

Tobias turns onto Seventh Avenue, desperate to shut his mind down and distance himself from all his rambling thoughts. He startles a squirrel in mid-meal as he approaches Casey's Hardware. It has a big bushy tail that sways as it furtively darts away with its slick oil-blot eyes set on a safe coordinate across the road it will never reach.

There is a slight screech of tires as the driver of a vehicle attempts to brake quickly, then the squirrel is nothing more than just another crushed bundle of fur and bone forgotten in a wake of exhaust as the vehicle thunders away. Just another roadkill pancake forgotten in the gutter among many others. Tobias gives the squirrel a cursory glance as he passes it by, a look that could almost be confused for sympathy if one didn't know any better, then continues up the block toward his primary destination of the afternoon.

A bell jangles as he sweeps past the threshold and into Casey's Hardware. Jackson is busy fumbling around behind the counter as Tobias approaches him, unloading clunky cans of primer from dusty boxes that look like they haven't seen the light of dawn in months.

"I'm surprised Casey isn't here," Tobias says as a means of conversational icebreaker. "I always figured the day Casey wouldn't be manning the register adding up merchandise on his old Burroughs would be the day I win the lottery and move to the Florida Keys."

Jackson chuckles, whether out of genuine amusement or under a societal obligation to appease could be debated. His double-chin jiggles vulgarly like gelatin in the dusty slant of sunlight. "Well, look what the feral cat dragged in," he intones. "Tobias Atwood, big as Billy-be-damned and twice as ugly. How the hell have you been? It looks like you've lost a few pounds. I wish I could do the same."

Tobias shrugs, tilting his head in a perplexical owl-like mimic, which could either be interpreted as *you know how times are* or *I find it difficult tracing how I got to be exactly where I am, but yet here I still stand.* "I've been better. Truth be told, I'm running kind of tight on funds, unfortunately."

To which Jackson chimes in like clockwork: "Yeah, you and everyone else I know."

Tobias hesitates, second-guessing whether or not his trip and objective is already in vain, then decides to go for the jugular as his father always did. "I guess why I came here today was to see whether or not I could sway you to help an old friend in need. You see, I'm in dire straits back at the farmhouse. We have no heat, and you know how winter has been coasting in as quick as a fox on the mating season prowl. Casey has been helpful with me recently, and I'm hoping the courtesy and charity runs as strong through your veins as it does the ones that brought you into this world. But I'm sure you're getting sick of me just skirting the issue, so I'll get straight to the point. I was wondering if I could put a portable propane heater on the tab I keep with your old man." Tobias raises his hands in the trained defense of one who is used to bartering and pleading with little qualms for remorse or humility. "I know it's a big chunk of change," he continues. "And I understand how quickly change can add up and get out of control and build into a mountain of debt, but just hear me out. I've got some money coming my way in the near future. I've got a few jobs sitting on the back burners just waiting to come out and light a fire under my ass. The checks are as good as cashed, is what I'm trying to say. You know I'm good for the investment."

The expression on Jackson's face makes it clear just how little he thinks the aforementioned statement resonates with truth. If Tobias had seen that look once, he'd seen it a thousand times. Jackson needn't have even continues speaking for all the words his look tells, and yet the fucker has the nerve to continue doing just that: "It's liable to set me back at least a few hundred for one of them portable heaters, and that's a few hundred further than I'm willing to extend myself right now. You're not the only one who's struggling, you know. This store has taken quite a hit these last few years with the recession being what it is and all. We can't really afford to be loaning things out. I'm not just saying this to be a dick, but my old man has already made it crystal clear to me that I'm not to agree to putting things out on loan. You know he's only done it in the past out of respect for your trying circumstances. As a good Christian man he's been willing to make some exceptions when looking at the greater good beyond these green pastures, but you've already rode him for a pretty hard ride, and he knows he can't afford to be putting the cart before the horse when there are larger problems at stake. It's nothing personal. It's just business."

Tobias has to restrain himself from lashing out. Every fiber in his being wants to tear Jackson's fucking intestines from his pelvis and make him lick them while pleading for mercy on his knees. "You can take your fucking good intentions for looking beyond these green pastures and stick them up your brown pasture for all I care, you crooked rotten skunk."

Jackson reacts to this bit of verbal lightning with an almost comical jerk of the head; the unexpected switch in temperament striking him as firmly as a fist or electricity. His expression toward Tobias is akin to a man who has heard rumors of sharks lurking below unexpected depths, but never having believed them until the fins made a hasty appearance and escape was futile. Perhaps he'd never seen a man who could be eclipsed by darkness with such dizzying quickness.

"You get the hell out of here!" Jackson screeches indignantly, his rage reverting him back to his awkward prepubescent voice that embarrassed him throughout high school and contributed to his unfortunate nickname Jerk-Off Jackson. "Me and my old man have done nothing short of pampering your ass when others would've left a washed-out old fool like you behind to hang to dry! You've got a lot of nerve, you worthless old kook."

"How very *Chris-tian* of you," Tobias spits as he backtracks through the entrance door. "You better pray to your God that you're not working next time I come back, cause you'll be in for quite the surprise."

He leaves Casey's Hardware behind, the vagueness of his threat lingering and building in sharp contrast to the dwindling of the bell chimes as the silence becomes charged by his departure and questionable futuristic intent…

24

A few hours pass and Tobias is still as livid as ever. He can't wash Jackson's repugnant self-righteous expression from his thoughts. His primary objective and reason for coming down to the cities, aside from the temporary relief of escaping Maggie's delirium, is now blown to hell and shot to dust and scattered with the wind, and Tobias finds himself wandering about aimlessly plotting vengeance and retribution and thinking of other ways he can salvage this trip so it won't be a complete bust. He manages to gather twelve dollars from a church collection plate during a noon mass he interrupts halfway through, not nearly as much as he'd make on an Easter or Christmas mass, but at least he doesn't have to worry about scrounging along the city streets gathering cigarette butts for stray tobacco so he can roll his own cigarettes later. He has a full pack of Camels and an icy cold bottle of Colt 45. He has a rusty Ford that has nearly a quarter tank of gas. He even has a part-time whore waiting for him and a roof and walls to go back to when the wind kicks up a fuss. Indeed, today is a day of luxury and excess. It could definitely be worse. It could always be worse. No need to keep dwelling on Jackson's cold-blooded refusal. No need to give away his power to anyone. He still has his freedom and his health. He still has his wits about him, and there are always limitless ways to gain a better position. After all, even a pawn can put a king in stalemate if taking the right path. Besides, being on top of the world is overrated anyway. There is nowhere to go but down. In the gutter, on the other hand, dreams thrive. In the gutter is where rats can grow to become lions.

He is still trying to convince himself that life isn't nearly as complicated and awful as he'd previously been ranting when he comes across a homeless man pandering on a street corner. The man is holding up a faded cardboard sign that is barely legible, aside from a few key lines that cover the homeless trifecta involving the key plea for sympathy having to do with some vague comment about falling on hard times, followed by the charitable aspect about needing money to care for his child, and ending with the final passage especially designated as a last ditch effort to pull at the guilt-prone heartstrings of the passerby by invoking the blessings of God and a good day. It is as calculated and to the point as a strategically placed Gideon in a seedy hotel used as a muffled plea for virtue and morality.

"Well, this must be my lucky day," Tobias chuckles sarcastically. "Not only do I get to witness a couple random jackasses bickering about political corruption and get turned down for a loan that could be life or death once winter rears her beastly haunch, but to add insult to injury now I have somebody else trying to burrow their wormy little fingers into not only my pockets but also my soul."

The homeless man glances at Tobias with surprise and suspicion. He stoops forward propping his hands on his skeletal hips, resembling a scarecrow in his blue and red checkered flannel. He's all loose-limbed and awkward and redolent of dirt. For some asinine reason Tobias is reminded of an old silent movie he saw in high school that bored him to tears as a youth involving Ichabod Crane.

"What's all this nonsense you're spouting about the soul?" the vagrant intones. His voice is raspy and hollow. It reminds Tobias of sandpaper grating against an empty casket. It's the type of voice that comes from years of dedicated smoking choked down with the more-than-occasional splash of whiskey.

"Well, excuse me for paying attention, but it seems to me that your sign is bringing God into the equation to guilt people into shelling out a couple extra bucks, and last time I checked God still has jurisdiction of the soul."

"Oh, a clever guy, eh?" The seriousness of the vagabond's gaze is almost comical. He squints his eyes in grimaced determination revealing distinct crow's feet that make him look almost distinguished, but for what he gains in gravity from the lines that trevail his face are easily cancelled out and counteracted by his eyebrows. They resemble big bushy caterpillars, and likely have never been acquainted with a razor or set of tweezers since Reagan was in office, if even then. "You think just because I'm standing here on a street corner instead of busting my hump doing construction or bringing in six figures pushing papers behind a desk that I'm somehow less of a man than you? Well, you don't know a damn thing about me and what I've been through, and what I still go through everyday."

"Let me guess, this is the part of the spiel where you cue your darkest memories involving a traumatic experience at war. Judging by the looks of you, I'd say Vietnam. Let me guess, you have a buddy who was blown to bits right in front of you by Charlie. Ever since then whenever you hear a car backfire you jitter and drop from a terminal case of shell shock. Is that roughly where this conversation was about to lead?"

The smirk that Tobias casts deepens the furrows around the homeless man's eyes. If someone had been passing by they likely would've been reminded of photos of old men in the aftermath of the Great Depression; all weathered and wasted. "You know, you're a real cynical son of a bitch," he replies. "But I'm sure you don't need me telling you that. You've probably gotten it enough over the years. And it's post-traumatic stress disorder and clinical depression, not to mention that Charlie has nothing to do with my experiences in Afghanistan. You guessed the wrong decade and the wrong hemisphere. If I was a gambling man, I'd guess you guess a lot of things wrong in life."

"That's rich," Tobias chuckles. "You mean to tell me you were part of the war in Afghanistan? Just how wet behind the ears do you take me for?"

"I'm not talking about Afghanistan *after* 9/11, I'm talking about the soviet war in Afghanistan. Ever heard of a man named Gorbachev, or does your memory not go back that far?"

Tobias is suddenly no longer smiling. He feels like he's dealing with Jackson all over again, and what little bit of amusement he's been gleaning from the conversation is quickly evaporating. "Cut the bullshit. This is all posturing. I know posturing when I see it. You're no better than one of those crooked politicians. I bet you aren't even homeless. At the end of a long shift, if you can even call it that, I bet you climb into your Cadillac and drive back to your loft off Lake Minnetonka and get a good laugh at all the dumbasses that are gullible and naive enough to fall for your act. Everything about you stinks of lies."

The bum is likewise growing decidedly unamused. "Your material is nothing new to me.

I know how all this bullshit works. I'm damned if I do or damned if I don't with people like you. Either I'm faking my experience living on the street just to swindle money or else I'm only spending it all on booze and fueling my disease. Either way I'm immoral. You can say whatever you like to justify not giving me a penny, whatever little lie helps you sleep through the night best beneath the comfort of your roof, but don't you dare call me a goddamn liar only looking for a handout! I wasn't always this way. I was once a young man with hope, but they pick young men to go to war because the youth never think death is something that can happen to them, and I was no different. Nobody plans to take a path that leads nowhere. Sometimes it just happens without a reason."

"Enough of this nonsense. You're never going to convince me of your sob story by raising your voice or shedding alligator tears. Everybody has a sob story to tell, you're nothing special or new."

The homeless man is relentless. Like everybody else Tobias has had the displeasure of coming across it seems like this man exists solely just to piss him off. "You called me a goddamn liar, and I don't take kindly to that. You want to hear my truth? The day I die, if I could afford a headstone, I'd have them inscribe *Best Day of my Life*. No shitting you. I've experienced horrors you couldn't believe. They haunt me every night before I close my eyes and every morning when I wake. Yeah, maybe some of the money used to go toward drugs and alcohol, but I've come a long way in cleaning up my act, because I now appreciate how death can come in many tempting flavors. Reverend Norwick helped me see the light. He explained how my addictions are like a cake fresh out of the oven always waiting on a windowsill, and taught me how they can dazzle from the shadows in moments of weakness. The draft from the window can be tempting, like a forbidden fruit from Eden, but when I find myself on the verge of caving in, I always remind myself that the cake isn't what it appears to be. It may offer temporary sweetness and relief, but its frosting is laced with arsenic. And just as Reverend Norwick explained, may he rest in peace, once I've taken a slice and allowed myself to give in to the constant hunger pangs, it may just end up being me the one that gets devoured. I don't fuck around with the poisons no more. I treat my body like a temple, the way it was meant to be treated. My faith keeps me alive. I let God carry me when I'm weak."

"Ahhh, such deep thoughts," Tobias laughs sardonically. "Had I known I was going to be graced by the greatness of the next Robert Frost channeling the light of the Holy Ghost I might've worn my Sunday best. But then again, you've got it all backwards I'm afraid."

The homeless man raises his ludicrous eyebrows in mock intrigue and gestures with his hands in a circular motion to proceed. "Oh, really? And how is that? Please enlighten me."

"You used to have the right idea, but now you're all clouded. You're as bad as those born agains that convert in prison on their deathbeds. You're too weak to own up to the truth."

"And what might that be?"

"Isn't it obvious? Haven't you noticed all the killing and raping and lies and manipulation, or are you just that ignorantly blind? There *is* no meaning. You want there to be answers to make this world seem fair, but this world has no soul. You'd do best just to accept that. There *is* no God watching over everything. You're just praying to a void. If anything, God is in the bottle and God is in the pills and God is in the dope. You should just go back to your old ways. It's the only real relief you'll ever find. I'd take real relief any day of the week over an imaginary friend."

And with that, Tobias moves on, despite the bums protests. He'd lost all interest in conversing with this simpleton. The day was wasting and so was his patience. What he needed was a way to come up with some more money. The collection plates hadn't provided him nearly enough. His buzz was wavering and fading and he needed another drink badly. If the weather was better he could go down to the lake and swipe whatever he could find on the beach from the pockets of wayward swimmers. Unfortunately, that wasn't an option. He could always go scrounging for metal and get money from the local scrap yard, but he was feeling too tired and unmotivated. He could break into foreclosed houses and steal the copper pipes to make money, but it was too early in the day and would likely attract attention. He had almost reached his truck when inspiration struck. He was standing on the sidewalk in front of a house that had one of those dime a dozen WE WATCH, WE CALL signs in the front yard when he noticed a bank in the distance and happened to catch the time. He recalled what the STS workers had been saying earlier and realized that the timing was perfect. The Vikings had a game that was starting in only two hours. That gave him plenty of time to get to the stadium. All hope might not be lost after all.

Tobias climbs into his truck and the engine chokes to life. As he drives past the bum he lifts his middle finger in salutation and chuckles to himself like a madman. Checkmate motherfucker.

25

He drives to a side street near Chicago Avenue and parks at one of the annoying downtown parking meters. He scrounges through his pocket and gathers as many quarters as he can find amongst the lint, which amounts to a whopping total of seven. He slid his first quarter into the slot and couldn't believe his fucking eyes when he saw how much time that bought him. Exactly three minutes. He figures it must be some kind of mistake, and slides a few more quarters in just to make certain. Surely the parking meters couldn't be involved in the conspiracy to piss him off as well? Now the meter taunts him with a lousy twelve minutes. He couldn't make it to the stadium in that amount of time on foot, let alone take care of his objective and make it back. What a fucking joke. He climbs into his truck and drives through the labyrinth of traffic. He sees several parking ramps that have Special Event banners announcing bargain rates of $40. People are absolutely everywhere. They disregard crosswalks and flock through the street in droves. They pat each other on jerseyed backs and call each other bro. Every second he slightly let his guard down some dipshit driver texting on their cell phone or applying mascara stops unexpectedly and forces him to slam on his brakes to the point where he is cursing with enough frequency to put a person with tourette's syndrome to shame. Every light he approaches turns red right on cue as if his car has a malfunctioning police receiver. He is about ready to scream or bash his head through the fucking windshield. Was every drunken obnoxious motherfucker this side of the Mississippi River going to this lame ass game?

After much huffing and puffing, Tobias arrives outside the parameter of the fascist parking ramps and Nazi meters. By now his buzz is entirely gone and he's struggling in the grips of a throbbing headache. He parks his truck on a plot of asphalt that doesn't come with a price tag and digs around in his glove box until he finds a flashlight. He reaches under the seat and comes up with an oily red bandana. He proceeds to put both items in his pocket and then makes his way back to the stadium on foot. When he arrives at the massive parking lot outside the stadium, the tailgating is in full swing. A couple guys have grills out and are cooking hamburgers and brats. Radios are cranked full blast playing the main hits of Guns N' Roses and Metallica and Queen, which apparently comprise the entire musical universe to jocks and that of their ilk. He watches the people getting out of their vehicles, waiting for the right victim. It takes nearly thirty minutes. By now most of the fans are starting to filter their way in through the main gates. His head is throbbing in time to the bass line of *Another One Bites the Dust* when Tobias finds his mark. It's a family of five. They are climbing out of a navy blue gas-guzzling Hummer, dressed in matching jerseys. The two boys appear to be around ten, and the little girl is barely in kindergarten at best. But it isn't the family or vehicle that has attracted his unwarranted attention. It's what they've carelessly left behind sitting out in the open that has sealed their fate. Tobias waits a few minutes until there's nobody around within seeing distance. He then takes the small metal flashlight out of his pocket and wraps the red Axl-approved bandana around it to shatter the passenger side window. He awkwardly reaches in and unlocks the door, thankful that the Hummer doesn't have an alarm system. He grabs the item he's been waiting for off of the dashboard and hauls ass back to his truck, cursing himself every block or two when he has to take a rest to let his lungs recuperate.

  Once he makes it back to his truck, he takes the item out. It's a small silver Garmin GPS. He turns it on and waits for a response. It takes a minute for the main screen to load. Once it does, he clicks the icon that might turn out to be his saving grace: HOME. The game should just be starting, so it should buy him a good three hour head start before the family notices anything amiss. By then, he'll be long gone.

  As the results for the search load, Tobias pulls another smoke out of his pack and proceeds to light it. He takes a deep drag and feels a brief head rush and comforting burn. The results come in, and the GPS quotes the arrival time at 12:47. It will take roughly a half hour to make the trip. Their house is in St. Paul. At 1076 Arundel Street to be precise.

Tobias turns the key in the ignition and the truck sputters, but doesn't start. He mutters fuck under his breath and takes another deep drag. He focuses all of his energy on the truck, trying to muster up as many positive vibes as he can manage, and tries again. This time the engine turns over, and once again life is okay. For the moment, anyway. A lot of things could still potentially go wrong. It seems like the entire family has gone on this expedition, but you can never know for certain whether somebody might still be at the house. He's done this twice before over the last decade, and while the former time had been an unequivocal success, the latter time had caught him off guard when he ran into an elderly woman drinking Caribou coffee at the dining room table. He can only hope that this break in won't be a replication of the last.

He arrives near the house a few minutes later than the GPS projected. He parks a few houses down from the intersection on Cook. The first thing he notices as he approaches is that the house looks way too small for a family of five. It's a charming enough two story, with siding a shade of yellow that looks so cheerful that whoever chose it surely must must have been on Prozac, but it was very compact. As he approaches the house a vision of the elderly lady sipping a mocha latte comes back to haunt him, but he's come too far to turn back now. Go big or go home, as the saying goes; or in this circumstance go big *by* going HOME. He'll be damned if he's leaving empty-handed. He refuses to allow this trip to become a complete bust. He has a propane heater that needs purchasing, and a smug expression to rectify. Mother nature doesn't wait for anyone, and he can't afford to procrastinate either. A long sloping driveway runs along the length of the house. The wide driveway is conjoined with the neighboring house which has extreme foundation issues. He walks around to the back and finds a window on the side of the house that is obscured by a privacy fence. He rips the screen off and is about to take his flashlight out and repeat the same process he did with the Hummer, when logic takes over and he decides to first check and see if the window is unlocked before taking drastic measures, banking on the fact that they were oblivious enough to leave the GPS in their vehicle without the slightest worry. His intuition pays off in spades. The window slides up without so much as a groan. He climbs into the house marvelling at his own stupid sudden change in fortune. He finds himself standing in a dining room, but thankfully there is no little old ninny getting hopped up on coffee this time around. The main level is silent and appears to be blessedly empty. Tobias searches everywhere on the main level, and to his chagrin he doesn't find practically anything that warrants taking. The kitchen is bare aside from the appliances, and the living room only has a worn couch and television. And it's a tube screen television at that for fucks sake! What are the odds of finding a place that hasn't bothered to upgrade to an LCD? And if they haven't bothered to upgrade even basic electronics, what are the odds that there will be anything worth making the trip?

In the bathroom vanity is the only place he finds anything useful on the main floor. Next to the toothpaste and floss are two bottles of prescription medication. One bottle is Adderall and the other is Tramadol, and they are both nearly full. He grabs them and heads upstairs. The stairway is one of the narrowest he's ever encountered. It isn't even wide enough to have a handrail. If a morbidly obese person were to come and visit they would be absolutely fucked. The top of the stairway dead ends on a narrow landing with a door on each end. He chooses the door on the right. It's a bedroom, and once again he is confronted with minimalism. The room contains only a dresser and bed and a cluttered nightstand. A dusty clock beside an imitation Tiffany lamp proclaims the time to be 12:47. Someone is halfway through reading a copy of Stephen King's *Full Dark, No Stars*. He searches through the dresser and nightstand and doesn't find so much as a debit card or box full of checks.Once again he mumbles fuck under his breath. He is on the verge of losing hope when he notices the closet on the far wall. He opens it and his heart skips a beat. Inside, amid the mountains of chaotic clothing, is a large eight gallon Culligan water jug filled almost to the brim with loose change. And most of the change appears to be quarters.

"Jesus-titty-fucking-Christ," he slurs in a rushed fever.

The jug is incredibly heavy, but Tobias is suddenly incredibly motivated as well. He hefts the jug up and is about to leave the room when he changes his mind. He sets the jug down and goes back and grabs the Stephen King novel. Maggie likes to read newspapers and keep up on current events. It gives her the affirmation she needs that the world is going to shit. He figures she might like reading the novel as well. If anything, it might help atone for smacking her on the porch yesterday morning. He tucks the novel under his arm and drags the jug out of the room and onto the landing. It's at this point that Tobias hears a noise. It's not coming from downstairs, but from the room across the landing he hasn't checked. It sounds like moaning. He presses his ear against the door and sure enough he hears it once again. It's definitely moaning. A second later he hears a young male speak. "I like the taste of you," he says. "Do you like the taste of me?" The response is quiet, and interrupted by a gag, but he doesn't have to be an astrophysicist to put the puzzle pieces together. The parents probably left, maybe bringing a niece or nephew to the game, because surely the house isn't large enough for all these people to live in such limited confines, and their son bowed out faking illness so he could have a little horizontal fun on the sly. Luckily they haven't heard him. Obviously they are too busy performing sexual acrobatics to give two shits about what else might be transpiring beyond the bedroom door. Tobias counts his lucky stars and heads down the stairs as inconspicuous as a cat in a room full of rocking chairs. He heads down the stairs and is out the window before either of them can reach climax. He makes it back to his truck with surprising quickness, only drawing the attention of a man with a blue backpack waiting at a bus stop. He nods at the man and the man salutes him without so much as a backward glance. He clearly hasn't drawn any unwarranted suspicion. He drives to the nearest liquor store, Broadway Wine & Spirits, and fills his pockets up with change. He picks up a case of Milwaukee's Best Ice and brings it up to a cashier dressed up in full Grim Reaper garb.

"Happy Halloween!" the Reaper intones. He swipes his scythe at Tobias good naturedly. "And a happy weekend to you as well."

Tobias starts taking his change out of his pocket and clumping it down on the counter. He looks up at Mr. Reaper apologetically. "Weeks end?" he jokes. "I didn't realize they did that. It seems like my weeks never end. Come to think of it, I even forgot it was Halloween until I saw you. I must be getting Alzheimer's or somethin. Sorry about all this change. It's laundry day."

"Don't fret a thing," Mr. Reaper replies. "Your quarters are silver enough for me. They do the trick." He scans the case of beer. "That will be $16.59."

Tobias fishes around through his change until he comes up with the correct amount. "Here you go. I figure 30 cans should hold me off until Tuesday or so."

Reaper chuckles. "Ah, a seasoned veteran. That's the spirit. I suppose I'll be seeing you soon then? I suppose I better start stocking up."

Tobias concurs that the Reaper is indeed right on target. He's about to leave when he notices a stack of Star Tribune's piled up on the counter near the exit. "On second thought, before I leave could I get one of those Sunday editions?"

Reaper grabs a copy and scans it. "It's a damn shame what happened to that Rutger girl," he exclaims.

Tobias pleads ignorance. Keeping up with the news has never really interested him. That's Maggie's gig.

Mr. Reaper points to the main headline on the Sunday edition. In dramatic bold 18-point font it states: **Authorities Fear The Stearns County Chameleon Has Struck Again.** "You can't tell me you're not familiar with the Stearns County Chameleon?" he asks incredulously.

"Oh," Tobias responds absently. His mind is already flashing ahead to fantasies involving swimming on the wrong end of a can or twelve. "Of course I've heard of him. He's been a boogey man since before Wetterling disappeared. Me and my friends used to always tease each other saying to make sure and not go wandering alone in the woods or else the Chameleon might find us. I just wasn't familiar with the Rutger girl. What happened?"

"It's a sad affair," Mr. Reaper replies woefully. "The little girl was camping with her family a few weeks ago at the Sinclair Lewis Campgrounds when she went missing. It was the 5th Annual Rutger family reunion. Her parents were preoccupied playing horseshoes and bocce ball with the other adults, while the teenagers and kids were hanging out back at the campsite playing board games and cooking hotdogs and telling scary stories at the bonfire. It was getting dark when the little girl, Veronica, left the site to use the restrooms. The kids forgot all about her, and it wasn't until the adults came back that they realized she was unaccounted for. At first they weren't worried, because Veronica had always been a precocious child and willfully independent. She had a habit of jumping from one hobby to the next, and her recent obsession had to do with horticulture. She loved studying plants and trees and said she wanted to work at one of the National Parks when she was older as a Park Ranger. They assumed she'd gotten sidetracked at the restrooms which bordered with the forest, and had gone off to collect and categorize different plants and flowers. But after searching everywhere within a mile radius without finding a trace of where she'd been, and with the sun starting to descend, they knew something was wrong. Veronica may be willfully independent, but she wasn't the type of girl to stay out past dark. They called for help, and it wasn't long before a search party was gathered. They traced every square inch of the woods that night, but had no luck. The next morning Sheriff John McCormack found the calling card that he'd feared might by lying in wait. You'll have to read this article. It's riveting."

"I'll do that," Tobias assures, heading toward the exit and sweet alcohol-infused escape.

As he leaves the store, he hears Mr. Reaper mumbling once again: "It's a damn shame what this world's coming to. A damn shame when an innocent child can't be left alone without having to worry about what some evil asshole might do to them."

Back in the truck, Tobias cracks open a can of Milwaukee and takes a gulp with delirious delight. He'd no more than finished his first few sips when a voice piped up inside his head. It was Maggie, of course, and Tobias was dismayed to realize that even his thoughts were no longer safe from her chaos: *Haven't you remembered anything you learned from AA? In particular, that night when Davis warned about how luck can be a fairweather friend? It seems to me like drinking in the middle of the afternoon behind the wheel of a suspicious looking vehicle in a crowded shit neighborhood constitutes just about every type of bad judgement Davis preached against. Are you trying to get the truck impounded and end up in the slammer or purpose? Wasn't it only yesterday evening that you gave me shit for taking the truck? How is what you're doing any better?*

"Fuck off," Tobias mumbled. "The last thing I want to think about is AA. Those 12 steps can lead off a fucking cliff for all I care, right along with that sanctimonious prick Davis. The fucking hypocrite gave me grief for my vices when all he did was just swap some of his out for others."

Tobias polishes off his first can of Milwaukee's Best Ice, or Beast Ice, as him and his friends call it, and punctuates the silence with a monstrous belch. He takes out a pocket knife from his glove box and grabs a second can. He tilts it horizontal with the pull tab pointing to the ground and the opening facing up. He cuts a hole roughly the size of a quarter near the base of the can, and cracks it open as he lifts the can vertically enabling the hole to meet his lips. The beer shoots out in a rage, and in five seconds flat the empty can joins the other Beast on the floor mat beside his feet. Once again, Maggie interrupts the brief moment of sanctity in the wake of cerveza dos: *You're pressing your luck. What makes you feel so confident that you're not going to get pulled over on the ride back north? You have well over an hour of driving ahead of you. All it would take is the slightest waver of the wheels and a state trooper could be on your ass like mold on bread. Do you really miss having whiskey plates that much? Or is there some other reason you wanna go back to jail again so badly? Do you have another girlfriend on the side? Do you like being some daddy's backdoor Betty? Can't get enough of those three hots and a cock?*

"Oh, fuck off," Tobias mumbles at the phantom Maggie once again. "I don't need to explain myself to a crackhead like you. I'm a grown ass man and can do whatever the fuck I want!"

As if to drive the point home, Tobias puts the keys in the ignition. The truck starts turning over with a rusty groan, and after a moment of indecision that suggests the junkyard might be the only trip left in its future, the Ford hesitantly sputters to life. Tobias reaches down and grabs a third beer. He pops the top and grabs his Camels from his side pocket. He simultaneously lifts the can with his right hand and takes a swig, as he fumbles a smoke out of the pack with his left.

"Now this is my kind of multi-tasking," he cracks to no one in particular. "If only Em could see me now, and how far I've come. It doesn't get much better than a Beast for breakfast, with a side of coffin nails for lunch. Fuck Michael Jordan and Wheaties. Fuck all the mindlessly void champions."

Tobias pulls out onto the street and five minutes later is heading down 94 west. All in all, he's satisfied with his little excursion to the cities. This might not end up being such a shitty winter after all now that his luck was finally changing.

26

    Maggie is sleeping when Tobias arrives back at the farmhouse, and he isn't surprised in the slightest. It has always been this way with Maggie. She's the type of person that lives life in one of two modes. In the first mode she is electric and on fire. She needs to constantly be moving. She'll climb the silo at night and name the stars. She'll rearrange furniture ten different ways, only to end up switching it back to the way it was in the first place. She'll have an insatiable appetite for sex. One moment she'll be fucking like a bunny and having orgasm after orgasm, and the next she'll be screaming about how all men are perverts and throwing pans at him and saying how he's no different than her grandfather. When her second mode hits her like a ton of bricks she slips into a state bordering on catatonia. She can sleep for days on end. She loses all vitality. She speaks in slurs and whispers and rambles about love gone sour and the ways the world has slighted her. She talks about her mother in Culver City and how much she misses California despite the cockroaches and memories that fester. She says at times she feels like her entire life is nothing more than the delusional creations of someone else's dreams. She says that her dreams sometimes feel more real than her real life. When she was younger she used to slit her wrists and suck at the blood that would seep through. It helped keep her grounded. She said she had an illness that came from a weak heart, and when she cut herself it helped sever the umbilical residue that was at the root of her pain. Once upon a time she had been a glamour child. Her mother had worked at Sony Studios and had deep-rooted ambitions of becoming an actress. After years of failed auditions and sexual rendezvous with men in prominent positions that failed to help her career gain any momentum, disillusionment had set in, and she'd vowed that if she couldn't bask in the glow provided by the twin spotlights of fame and adoration, then she'd make damn sure that her daughter would continue the path from where she'd fallen by the wayside. Madeline had started enrolling Maggie in pageants shortly after her third birthday. She'd funnel all her meager earnings into ballet lessons and hair extensions and personal tutors. Yet, try as she may to please her mother, Maggie was always stumbling down and falling far short of expectations. She'd watch the other girls pirouette with a regal grace that came flawlessly, and she'd practice in front of the mirror for hours on end to try and capture their essence, but her maneuvers came across as gangly and self conscious, and the beauty of the other dancers consistently eluded her. She'd explain to Madeline that her limbs weren't right for dancing, but Madeline refused to hear it. The talent portions of the pageant were the worst. She'd see her mom in the front row mirroring her moves as she'd dance, and inevitably she'd buckle under the pressure and watch as her mother's warm gaze of approval melted away and was replaced by icy daggers that could pierce to the core. After failing several talent segments, Madeline finally admitted to herself that dancing was futile for Maggie, and instead decided to enroll her in piano lessons. For awhile, it seemed like piano lessons were doing the trick. Whenever Maggie was in her room practicing alone she could play adequately. Sure, she'd never be Tori Amos or Elton John, but she could maintain a good rhythm and had excellent timing. The second she stepped in front of a crowd, however, everything buckled and fell to pieces, and she couldn't remember any of the notes she'd rehearsed for the life of her. It was as if she had selective amnesia that hinged upon Madeline's proximity. Madeline would get furious every time she'd falter She'd remind Maggie of the life she'd sacrificed because of her. Then the next week she'd enroll her in some new cockameemie endeavor and inevitably everything would fall to pieces once again. Eventually it got to the point where Maggie lived just to spite her. She started playing topless piano at an adult tiki lounge with the aid of a fake ID when she was only seventeen. She put all her ballet routines to good use by giving lap dances and gyrating on poles at The Eager Beaver under the alias of Violet by the time she turned eighteen. Stripping led to a string of bad boyfriends that beat her down, followed by mirrors filled with lines of coke that helped bring her back up. Strangely enough, it was her drug habit that temporarily helped fuel her sense of self-confidence. Whereas she'd felt gangly and awkward when she was a little girl dancing at the pageants, she felt liberated and unrestrained dancing in her panties and grinding her crotch in the faces of anonymous frat boys in polo shirts. She started sleeping with anyone who wanted to take her home, and her reputation became popular enough to where she ended up getting vetted by Frankie from The Meat Market in Las Vegas on her nineteenth birthday. Frankie was a portly old man who had a perpetual sweating problem. When he sat in the front row and watched her dance, Maggie worried that she might buckle. While trying to maintain the focus on her routine, she kept getting distracted by the way the light reflected off the gaudy gold chains Frankie had a penchant for wearing. She felt like she was five again with her mother breathing down her neck. There was one point in her audition where she attempted doing an inverted helicopter spin and ended up falling ass over teakettle, further solidifying her thoughts that the audition was in vain. After her routine she tried talking to Frankie to see if she'd made the cut, but one of his bodyguards, a real meathead, intercepted and explained how Frankie didn't like interacting with his potential prospects and would have somebody get back to her shortly if he was interested. She'd all but written off The Meat Market as a doomed proposition when a week later she received a call from Miguel. He told her that she had an hour to pack her bags and get on a flight from LAX or she could kiss this opportunity goodbye. He explained that further accommodations would be provided upon her arrival and to pack lightly and keep her farewells brief and to a minimal. She did as she was told. She didn't even bother saying goodbye to anyone, not that there was anyone worth saying goodbye to. When she landed in Vegas a man was waiting for her. He was holding a cardboard sign with her name on it in his hand, which, as it turns out, happened to be his only hand. His other arm was nonexistent, as were his legs below the thigh. Yet, surprisingly, despite his limitations, or maybe perhaps because of overcompensating for them, he was built like a brick house with a full set of washboard abs, and his solitary arm was roughly the width of a tree trunk. He vaguely resembled Omar Epps, and so it was a surprise to Maggie when he identified himself as the man she'd been speaking with on the phone. After all, she'd never met a black man by the name of Miguel before. But she was soon to discover that abnormalities were the rule and not the exception when it came to The Meat Market.

Tobias discovered first-hand how strange the place could be after going down to Nevada on a whim. Clint had been the one that talked him into it, after tiring of seeing him obsess over Emily in the months following their not so amicable split. He'd persuaded Tobias to follow him down to the land of sinful decadence, and instead of bringing him to the Bunny Ranch to fuck his woes away, he'd brought him to The Meat Market to channel his inner demons. It was like falling through a rabbit hole into a weird Wonderland yanked straight from the pages of a Lewis Carroll novel. Only in this Wonderland, instead of stumbling upon a hookah-smoking caterpillar or a crazy tea enthusiast spouting riddles, he came across men and women dressed in latex and torn fishnets smoking from crack pipes and sporting ratty dreadlocks and pierced genitalia. There were meat hooks dangling from the ceiling along the central corridor for as far as the eye could see. There were men and women with body modifications in various states of suspension. He saw a man with a shaved head and a flayed tongue and horn implants hanging limply like a suicide victim from a pair of meat hooks that were pierced through the flesh near his shoulder blades. He saw women being suspended horizontally by meat hooks that penetrated their legs and arms. One was moaning and appearing to be in the throes of an intense orgasm. The doors to the left and right of the long central corridor were labeled with every imaginable fetish and vice known to man. There were rooms designated for basic garden-variety S&M near the entryway. There were rooms featuring barely legal girls dressed up in perverted Catholic school garb. The deeper you walked down the corridor the more perverse the fetishes became. There were rooms featuring trannys and rooms featuring men dressed up as women and women dressed up as men that Clint and Tobias avoided like the plague. They entered a room featuring beastiality and Tobias nearly lost his lunch, knowing that he'd never be able to look at a horse in the same way again. They visited a room featuring little people grinding on stripper poles and being tossed into pools, which seemed harmless enough, until he realized the pools were filled with blood. There was a room dubbed the Squashing Room that made Tobias squirm. In it, he saw a group of naked men and women that were roughly the size of Volkswagen Beetles. They were so huge that their genitalia was lost under the pouches of their belly fat that hung low like over-bloated waterbeds on the verge of rupturing. They took turns climbing on top of extreme chubby chasers, smothering them within their many layers of flab and musty folds. One of the joyous participants compared the experience to reliving life as a fetus. He said he spent his entire week working at an investment firm pining for the weekend so he could get back in touch with his primal roots. Under the layers of fat all senses were cut off, and if he paid them extra they would turn on a vacuum to replicate the gentle lull of the womb. His persuasions to experience pre-birth via squashing fell on deaf ears, as Tobias explained to him that he'd rather have a skinny thermometer wedged into his urethra and shattered by a hammer before suffering the indignity of suffocating under a landslide of lard. They opted to check out a room catering to burn victims and amputees instead. Unsurprisingly, it wasn't any less unsettling. Stumps were being inserted in places where they didn't belong.

Tobias and Clint were on the verge of hitting fetishism rock bottom when they decided to give one last room a try. It was the Wet Room, not to be confused with the Moist Room, which is probably best not to elaborate on. This is the room where Tobias first met Maggie. He was sitting in the front aisle next to the stage, which in most normal stripclubs would be known as Sniffer's Row, but in this decidedly abnormal freak show was aptly enough nicknamed Dripper's Row. When she came out he was drawn to her in a way that the other performers hadn't been able to evoke. There was something borderline illusionary about her that made her stand out from the other girls that he couldn't quite put his finger on at first. She was wearing what looked like a vintage wedding dress that had yellowed with age. Her bleached blonde hair was absolutely glowing beneath the harsh stage lights, transforming her into a feral wraith of sorts. She strutted across the stage in her pointy stiletto heels and squatted down in front of Clint, but her gaze was solely honed in on Tobias all the while. She gingerly lifted up her dress revealing her shaved nether regions and cesarean scars and proceeded to start urinating. It was at this special moment, not quite When Harry Met Sally, but who really gave a fuck, that Tobias realized what set her apart from the rest of her cohorts. She was absolutely un-self conscious and unrepentant about what she was doing. She exuded supreme confidence, and possessed a rebellious air that the other women were lacking. You could tell that despite her humiliating circumstance she wasn't allowing her spirit to wither. If anything, she seemed to be thriving on the dominance she held over the contemptible men that surrounded her like ants drawn to sugar. If this was Wonderland, she was certainly the walrus leading all the naive oysters to doom.

After her performance ended Maggie led Tobias to an outdoor patio where many smokers were congregating. She took a hit from a delicate glass pipe that resembled a penis and exhaled a wide plume of weed smoke. She passed it to Tobias who was more than happy to partake, despite the homo-eroticism of the pipe. Next to her, a man dressed up in a full-body latex suit with assless chaps began coughing boisterously from within a bedazzled gas mask bong that was strapped to his face. Waterfalls of tears began streaming from his eyes. A friend of the man, a scrawny little wisp of a beanpole, commented on how he looked like a futuristic anteater with a sinus infection. In response, the rest of his weed-head friends began laughing hysterically. Turns out, they had just gotten back from a trip to Amsterdam and still felt the need to emasculate one another by proving they were still the King of Cannabis Palace. But, as the saying goes, heavy is the head that bears the crown, and this was no exception. King Chronic's coughs underwent a sudden transformation as they shifted into a snarled gasp which was momentarily followed by a liquid spurting as he began to spatter the interior of his gasmask with a strange vomit that vaguely resembled the pea soup spewed up by Reagan from The Exorcist, albeit slightly chunkier and more of a milky liquified hybrid of snot.

Maggie, despite her familiarity to the grotesque, had had enough. She grabbed Tobias by the hand and led him out a side door. They lit a cigarette under the harsh glare of a street light. The alleyway was empty, aside from a curious raccoon that was scavenging for whatever passed as nourishment in a nearby dumpster. They could still hear the scatterbrained laughter coming from inside the club. It was at this point, safe from prying eyes, that Tobias offered Maggie something a little stronger than weed. She put out her smoke and was quick to accept his pipe, which was decidedly less phallic than hers. As she lit the flame below the glass bulb, shifting the stem of the pipe left and right between her thumb and pointer finger to prevent the bulb from burning the glass and wasting the meth from overexposure, Tobias explained to her his intentions of heading out to Burning Man with Clint. Truth be told, he hadn't even brought it up to Clint, but he'd heard Old Man Jones rave about his previous experiences, and he really wanted to get to know Maggie. He needed someone to replace the void left behind by Emily, and if Clint decided not to go along so be it. If he could get Maggie to come along he didn't really give a flying fuck what Clint decided to do. He had barely started elaborating on the debauchery of Burning Man when a tall bald man with bulging muscles opened the door. "Back inside," he intoned. "If Frankie knew I let you come out here unsupervised, and with another man at that, my balls would be mailed back to my family in a knapsack, and you know that."

Maggie didn't even try to protest, which caught Tobias by surprise. In fact, her non-reaction made it perfectly clear that she was used to being led along like a dog on a short leash. Tobias had expected her to go off like a nuclear reactor. He'd seen the flames burning in her eyes onstage. Her sudden meekness made him reevaluate his intuitions, and for the first time in a long time, even question if perhaps he'd been hitting the pipe a bit too much as of late. But Emily was lost in the rearview mirror with no signs of ever returning, and his childhood farm had also gone belly up. After all, his mother could no longer function on her own anymore after having a stroke that left her looking like a zombie extra straight from the set of The Walking Dead, let alone maintain her job of caring for another as a PCA. And as for his father… well, fuck that worthless waste of sperm and egg. If he ever saw that shitbag again he'd kick his teeth so far down his throat he could start chewing with his asshole.

"Hey, what are you doing back here?"

Tobias jumps and twists to see Maggie standing beside him, a quizzical expression on her face. The *here* she is referring to is the back hallway that runs along the stairwell leading upstairs. Tobias feels like a kid caught with his hands in the cookie jar, or a homophobic republican caught with a cock between his lips.

"Jesus Christ woman," he replies. "When did you suddenly learn to get so sneaky?"

As if reading where the residue of his thoughts had been Maggie says: "Being sneaky was a way of life navigating The Meat Market with Frankie around. He was bi-polar and always liable to freak out over something that never amounted to much. He had all us girls walking on eggshells, paranoid a landmine was around the next corner. He was our judge, jury, and executioner, and best believe you-me he wasn't afraid to flaunt the power he held over us. Now back to my question, what are you dinking around with back here?"

"There's a damn draft that's been kicking up a fuss and driving me crazy," Tobias says. He gestures vaguely behind him at the haphazard stack of wooden planks that are strewn against the wall like a Jenga tower on the verge of collapse.

"You never cared one way or the other about drafts before," Maggie replies. "I guess I started learning to be so sneaky at the same time you started giving a damn about the upkeep of this haunted house. How did your trip down to the cities go? Did you have any luck?"

Tobias grins a classic fox in the henhouse smile. It melts at least a decade off his age. "I had a bit of luck," he concedes, after pausing to rearrange the planks against the wall in a fashion that apparently served as a better barricade against the pesky winds of winter. "I made some money from the collection plate. Enough money to buy some liquid courage and a pack of coffin nails, anyway, but not a whole hell of a lot extra."

"So in other words, the trip was a bust." It's supposed to be a rhetorical question, but comes out sounding more like a statement. He can see the resignation in her eyes as something she's grown used to. It's the same look children make after being disillusioned with the truth that the only fat guy in their neighborhood entering their house isn't coming down the chimney to bare gifts, and is only likely to grow jolly after forcing his hand down their pants.

"Jesus, Tobi, I needed something to keep me going. I'm burning out on life. My flame is flickering. I don't have the motivation to make it through the day on my own. You know I fade without my shit."

"Sorry Magpie," Tobias says. "I wish I had better news for you, but I don't. I've got a little bit of weed that I stashed away for a rainy day. It's in my mom's old music box. You know, the one with the dancing ballerina? It's probably stale as day old dog shit, but any port in a storm, I suppose."

Once Maggie leaves the room, Tobias rearranges the loot behind the partition. His hands are trembling with excitement. He can hear the hollow thud of Maggie's clogs as she heads upstairs. Once he is certain that she's far enough out of proximity and the coast is clear, he takes the glass pipe he's been coveting out of his pocket and enjoys a deep drag. The smoke is bitter and strangely silky. It tastes of floor stripper and battery acid, and gives him the familiar floaty feeling in the head that keeps him crawling back. All of his burdens leave him behind as he rises beyond and above everything with the freedom of a hot air balloon freshly untethered, It's truly a poor man's paradise; poor in spirit, poor in body, poor in soul: and he appreciates every second he's allowed a reprieve from the cell he's been cursed to inhabit.

By the time Maggie has returned, his pipe is once again safely stowed away in his pocket and he feels pins and needle accompanied by a trembling chill that traverses up and down his arms and legs like an army of fire ants disoriented and treading in circles. All in all it's a pleasant sting.

"You must think I'm a complete idiot," Maggie says upon meeting Tobias at the base of the stairwell. She brandishes the bag of weed like it's a soiled diaper or used tampon that's been left out in the sun for a week to clot and congeal. "You send me upstairs for this shwag that has more seeds and stems in it then can be found in a greenhouse, and think I won't notice you've been holding out on me when I get back? You of all people should know better than that. I've got the nose of a bloodhound, Tobi. In my past life I was probably a drug sniffing dog. Where did you put the shards? It reeks like a fucking meth lab down here."

"Alright, guilty as charged. I'm not completely dry. I was just-"

"Holding out on me," she interrupts. "Being a greedy prick and holding out on me, after all the things I do for you."

"If by things you're referring to driving me crazy, you've been most charitable. Every time I've let you smoke lately, you've been acting nuttier than a squirrel's shit, and I'm tired of it. Tired of dealing with your lunacy and delusions."

"That's not fair," Maggie interjects. "If you'd been through half the things I've been through you'd be twice as unstable. Not everybody has had the luxury of living under one roof for most of their lives. You complain about your father, but at least you've had a male influence in your life."

"If by influence, you mean being completely neglected to the point of doing anything for attention, and savoring the feel of a belt being slapped against my ass because it's at least some form of being noticed, then yes, I've had wonderful influence over the years. My dad was too busy obsessing over and stalking my mom to care about anything else. She couldn't leave her house without him watching the clock and making sure the mileage hadn't gone over on the car. We were prisoners living on this farm. That's why I empathized with you when we met at Frankie's. I understood what it meant to be confined. My dad was just a two-bit con man and a coward to boot. You've got a lot of nerve acting all high and mighty like your suffering has been so much greater than mine. As if it's a fucking misery competition and you're fighting for your place in the top ten in the charts of pain. You don't have a monopoly on sorrow. Get over yourself."

"Fuck you, Tobias. Fuck you." Maggie's eyes have suddenly transformed into molten lava and her tone is jagged glass. "It's not about milking it for all it's worth. It's just about getting a little bit of sympathy every now and then. It would just be nice to know that you give a flying fuck about me beyond getting a side of pussy every now and then, when you can even get it up."

"C'mon now, Magpie. You know it ain't all like that. Sometimes you just push me to my breaking point and I snap. It's only natural. Every action has an equal reaction. You of all people should know that."

"I don't know about anything in this world, much less about that," Maggie says. Her eyes are cooling, and the jagged edges of her tone smoothing out, but Tobias knows better than to press his luck. "Maybe if there were life on Mars it would have rules that apply and make sense, but so far as I know Life on Mars is just a David Bowie song, and justice is equally fictional."

"How about a peace offering?" Tobias suggests, now that she is starting to neutralize. He holds the pipe up to Maggie, a dusty shaft of sunlight piercing it and scattering prisms that dance and twist upon her bleached hair like psychedelic suicide victims jitterbugging from fiber optic ropes.

"I'll let it slide for now," Maggie says. "But don't try that shit again. I never hold out on you, so don't try flipping the script on me."

Tobias' gaze becomes evasive, so Maggie leans in like a prosecutor trying to instill guilt in a wavering defendant. "Is there anything else you're trying to hold out on me? Speak now or forever hold your peace."

Tobias changes the topic as Maggie accepts the cylindrical glass olive branch of sorts, making a mental note to relocate his hidden stash before Maggie really discovered the extent of his success this afternoon. If that were to occur, she might be liable to hightail it out of this town and his life for good, and if anyone is going to be instigating the exodus he has every intention of being the one who holds the reins. He's had his share of being walked out on and forgotten in his greatest moments of need. Never will he allow himself the weakness of caring too much again- of growing pale in someone's shade that only cares about stealing and hoarding the sunshine for themselves.

After Maggie has satiated her chemical desire, Tobias further solidifies himself in her good graces by offering her the Stephen King novel he'd hawked earlier, along with the newspaper article chronicling the highlights (or should it be considered lowlights considering the circumstances?) of the Chameleon's illustrious career.

Her reaction to the reading material is decidedly better than her reaction to the ancient bag of weed. She jumps into Tobias' arms like a pet that underestimates its size. "Eww," she gushes. "Now I can get my daily dose of drama without having to visit the latest murder scene over North."

"That you can," Tobias agrees.

Maggie glances at the newspaper headlines and her eyes become anime-sized. "The Chameleon is up to his old tricks it would seem," she observes, hmmphing in a dismissive some-things-will-never-change kinda way. "I can't believe he's still at it. How long has it been? Christ, it must be pushing three decades. I remember hearing stories about him in Culver City when I was a girl. His story went big time national."

"Why do you keep assuming the Chameleon is a *he*?" Tobias questions. "It could just as easily be a woman. They have no evidence to prove either way."

To which Maggie chimes: "Oh, give me a break, Tobias. There's no way it's a woman. Women are more passive when they kill. They're more likely to kill by smothering or poisoning or using pills. Don't you remember Annie Wilkes?"

Tobias laughs in a carefree way he wouldn't be able to manage if it weren't for the drugs. "Annie Wilkes is fictional. And if my memory serves correctly there was a hobbling scene in that movie that didn't seem particularly passive by female standards. And you're assuming that the Chameleon is a killer. We don't know that. All we know is the Chameleon takes people in the neighborhood and they're never seen again. The Chameleon doesn't discriminate between race or age or sex. The people just vanish and aren't heard from again, but we don't know that murder is what happens to them. You're just assuming, and as the age old saying goes, when you assume you make an ass out of both you and me."

"Maybe you can remember your movies alright, but you can't remember news stories for shit. It's sad it takes a Cali girl to remind you of what was going on in your own backwoods. Don't you remember that Berryhill girl? I can't remember her first name, but it said in the papers there was a struggle that went down. She was out doing her paper route. Do you remember? Her brother came home from football practice and was worried because she hadn't made it back and she was always punctual. He retraced her newspaper route and found her bike lying on its side at the end of their block. There was a pool of blood left at the scene and his calling card, but no witnesses. The authorities said it was unlikely she had survived considering all the blood left behind. And she wasn't the only missing person that left a trail of blood behind in her wake. Whoever the sadistic fuck involved in all the disappearances is, there's no chance it's a woman. Some serious violence was involved, and most women are about as harmless as wingless gnats."

To which Tobias can't resist but add: "With similar brain sizes, too."

Maggie is leaning in to punch Tobias in the arm for his quip, when her mouth drops open in shock. "Christ," she says. "Your breath smells like it's hundred proof. Please tell me you weren't driving back from the cities drunk again."

Tobias' response does little to put her mind at ease: "I can handle my liquor, Magpie. I don't need you lecturing me like I'm a goddamn child right now. Can't we go five minutes without griping about something stupid?"

"You're right. We *are* talking about something stupid. Drunk driving is something I'd consider *incredibly* stupid. You've had to take classes because of this shit. Do you really miss A.A. that badly? If you get busted again they'll throw the fucking book at you!"

"They aren't going to catch me again! It's been years since I last had an issue. I'm more alert to my environment now than I was back then. I've learned from my mistakes."

Maggie shakes her head adamantly in disagreement. "If you'd really learned your lesson you wouldn't be playing these games. It's only by a complete fluke that you haven't been involved in an accident or killed someone yet. But luck only lasts so long before it runs out. It's a fair weather friend. You'd do best to keep that in mind."

Maggie stomps out of the room in a huff. Tobias has to fight off an urge to chase her down and tackle her to the ground. Emily used to push him to the very same limits. She'd go out of her way to find something to complain about, and was never satisfied with any of his attempts to pacify. He remembered one Valentine's Day when he forgot to bring her flowers, and the way she'd acted like he'd fucked her best friend Becca who was an incredible slut. So when the next Valentine's Day rolled around he'd been careful not to repeat the same mistake again. He'd gone out of his way to bring her not only a dozen red roses, but also a box of her favorite truffles. Instead of gratitude, or a well-deserved blowjob, she'd instead reacted exactly the same way as the previous year and reamed him a new asshole, complaining about how he shouldn't have wasted so much money on superficial nonsense when they were so tight on funds, and besides, could he get any more *cliche*? Chocolates and roses? *Really?* Didn't he have even an *ounce* of creativity? Becca's boyfriend had taken her out to Minnehaha Falls for ice skating and they'd shared hot chocolate spiked with Peppermint Schnapps. Becca's boyfriend had also taken her to an amazing Jeremy Messersmith concert at Coffman Memorial Union on the East Bank and out for pizza at Mesa's afterword. Yadda, yadda, yadda… He'd gotten so sick of dealing with her perpetual need to complain that he did the only thing that seemed halfway reasonable after spending a night on the couch and downing a case of Milwaukee's Best Ice: he invited Becca over while Emily was at work and he *did* fuck her. And not only that, he *did* get his well-deserved blowjob as well. In fact, her slut friend was twice as good at giving sloppy head as Emily was on even her best day. Of course, when Becca felt guilty and had a change of heart and Emily found out all the sordid details, Tobias had feigned regret and come up with a litany of excuses for his bad behavior, as cheaters always will, but his *real* regrets only extended so far as having been caught and dealing with her subsequent mood swings and paranoid badgering.

    A knock at the door interrupts his reverie. It is loud and authoritative: not the usual timid rappings of the local Jehovah's Witnesses that periodically stop by to save their souls and earn brownie points for paradise. Tobias chooses to ignore it. One of the perks of living relatively off the grid is not having to deal with any of the typical daily trappings that normally befall the domesticated. Not having to worry about his yard falling to waste, or the siding and windows requiring updating is one of many blessings. Not having to worry about annoying visitors showing up unexpectedly and overstaying their welcome is another gift.

The knocking continues, and Tobias has to choke back the anger that is rising like bile in the back of his throat. Despite the fact that the knocks aren't timid, he's certain it must be the annoying Jehovah's Witnesses anyway. They'd left a Watch Tower pamphlet by the door a few weeks earlier talking about God's Kingdom and the 144,000 devout followers of Christ that would make it through the gates and bask in the paradise of God's glory, while everyone else blipped out into nothingness. So when the knocking is repeated yet again, he's thankful that he doesn't have to answer.

Except, whoever is knocking at the door is being ruthless and relentless, and eventually their persistence pays off in spades. Tobias crosses the entryway in five long strides and throws the door open with enough force to knock it aslant from its hinges, his voice echoing with the force of Cecil B. Demille parodying a wrathful God: *"What in the flying fuck is wrong with y..."*

He cuts off in mid sentence upon noticing who it is at his stoop. His mouth drops open in astonishment.

"Now is that any way to speak to an old friend?" asks the wiry man standing before him. Tobias hasn't seen him in at least four years, so it takes a second for his mind to put the pieces together and register who he is. It doesn't help that the man has lost at least twenty pounds and is covered in the type of sores that come from years of dedicated drug-addled addiction and despondency.

"Jesus Christ," Tobias intones, as the man steps forward. "Vance, *is that really you?*"

Part 3

The Calm Before the Storm

27

Despite the fact that Maggie Singer didn't know the man who'd been knocking at her door, instinctively she didn't like him. And she had plenty of reasons not to. Her first impression, the one that had caused her to do a double-take, was that he was Tony Oscar, and Tony was not the type of guy one wanted to be associated with. Not the type by a long shot.

Tony had been one in a long string of men at Sony Studios her mother had briefly dated. He'd been the first to fill her head full of false promises with his slick silver tongue and cinnamon lips, but he certainly wouldn't be the last. He'd wooed her with his impressive luxury vehicles, taking her to the fanciest clubs and exclusive parties. He'd impressed her with his knowledge of films and music and literature, and taken her out to ten course meals that would've cost her entire paycheck if she'd been the one fronting the bill. In fact, he'd been the one to introduce her to her lifelong passion for squid ink caviar with crab salad, and for that she would forever be grateful, if for little else.

Tony had lived in a lavish bachelor pad on the Hollywood Hills. He'd attained the place with help from his father who was a bigwig at Sony and had helped him get the position as a talent scout. Tony liked to brag about how his Spanish villa had more bathrooms than bedrooms, and how that was a telltale sign of success in tinseltown. Surprisingly, it didn't seem to bother him that he'd gotten his big break by standing on daddy's coattails, and it didn't bother Madeline either because nothing was going to dispel her illusions that she was on a fast track toward achieving that ever-elusive whore known as fame, and Tony would be her meal ticket as well. In Hollywood, she realized, it wasn't what you knew so much as *who* you knew, and her social circles were expanding admirably.

Tony helped Madeline get a few bit parts in B-grade movies that would've won Razzies had the awards been around at the time. Most of these parts didn't require dialogue. Usually she just stood in the background at pool parties or at posh gatherings with a drink in her hand while pretending to carry on titillating conversation with some random hunky extra, as the higher profile actors messed up their real lines forcing everyone to do endless retakes. The best part he'd provided her during their courtship, her only real claim to fame worth mentioning, had been a role in an obscure Woody Allen movie where she'd played a waitress at a cafe in Spain. In the movie the main protagonist orders a beer from her, while his significant other debates ordering Anis del Toro. She goes to the table three times throughout the scene, always at the most socially awkward moments, while the couple bicker and speak in hushed tones. The male wants the female to board a train and do a favor for him. The female focuses on the landscape, rarely making eye contact as he continues his propositions. Her intentions are unclear. The scene clearly pays homage to Hemingway's short story *Hills Like White Elephants*. It was this bit part, one of her few involving dialogue, that filled Madeline with delusions of grandeur. She'd go to cocktail parties and brag about how Woody Allen had such dreamy eyes that the cameras gave no justice to. She'd attempt to bedazzle bored trophy wives with made-up tales of encounters with A-list celebrities that involved flirtation which she'd modestly evade, ever protective of her virginity. Her favorite story involved Richard Burton at the Chateau Marmont. He'd supposedly seen her having a martini at the swanky bar in her favorite slinky red dress and had pulled her aside, asking her how much it would take to sway her into escorting him back to his hotel room for a "gentleman's evening" alone with him. She'd politely declined, explaining how Tony was waiting for her back at their garden cottage. Richard had been indignant at being turned down, apparently being unaccustomed to the experience, and had told her that the least she could do is provide the common courtesy of being discreet about his proposition considering she wasn't going to follow through with it. He'd left her with a vague veil of a threat that she'd be blacklisted if she didn't comply with his request. "And he'd been married to Elizabeth Taylor at the time," she'd scoffed, rolling her eyes in a *can-you-believe-the-nerve* type of way. "For the *second* time!"

But her moments of happiness with Tony were to be ill-lived, as so many moments in life tend to be. He developed a fondness for nose candy, and it didn't take long before his habits escalated to the point where he snorted everything of value away through his nostrils, including her infatuation with him. As his morals disintegrated in proportion to the increase in his habits, Madeline started growing desperate. She knew he was seeing other women behind her back, and she'd been willing to turn a blind eye for the greater good of the future they'd have together, but when she walked in on him in a bathroom to the sight of another man going down on him while he sat on the upper deck of a toilet tank with his pants pulled down around his ankles she was all but emotionally spent. Unfortunately, it was at this moment, at the point when she was most ready to leave and move on, that Madeline, in the immortal words of Sylvia Plath, discovered she had eaten a bag of green apples and boarded the train there's no getting off of. She'd become pregnant. And this man, the one whose apples of sin and temptation she'd succumbed to, was no longer interested in being around. She tried tethering herself to someone else's ship, but no one was willing to stay anchored for very long, and once Maggie came into the world, in the spring of 1977, after a complicated birth that lasted over twelve hours and required cesarean section, her dreams were all but vanquished. She'd put on an ungodly amount of weight during the pregnancy, and the marks left behind from the surgery did little to encourage potential suitors to stop by her port for a visit and hopefully stick around. She'd gone back home with her tail tucked between her legs, humbled and embittered and forgotten in all the ways that mattered. And it was all because of this man she'd allowed into her life, this dope-head Tony Oscar who'd brought her to heights she'd never fathomed only to plummet her to lowly depths where only the snakes and dust were left for company, that she'd turned Maggie into an experiment to recapture dreams that never brought any satisfaction.

Sometimes people don't grow up because of their parents, but in spite of them, and as Maggie hears Tobias talking to this man that reminds her of Tony's doppelganger as he leads him across the threshold into the living room, she can't help but feel a little leary.

"You owe me a new door," Tobias tells him grudgingly.

It's then that the wiry man notices Maggie and extends his hand. "Nice to meet you," he says, but his eyes are shifty and salutations seem like the last thing on his mind. "I'm Vance," he explains with the same level of detachment that his eyes suggest.

"I'm Maggie," Maggie says. She gestures around the room with a broad sweep of her arms. "I'd offer you to make yourself at home and have a seat, but as you can see we're a little shy in the furniture department at the moment, and anyway, I'm afraid the mattress is off limits. I have to know a guy at least five minutes before I let him take me to bed. It's just basic feminine mating etiquette,"

Vance looks taken aback, like he's not quite sure how he should respond.

"It's all good," Tobias replies. "I have something you'll like even better. Besides, you don't want her goods. They'll rot your cock off. Follow me."

He leads Vance into the kitchen and motions toward an icebox sitting in the corner on the counter. Vance opens the lid and peers inside. The icebox is primarily filled with water. A scattering of half-dissolved ice cubes are floating on the surface in a futile battle against time. Below the surface a package of congealing baloney is drifting amongst a random assortment of condiments which have clearly been neglected in favor of Tobias' main love, which is, of course, a case of Milwaukee's Best Ice. They crack open a can each, and Tobias asks Vance the pertinent question that's been eating at him: "Not that I'm not happy to see you, but what brings you up to the sticks after so long? Last time I saw you, you were still down in the cities pal-ing around with Trev. Didn't you guys go down to Burning Man with Old Man Jones and Clint last year?"

Vance shakes his head. "I've never been there before. Clint kept talking about going, but it never amounted to anything. You know how Clint is, a whole lot of talk with very little follow-through. He always has some crackpot idea or flavor-of-the-week dream that he barely begins and instantly grows bored of. He never finishes anything he starts. I don't think he has the discipline. Either that, or he's just horribly ADHD."

"Hey, everybody has a label now days," Tobias says, taking a big swig. "You gotta keep the pharmaceutical companies in business after all. Me personally, I'd rather medicate myself with this," he indicates, swinging the can in Vance's general direction. "And it doesn't even require a copay."

"Speaking of medicating," Vance says, with a glimmer in his eyes that wasn't there before he started drinking.. "I have to tell you about this black girl I met a few months ago. She was at this house party off of Blaisdell and you'll never believe what she told me."

"Judging by the look on your face, I can only imagine," Tobias replies. "Do I even want to know?"

"She was telling me about her kids. She said she has a daughter named Allegra. Can you *believe* that? Allegra! Like the fuckin allergy medication. And that's not even the real kicker. She has a son she calls Suda. Care to wager what that's short for?"

"You've gotta be kidding me."

"I shit you not. Her son's name is Sudafed. The bitch is working on opening her own pharmacy!"

"Damn." Tobias shakes his head in bemusement.

"That's nothing," says Maggie, entering the room. "I once knew a girl who named her daughter Secret. And she was telling me she wasn't quite sure how to tell her man that Secret might not be his. And the girl's name was Victoria! Like, Victoria's Secret!"

"I call bullshit," Tobias responds.

"You can call bullshit all you want," Maggie says. "But that doesn't make it any less true."

Vance is drawn back to the cooler like it holds gravitational force over him. He grabs a second can of Milwaukee's Best and downs it in six monstrous gulps. His hands are trembling as he motions to Tobias, and it's clear that his jovial mood is shifting.

"Not to be a prick or anything," he says to Tobias, "but do you mind if we go outside for a moment and catch up? Just the two of us? I have something important I need to ask you, but I need some privacy."

Maggie waves a hand dismissively. "Oh, you boys and your need for secrecy. Afraid to say something in front of a lady, cause you think we're all just delicate flowers just waiting to wilt. I know how this goes." She walks out of the room and drops down on the mattress. She wraps the quilt around her until she's comfortably cocooned and starts reading *Full Dark, No*

Stars as Tobias follows Vance outside. They circle around to the backyard and stand in the shadows of a silo, looking out at the clotted humps of soil and brittle corn stalks that have faded and gone to waste. The sun is setting in the background, tinting everything golden and somber with its silken glow. They sit in a contemplative silence that lasts long enough for Tobias to smoke a full cigarette before Vance speaks: "It feels strange standing here again. I've forgotten how open everything can be. It makes me feel dizzy and small. And this sunset... Man, we don't get sunsets like this down in the cities. You can actually feel the weight of the sky."

"You can definitely feel the weight," Tobias agrees, lighting up another cigarette. "Speaking of which, what's been weighing on you, because judging from the look on your face you're obviously not just talking about the sky."

Vance remains silent, just staring out into the field. It's as if he hasn't heard a word Tobias has spoken. Something else is absorbing his attention. After a minute of silence he continues talking, his train of thoughts continuing where they left off without missing a beat: "Have you ever noticed how similar life is to the changing of the day and the seasons? In the springtime a new day dawns, and the days are longer and filled with hope. But the season continues rolling along like a wheel, waiting for nothing, and ready to crush whatever stands in its way. The days become shorter as the end of the season approaches. The blandness of life, the blueness of the sky, changes as the evening approaches the dusk. The endless light of spring, the long days of youth, speed faster towards darkness, and we can only imagine what lies on the other side of the shadows as the transformation comes to a close."

Tobias has been listening so intently to Vance's rhapsody about life and death that his cigarette has become nothing more than a teetering cylinder of ash. If he'd been asked a week earlier, hell, even ten minutes prior, whether Vance had the capacity or even presence of mind to delve into the metaphorical realm, he would've undoubtedly said there wasn't a snowball's chance in hell. Vance had always been a hot head debater whose words were composed of gold, and only a glutton for punishment would try to convince him otherwise. He was good for an entertaining fistfight, but not known for wasting effort on deeper contemplation. Yet, here he stood in the flesh, this ludicrous Mike Tyson throwing his towel in the ring, only to reappear dressed as a pageboy attempting soliloquies like some half-assed Shakespeare. It was almost too much for the mind to process. Obviously something terrible had happened to bring him to this tipping point, and clearly this random appearance had little to do with nostalgic pining or sentimental leanings. Something larger was at play.

Vance turns toward Tobias and his cheeks have become the shade of a cherry tomato. He's never been able to hide his inebriation well. Even as a teenager he'd always had to carry around a bottle of Visine with him because his eyes betrayed what was going on beneath the surface. "I have to tell you something important. I need you to promise me that you'll follow through with what I'm going to ask."

Tobias nods his head complacently. "Whatever you need, man. You know I've got your back. I always have and always will. Shit, we've known each other since cradle school"

"Some bad business has come my way," Vance begins. He hesitates, before amending his statement. "*I've gotten myself* mixed in with some bad business, I mean."

"What kind of business?"

"The specifics don't really matter. You'll hear all the details soon enough. I just want you to know that I own up to my end of everything. God, it still feels like a dream that happened to someone else. I can't believe it's real."

"Jesus, Vance, what the fuck have you gotten yourself involved in?"

"I let my desperation get the best of me and made a stupid choice that can't be undone. But unfortunately, that's not why I'm here. You see, it's not just about me."

Tobias knew what Vance was going to say before he even said it. "Something happened to Trevor. That's why he's not here with you right now."

Vance's silence spoke louder than words.

"Is Trevor going to be alright?"

Once again, Vance's lack of response tells Tobias all he needs to know. The oppressive silence stretched like taffy, and Tobias is grateful when a Ford Explorer comes trundling down the road. It has a spider-webbed windshield and the noise erupting from its damaged muffler is deafening, but not nearly as loud as what came before it. The driver behind the wheel, who looks of Native descent, is preoccupied with his phone and oblivious to the road. The Explorer is weaving as it approaches, getting perilously close to the ditch before the driver notices and over-corrects. Vance, however, doesn't notice the obliviousness of the driver, and instinctively takes two steps backward, his eyes darting nervously in the direction of the vehicle, until he is swallowed by the shadows of the silo, and it's then that Tobias realizes just how dire the situation is.

"You don't want to be seen," he exclaims incredulously, his tone making it clear there's no room for debate. "People are looking for you."

Instead of trying to deny it, Vance's eyes suddenly well up with tears.

Tobias finds this sudden display of emotion off-putting. It reminds him of the first time he ever walked in on his father in a moment of despair. Hank had been crouched over the kitchen table with his head cradled in his arms amid a scattering of poker chips and crushed beer cans, big gulping sobs racking his frame. The awkwardness and intimacy of his tears had bordered on the obscene; even worse than the time he came home early from a hunting expedition with Clint to bust Hank balls deep in his mother. What had alarmed Tobias the most, and made this worse, was the way Hank had never even hinted at the possibility of any inner vulnerability. If anything, he'd always discouraged it in his kids. He pretty much let Tobias do whatever he felt like doing, and rationed out his communication like it was the last flask of water after struggling through years of drought. Hank had always been gruff, abrupt, distracted. Always seeming like he was in the wrong place at the wrong time with no idea how he'd arrived there, like a traveller with Alzheimer's. He spent more time fading out in front of the television watching sports recaps then he did on either Tobias or his younger sister Krissi. Hell, he probably spent more time watching the commercials between quarters and innings, let alone the games themselves. On the rare occasions when he gifted them with attention, it was usually allotted just to point out how disappointed he was at something stupid they'd done. He'd bark commands on ways they should alter their behavior from the couch like a general prepping for doomsday, but would never follow through with any discipline. Tough love was the only type of love he expressed, and whenever they accomplished anything that a normal parent would be proud of, like the time Krissi brought home a small glazed bowl she made in pottery class that she decorated with an underwater theme feauturing dolphins frollicking with seahorses, he would always find some reason to discredit them and find fault. ("What am I supposed to do with this? The seahorses look like fetuses, and it's all girly pink. I don't want my friends to come over and think I'm a faggot. You're just like your mother, always trying to find some way to undermine me.")

Hank's delusions of being undermined knew no limits. It was a regular occurrence in the Atwood residence to be affronted for doing next to nothing. Tobias remembers being yelled at one time for leaving an almost empty glass of water on the counter instead of putting it in the sink where it belonged, ("You trying to rub it in my face that we can't afford milk or juice like the other little spoiled shits at your school? Well, guess what? Sometimes life isn't fair. Deal with it! I don't see you contributing anything of value to this place. Don's boy is out mowing lawns from dusk til dawn for his old man. Feel free to get a job of your own, unless you're too scared of breaking your purty little nails and getting dirt on your hands like a real man!") or the time when Krissi left her backpack out in the hallway shortly after starting college at St. Cloud University. ("Well, don't you think you're something special, working on your fancy degree. You must just love leaving your backpack in the hall to show off. Think you're better than the rest of us, young lady? Well, I've got a newsflash for you, little miss shit-don't-stink. I know lots of people who've gotten degrees, and they're nothing but educated idiots at best. A piece of paper don't make you any better than me. I made it all the way through tenth grade without ever having to read a book, and I know a thing or two about an honest day's labor. You should try it yourself. You might learn something of value that your silly books can't teach.") He'd spit the word *books* out like it was something distasteful and decadent that left a bad taste in his mouth.

And he treated their mother, Patricia, just as poorly. It was like that line in the Miranda Rights: anything she said could and would be held against her. Patricia had learned the hard way that it was best to just leave well enough alone. She kept her communication with him to a minimum, following the same example he set with the kids. She knew better than anyone the way he'd manipulate and twist words around to use them against her. They rarely spent time together in the same room unless it was absolutely unavoidable. He'd been hard to handle to begin with, but ever since he lost his 9-5 at the manufacturing plant he'd worked at for the past three years, he'd become all but unbearable. She preferred him fading away on the couch with a beer as opposed to having to deal with his random pissing and moaning fits. That went the same for Tobias and Krissi. It was easier watching him sulk and wallow and being a petty asshole then it was to suddenly have to humanize him and be forced to deal with the messy conflicting emotion of pity.

    That's partly why walking in on him that sunny afternoon many years earlier had filled Tobias with such unease and disgust. He'd had it hammered home to him time and time again the importance of never letting his weaknesses show, and seeing Hank in the throes of a full-on meltdown had felt like a betrayal that was unforgivably hypocritical. Tobias didn't have room in his heart to waste on this excessive softness. His heart had hardened years ago to Hank, and he'd rather Hank just stay the same old reliable asshole he'd always known and loathed. It was easier that way, as hate often is. Finding compassion was far trickier.

    Vance wipes the trickle of tears that look like liquid diamonds from his cheeks and takes a big shuddering gulp of air. "You know what's funny?" he says, trying to regain his composure. "When I was a teenager I thought I knew everything, which is kinda par for the course. I remember one summer when we went to a family reunion up near Duluth. My parents rented a fancy cabin off of Lake Fiona, where the reunion was set to take place, and we stayed there over the big Memorial Day weekend. I was seventeen and lanky. A toothpick with arms and legs. I guess some things never change. My figure certainly hasn't. I guess that's one of the perks of finding the crystal fountain of youth," Vance says, chuckling. "That was the summer I was dating Sasha. God, how I worshipped the ground that girl walked on. I pestered my parents into letting her and Trevor come along with us for the trip, and man did that take some work. I wish I could say it ended up being worth it, but you know how wishing goes. On the day of the reunion I met up at the pavilion down by the park around noon where everyone was starting to grill hamburgers and brats. The larger branches of the family were dominating all the planning. They set up the different activities for the day: bocce ball, croquet, ladder golf, bean bag toss, the potato sack race; all the happy horseshit you could imagine. I left with Trevor and Sasha on a nature hike around the lake. We had a flask filled with vodka that Trevor had pilfered off Old Man Jones. There were lots of dragonflies and wasps I had to protect Sasha from. You see, she had allergies, but that's beside the point. We walked along a path that led around the lake until we came across a cemetery. The newer plots of the cemetery were decorated with wreaths and flags and vibrant bouquets of chrysanthemums and orchids. It was beautiful under that perfect sunny baby blue sky. Crazy as it sounds, it seemed more lively there than back at the pavilion with my family. I remember feeling really insecure because Sasha had been giving me the cold shoulder for the past few weeks, and the day at the reunion was no exception. As we walked through the newer section of the cemetery she kept trying to shrug my arm off when I'd attempt putting it around her, slapping at it like it was annoying insect she couldn't stand. I asked her what was wrong, and she said exactly what I was afraid she'd say. She told me that she really didn't think things were working out between us and thought we should take a break. Man, was that talk a blow to the dreams I'd built inside my head. You see, I'd been obsessed with her for years. The day she agreed to date me I felt like my life finally had meaning. I felt validated, because if she could find something special in me in the same way that I did for her, then surely I had a place in life that mattered. Her denial of me cut to the bone. I walked away, with my thoughts weighing down on me like the rock-filled pockets of a man jumping into an icy river. I needed some time alone to absorb what she'd told me. I entered the older section of the cemetery where the plots had fallen into neglect and rested against a headstone that had crumbled away until the lettering on it was no longer legible. There were no chrysanthemums, no orchids, no flags. Time had swallowed everything in this barren corner lot, and I felt that it suited me perfectly, because without Sasha in my life everything would be as aimless as a letter without a postmark, and having the hungry Earth open up beneath me would be a blessing I'd gladly take, because I didn't want a life without her in it. I didn't want a house or my own family or anything normal. And I didn't want to settle for anything less than normal. You know how dramatic things can be as a teenager. The littlest things can mean life and death." Vance paused, as if debating whether he was revealing too much. Just when Tobias figured the conversation was finish, Vance continued, with his eyes glued to the horizon: "Anyway, I finished off that flask of vodka under the powder blue sky and thought about how easy it would be to slip into death. I went back to the family reunion and tried to focus on the fun of all the activities taking place, but all I could think about was that forgotten corner of the cemetery where the visitors no longer existed. I looked at my immediate and extended family, and thought about how each dynasty would eventually amount to crumbled monuments, nameless and forgotten. I think that was the day I fully lost God. You see, God mattered more to me before I was eaten by grief. It's easier to believe in meaning when everything is works and makes sense. I mean, especially if you have kids and grandkids. You have to believe in something important, because otherwise you'll be left with the guilt of bringing lives into a world that doesn't hold any meaning or truth. The ego needs something to cling to so we won't feel adrift in an ocean without any anchor or port to come home to. Otherwise, we'd have to accept that the waves striking us down hold a raw power that exists without purpose or meaning."

Tobias doesn't know how to respond, so he just asks the obvious: "So, whatever ended up happening with Sasha?"

Vance grins mirthlessly. "Oh, she left me for Jerome. Go figure she ended up being a fuckin nigger lover. But that's alright, because I found my own lover in drugs. That was half a lifetime ago, and look at me now. You know how sometimes you can go to a movie and it's absolute shit? You sit through the first half and leave because you know the other half won't be getting any better. Well, that's my fucking life. The only constant I've ever had worth mentioning was Trevor, and look how that turned out."

Tobias looks into Vance's eyes and tries finding the compassion he's purposely been evading for years. "When did Trevor die?" he asks. He tries being understanding, just to spite his dad, but comes across unintentionally gruff and abrupt, due to his voice being about as soothing as a payload of gravel and broken glass being crushed in a compactor. Smoking endless cartons of Camels and gargling enough whiskey to fill a swimming pool will have that effect.

"It happened today," Vance responds. "And it's my fault. Trevor didn't want to get involved with my plans, but I kept pushing him and pushing him until he caved. If it hadn't been for me trying to feed my selfish needs he would still be alive. I need you to talk to Old Man Jones for me. I need you to let him know how sorry I am about the way things played out. He was like a second father to me."

"Can't you just tell him yourself?"

"I would if I could," Vance says. "But I'm gonna have to lay low for awhile. I can't have anything to do with the Twin Cities until I'm under the radar. I'm heading out to Winnipeg. I have a few friends there that will take me in. Can I trust you to talk to Blaze for me next time you see him?"

Tobias confirms with a subtle nod. "You've got my word, man. But you've gotta promise me something also. Don't let his death eat at you. You can't blame yourself for something that was beyond your control. Life's too short to live in regret. Whether you were pestering him or not doesn't matter. At the end of the day he's a grown ass man, and it was his decision to go along with you."

Tobias lights another cigarette, noticing to his chagrin that his pack is almost depleted. His bladder, on the other hand, is fully alive and kicking. He finishes his cigarette and excuses himself, stepping out from the shadows of the silo. He makes his way across the back lawn, which has been overrun by renegade crabgrass and a cesspool of weeds, and enters the outhouse. As he walks through the creaky door, which like everything else in the vicinity is neglected and in dire need of a fresh coat of paint, he's suddenly struck by a strong bout of vertigo. His legs turn to jello as the room begins jittering, and he can feel the vomit rising at the back of his throat. He stumbles down onto the outhouse seat, the scent of lye mingling with dank shit assaulting him like a fist to the face, and gags and swallows, forcing the vomit back down. He'll be damned if he's going to suffer the indignity of tainting one of his last clean shirts with a tie dye vomit stain that'll end up making him look like a Dead Head. The seat is cold against his ass as he shimmies his jeans down to his ankles, and he's struck with the irrational fear that always rears its ugly head when he's in the outhouse: that there is something lonely down below waiting in the hole, gnarled fingers writhing in impatience, just waiting for the right moment to claw forward and bring company to join it down in the waste.

Tobias finishes his business in a hurry, feeling a sheen of sweat breaking out on his flesh. He swipes his hands through the stringy rat's nest of his hair, which has become so greasy and clumpish that it almost resembles dreads, and takes a deep breath. He wills the room to stop its demented jittering, but the outhouse is still rocking like a rocket launching into space. Apparently he's been gone too long, because Vance starts rapping at the door.

"Hey man," he says. "Are you alright in there? Do I need to call an ambulance?"

Tobias chuckles despite the chills he feels scampering up and down his arms and legs with the nimbleness of mice feet. "You don't need to worry about me. I have no intention of leaving this world on the shitter. I'm not Elvis. I'll be out in a few. I just need to collect my thoughts."

"That shouldn't take long. If thoughts were butterflies, you wouldn't have much of a collection," comes Vance's response.

"Yeah, go fuck yourself," Tobias deadpans.

It takes a few more minutes, but eventually the chills and tilt of the room subside, and Tobias cautiously gets to his feet. He pulls his pants up, staring out through the narrow crescent moon opening carved through the door. He can see Vance in the distance pacing on the porch, the way Maggie does when she's in one of her manic phases, and the barn beyond that. He hasn't been in the barn in at least a month. It really doesn't have much to offer aside from some rusting antiquated farm equipment that was left behind by the previous owners before his parents, when the farm had actually been a fully functioning entity, complete with freshly tilled corn fields, a hen house, and cows for milking and slaughter. It did, however, feature an outstanding hayloft. It had been in the hayloft where he bedded Maggie for the first time, although bedding was a bit of a mild term for what had actually conspired between them. It had been nothing short of a rough power struggle of a fuck, which wasn't surprising considering the road trip back from California, which had been filled with the kind of sexual tension you could cut with a knife. He remembered how eager they'd been that first night when they arrived back at the farmhouse. The tearing of clothing and scattering of buttons. The way he'd thrown her down in the hay in reckless disregard, his cock throbbing with a hardness that felt powerful enough to crush diamonds, and how she'd narrowly avoided being punctured by a row rake that was barely visible beneath the hay; it's rusted tines poking through hesitantly like a row of gator teeth hungry for flesh. Her face had briefly turned fish-belly white with the realization of the close call, but her overwhelming horniness had driven her on as Tobias removed his pants, his erection thrusting out like a missile, and he worked his fingers into her panties to discover she was as wet below as the grounds of a slaughterhouse. In a younger couple it would've seemed more passionate and natural, but for them it just felt rushed and desperate and sad. Her breasts were still amazingly perky, despite her age, with nipples the size of half dollar coins that had the earthy taste of sweat and dirt. When he entered her, thrusting with the abandon of a bucking bronco, she let out a gasp and clung to him like something that had been lost and long forgotten. It was not so much an act of mutual pleasure, as it was an act of taking and pillaging. A ravaging between two souls that had been emptied and were fighting for jurisdiction to fill a void. By the time he came they were both covered in a criss-crossing grid of scratches from the hay, and he felt cheated and vaguely repulsed. The chase had been enticing, and now that he'd gotten what he wanted, he felt strangely blank and gazeless. Their union had been utterly meaningless, and he felt the ache for something of consequence straight down to his bones. She couldn't take the place that Emily still held captive, and he knew that likewise she was just as dissatisfied. Yet, now, after a day of extreme fortune, he suddenly felt the need to recapture that moment of intimacy and breathe new life into it, reviving the corpse they'd become. But first, of course, he'd have to square things away with Vance.

Tobias leaves the outhouse and shuffles over to Vance like an old man after a hip replacement. Vance is still just as morose as ever, hardly acknowledging Tobias' presence.

"I need something to take this edge off," Vance says. "This beer isn't cutting it. Do you have anything with more of a kick?"

"How much of a kick?" Tobias asks. "The kick of a baby billy goat, or the all-out running of the bulls?"

"You know what I'm asking for. Don't play naive with me."

Tobias digs around in his pocket until he finds his pipe. "There's still a little left. The rest is in the house. This should be enough to get your kite spinning high. And to think, you don't even need wind."

"That's good. I've already been in the eye of the tornado. I've had enough wind for one day." Vance accepts the pipe and takes a drag. He can feel the silky smoke gathering in his chest, snaking out and filling all his hollow crevices. He feels a brief headrush, and suddenly the world seems brighter and more highly defined. His thoughts sharpen and narrow, and Trevor and the afternoon suddenly seem like a distant memory that happened to someone else, fading away as clearly and completely as the honeyed dusk which has transformed to a plum wine. "Ahh, God, that's just what I needed. Fuck."

"Glad I could be of service to you."

Vance is still enjoying his head buzz when Maggie comes out and joins them on the porch. "Hey boys," she says. She's changed into a vintage black cocktail dress that could've been hawked straight from the set of *Mad Men*. "Have you guys had enough time to air out your grievances?"

"Well, actually…" Tobias starts, but Maggie cuts him off: "Well, actually, I really don't give a fuck. I have something more important to ask you, but first, give me a drag."

"I would," Vance says. "But it's out."

Tobias turns to enter the house, but Maggie stops him by grabbing his sleeve. "Where do you think you're going?"

"You said you wanted some shit. I was just going to grab you some."

"Oh no you don't," Maggie says. Vance doesn't know her well enough to read the look in her eyes, but her tone says all he needs to know. "Didn't you hear me? We need to have a talk."

"Well, it must be pretty fucking important if you won't even let me get drugs first," Tobias says with a smirk.

"Oh, you could say that."

Vance shifts on his feet, clearly uncomfortable. "Do you guys want me to leave and give you some space?"

"Naw, fuck that," Tobias says. "I haven't seen you in a long ass time. I'm not going to let one of her random little mood tantrums force us to cut things short. Whatever she wants to say she can say in front of you."

Tobias turns to Maggie with an exaggerated expression of annoyance. "Well, what suddenly got your panties all in a bind? Feel free to elaborate."

"Actually, I'm not wearing any panties, but that's beside the point. Remember that time you told me the story about Clint and Adele?"

Tobias looks at Maggie with suspicion. "What are you getting at?"

Vance laughs. "You know about Adele? She was that french girl he was supposedly dating that had the big tits, right?"

Maggie ignores Vance and continues glaring at Tobias. "Supposedly is the key word. Remember how you laughed about his mystery girlfriend?"

"Of course," Tobias says. "It was a laughable story. I mean, come on, no one ever sees this mystery girl and she dies under ridiculous circumstances."

"Wait, wait," Vance interjects. "How did she die again? I'm getting foggy around the edges."

Tobias chuckles. "How could you forget? She was a heavy smoker. She loved smoking clove cigarettes. Every day after finishing her shift at the cafe she worked at she stopped at the tobacco shop and would buy a pack."

"Oh yeah," Vance says. "Now I remember. She tried quitting smoking, right?"

"Oh yeah," Tobias agrees. "She decides to up and go cold turkey for the first time and drives straight home instead of stopping at the Smoke Shack and…"

"Gets t-boned by a semi truck," Vance finishes. "How could I forget?"

Tobias laughs again. "Quitting smoking killed her! Oh, the irony. And do you remember how earnest Clint would get whenever telling the story. How could he possibly believe anyone would buy such bullshit? It's insulting, really."

"Yeah, it was insulting," Maggie agrees. It's Tobias' turn to start shifting, because he knows that Maggie agreeing with him during the start of an argument is a bad sign. It usually means she has an ulterior motive and is about to put her foot down. "I couldn't put it any better, Tobias. I really couldn't. It was really insulting. Now, is there anything you'd like to tell me, while we're at it? Speaking of insulting lies."

"Oh Christ, Magpie," Tobias complains. "I don't know what the fuck you're trying to get at. Could you quit beating around the bush with this passive-aggressive nonsense and just get to the point?"

Maggie harrumphs. "I should've figured you wouldn't have the balls to own up to your lies."

"What lies!?" Tobias shouts. He can't stand the way she treats him like a child. Especially with Vance witnessing everything.

"What about the money?" Maggie growls. "I thought you didn't have any luck when you were down in the cities? Where the fuck did all the money come from?"

Tobias' face drains of all color.

"You didn't think I'd figure it out, huh? How weird you were acting when I busted you by the stairwell?" Maggie spits. "You thought you could just keep it without me ever noticing, huh?"

"Listen, Mag-" Tobias starts, but Maggie doesn't let him finish.

"You asshole," she says. "You *selfish fucking little arrogant prick*! Everything I've earned I've shared with you. We had an open agreement! What's mine is yours and yours is mine! Or did you forget? I've sucked cock for you, and you don't think it's fair to tell me about that big fucking jug of change you got hidden in the wall?"

"I was going to tell you," Tobias says, the color coming back to his face. "I swear. I got it today when I did one of my GPS numbers. I was going to-"

"Like hell," Maggie interrupts. "I thought better of you, Tobias. I didn't think you were going to play these silly games with me like all the others. But I guess I know where we stand now... Don't think I'll forget."

Maggie turns heel and goes back into the house, slamming the busted door behind her with enough force to make the windows rattle. Tobias raises his hands to his sides in a mock damned-if-you-do-damned-if-you-don't surrender.

"I should probably leave," Vance says.

"Oh, man, don't go now. We're just getting warmed up."

"It's nothing personal. I just don't handle awkward situations well. I never have. I had a few too many awkward encounters with my parents over the years, and I'm not big on reliving them. And anyway, it's gotten dark out. I really should be moving on."

Tobias waves his empty pipe in Vance's face like a bully taunting a kid with a candybar held just out of reach. "C'mon, man. I just smoked you up. You're not just going to scavenger my ass, are you?"

"It's not like that, Tobias. You know I wouldn't normally play you like this, but I have a busy night ahead of me, and these next few days are going to be chaotic at best. Why put off for tomorrow what you can get done today, right? You've heard the Boy Scout motto: be prepared, and all that jazz."

"So, you gotta go now, huh?"

"I'm afraid so. I appreciate everything you've done for me over the years, but I really need to hit the road before the road hits me. I'll see you around."

Vance steps off the porch and starts walking away. He's nearly down to the road when Tobias shouts after him, "I'll pass on the message to Old Man Jones, but just remember, next time you come to see me, don't bother coming through the door unless you bring me a goddamn new one!"

28

Maggie is curled up on the mattress and once again reading her Stephen King novel when Tobias lets himself back inside. She has a semi-circle of candles set up around her, all shrine-like, and the glow from the flames brings a creamy youthfulness to her face that normally isn't present. She has the patchwork quilt pulled up around her chest, and the track marks on her arms are barely discernible as she flips to the next page of the novel with her brow furrowed in concentration. A tendril of bleached hair dangles against her cheek and in the deceptive lighting it looks almost cherubic and innocent instead of bleach-damaged and ravaged.

"Hey Magpie," Tobias says.

He half expects her to ignore him, but she looks up from her book, her smoky eyes and sultry lips piercing him to the core. "Tobias," she says, all no-nonsense, with a briskness like a teacher addressing a pupil who hasn't been listening.

"I really am sorry," Tobias responds. She puts her book aside and raises her arm to indicate he should quit while he's ahead.

"Let's not talk about that right now," she says. "I really don't want to fight. Sometimes I just find it hard to control myself. You know how I can be. The words are out of my mouth and my foot is in it before my brain can even register what's being said. I'm like a raw nerve in that way. I just react on impulse."

"That's why we connect so well. Neither one of us knows when the fuck to shut up or how to filter what we say."

"I suppose you could say that."

Tobias climbs down onto the mattress and pulls Maggie up against him, relishing in the warmth she brings. "How's the book?"

Maggie smirks. "I just got to the part in the story where the woman realizes the man she's been living with is a complete fraud, so I guess you could say it's art imitating life."

"Now, now," Tobias says. "Let's play nice."

Maggie wraps her arms around him in a tender embrace, craning her neck to look him in the eyes. "In all seriousness, I shouldn't have bitched you out like that in front of your friend. It wasn't a huge deal. I overreacted. Who am I to judge, with the skeletons in my closet?"

"How do you mean?" Tobias asks.

"You know," Maggie responds. "My life hasn't been all peaches and cream. I spent most of my childhood living for my mother instead of myself. I spent a lot of years in denial, trying to pretend that what happened with my grandfather was just in my imagination. You know, there's nothing worse than being a child beauty queen living in a house with a pedophile."

"I know, Magpie," Tobias whispers reassuringly. "And I'm sorry that ever happened to you. If he hadn't died of a heart attack I would've killed him for you myself. People like him don't deserve to live. You deserved better, and for that I'm sorry."

"Sorry?" Maggie reiterates, raising her eyebrows. "No need for that. Sorry laid its mat down at my dooryard a long time ago and never had the decency of moving on. Sorry people. Sorry places. Sorry circumstances. It's got so expecting the worst has fed me fat while hoping for anything better has strung me along gaunt. No use for crying for a baby with a weakened heart, or an old man with creeping hands, cause things have gone exactly according to plan. Cause God has a special plan for all of us, right? I guess he put me down in the gutter on my back just to give me a view to remind me just how bright the stars can be. Gotta love a wicked sense of humor."

Maggie chuckles sardonically.

Tobias leans down and kisses her on the lips. "You've always got me, Magpie. We'll always have each other, but what do you mean by a baby with a weakened heart?"

"Like I said, Tobi, we've all got our skeletons in our closets, and I haven't been completely honest with you. There's something you need to know. Those cesarean marks on my stomach, and that story I gave you about the baby that died stillborn from an ex-boyfriend weren't true. I gave birth to a baby girl. Her name is Lily. She's still very much alive and in California."

Tobias pulls away from Maggie like she's a live wire. "Why would you lie to me about that?"

"It's complicated," Maggie responds. "You see, I was worried about what you might do if I told you the truth. Lily's father is Frankie."

"Frankie!? That sack of shit from The Meat Market?"

"The one and only."

"I don't get it. What happened to Lily?"

"As far as I know Frankie still has her, and she's not the only baby from a stripper that he's taken. It was a prerequisite of his to dip into his products, as he liked to call us. He dined us with designer drugs and alienated us from our families. He forced himself on whoever he pleased, and if anyone disagreed they had a habit of disappearing."

"Disappearing? What are you saying?"

"You get the idea."

"But why didn't anyone go to the police?"

"Are you kidding me? Half of the precinct was in his pocket. They were crooked as fuck. We were too scared to try and escape. He kept us in locked quarters at night like fucking livestock. That's why when I met you I was so eager to leave and start a new life. I knew that if I didn't leave soon I would end up vanishing like some of the other girls, because, you see, I wasn't just any girl to Frankie. I was sort of his main squeeze, if you catch my drift."

"So you're saying that he wouldn't have let you leave with the baby alive?"

"That's a certainty. Why do you think I was so happy to live off the grid? Did you think I enjoy having to go out to the outhouse in the middle of winter to take a shit, or having to save up enough money to get a seedy room at a hotel for an hour just to shower? Don't take this the wrong way, Tobias. I'm incredibly grateful to be here with you now that I've gotten used to the lifestyle, but when it first began, if I hadn't been in the predicament I was in I probably wouldn't have stayed more than a week. But Frankie has probably tried finding me. He could be having people looking for me still. He's not the type to let someone get anything over on him. As far as he's concerned, I'm still his property."

Tobias sits up on the mattress feeling shell-shocked. "Fuck, Maggie. I don't know what to think. You've been holding onto this that long? Christ, is there anything else I should know?"

"Only one other thing. Someday I intend on getting Lily back, consequences be damned. And I intend on making Frankie pay for everything and everyone he's affected. But I never want to leave you. I want you to still be here and raise her with me. She's four years old now."

"Christ, Magpie, this is a lot to take in. I don't know how I feel about all this. It's like a nuclear bomb being dropped on my head."

"I understand. I should've came clean with you a long time ago. I'm sorry I held it all in. I just didn't want to burden you. We've had it hard enough just scraping by on our own. I know throwing a kid into the mix would only complicate things even further."

Tobias climbs up off the mattress and starts pacing the room, his arms swinging back and forth like an erratic pendulum. "Christ, Maggie. I didn't know things have been so hard for you, and yet you barely let it show."

"Well, when it's a hard world you have to get even harder. All things considered, I feel like I've fared pretty well. I know many girls that have crumbled under the pressure of half the things I've been through. So, where do we go from here?"

Tobia stops pacing and stares blankly ahead.

"What are you thinking?" Maggie asks. "Are you okay?"

"I'm thinking about Frankie."

"And what?"

"I'm going to kill the son of a bitch for you. That's what. I'm going to give him a taste of his own medicine and see how he likes disappearing."

"Oh, Tobias."

Maggie reaches down, cupping his crotch.

"Wait a second. There's just one more thing I need to tell you before we get to business. Since you've been so open about everything, I want to give you reason to trust me also. There's something I need to show you."

Tobias leads Maggie to the hallway and heads back to the opening in the wall. After a few seconds of fishing around within the opening he reveals to Maggie the other secret he's been hiding from her.

"Jesus Christ, Tobias. Are you fucking serious?" is all she can manage to say.

Part 4

Nothing Gold Can Stay

29

The trek back to Jacob's house takes about fifteen minutes. Vance moves through the shadows with ease, staying to the side of the road in case anyone comes driving along, but as it turns out his precautions are unnecessary. Upon coming to the back sliding glass door he notices that Jasper has brought another contribution to the household: this time a dead cardinal. Its blank eyes stare glassily into the evermore beneath its crown of red feathers, with reflections from the moonlight causing them to shimmer like marbles submerged in water. Its stomach has been torn open, and small strands of intestine dangle out like angel hair pasta, attracting opportunistic flies. Vance sidesteps this new conquest and enters the house. All is silent within. If Vance didn't know any better he'd figure that nobody was home, but considering tonight's endeavor, the likelihood of Jacob being gone are slim to none.

"Hey, Jacob," he calls into the shadowy confines. "Where the fuck are you?"

He swipes his arms along the wall looking for a light switch, but to no avail. His feet echo on the wooden floorboards as he enters the darkness.

"Fuck," he mutters, banging his thigh against an end table in the living room. He rubs his leg as the lights cut on.

Jacob is sitting beside the coffee table in a plush Lazy Boy giving him a strange smile. "Having troubles?"

"Why are you sitting in the shadows like a cannibal?"

"I just woke up from a nap. Shit, what time is it?"

Vance shrugs his shoulders. "I have no idea. Probably around nine or so. How can you find the time to sleep with all the craziness we experienced this afternoon?"

"You'd be surprised how easy it is to sleep when you have a kid at home. Harvey keeps strange hours, and whenever I can get the place to myself I enjoy whatever luxuries I can afford. It's one of the perks you take for granted when you're younger and single. That, and being able to walk around in the nude, of course."

"Well, thank God for small favors. It's dark outside now. Are you ready to make the pickup?"

"Of course. These walls and roof depend on it."

Jacob climbs out of the Lazy Boy and walks over to the kitchen table in the dining room. He takes a seat and stretches, several vertebrae popping along his spine like acorns roasting in a bonfire. He lets out a monstrous yawn as he slips his weathered suede Pumas on.

"Oh, by the way," Vance casually mentions. "Jasper left you another gift outside by the sliding glass door. Be careful not to step on it on the way out. Or what's left of it, anyway."

"Oh, shit," Jacob mutters. "That cat is going to be the death of me. I'm going to leave the mess out there for Tori to take care of. I'm tired of always having to be the one cleaning up after all the bullshit he leaves behind. They need to learn how to remember to close the goddamn door behind them when they go out. But, of course, why would they give a shit? They're not the ones paying for the A/C. But trust me, if I put my foot down and started making Tori pay for the electric, you can be damn sure she'd start remembering basic energy conservation skills in no time. Funny how that works."

Jacob opens the sliding glass door and steps outside, a brisk wind causing his black and blue checkered flannel to ripple like the surface of a pond after the skipping of a stone. Vance joins him. The cardinal lies dead between them, with an army of ants struggling beneath it, making tentative movements, to carry it back to their domain for dinner. Scampering in unison against the weight of the cardinal, they remind Vance of pallbearers in a funeral procession paying their respects to a powerful fallen martyr.

Jacob walks over to his Monte Carlo and unlocks the doors. He gets behind the wheel and adjusts the rearview mirror as Vance climbs in beside him. The ride to recover the money passes in silence. They take the highway until the exit near the recovery zone creeps up, then Jacob pulls off and follows an old dirt road that runs parallel to 94 and parks the car on the outskirts of the old Dahle residence, where they continue on foot. In the silence of the night, every sound is amplified. The breaking of a twig becomes the cracking of a bone. The bubbling of a brook becomes the roar of a riptide. They cut through the forest until they reach the tree-line that runs along 94. They follow the tree-line, listening and looking for the slightest signs that someone might be tailing them, as alert as mice to the possibility of prey swooping in. They examine the perimeter of the site with the deliberate exhaustive care of a crime scene investigator, until they feel as comfortable as they can given the circumstance. Jacob stops upon reaching a mile marker that's surrounded by a tangled thatch of primrose bushes and a quartet of yellow birch trees.

"This is the spot," Jacob says. "This is where I tossed the bag that wasn't ruined by ink."

He crouches down and starts shifting through the foliage of the nearest primrose bush. His top half is obscured by the branches that grasp at him like the greedy hands of spoiled children, and the knees of his jeans are covered in dirt.

"Do you see anything?" Vance asks.

"Not exactly," comes Jacob's response. "It must have gotten twisted up deeper in the brush than I thought. Care to join me, or are you just going to lollygag all night?"

"Lollygag? Where the hell did you learn that word? Been hanging out at nursing homes a lot lately?"

Jacob thrusts his arm out from within the bush and gives Vance the finger.

"I guess lollygag is an appropriate enough word for you to use," Vance relents. "What with you playing around in the dirt on your knees. All you're missing to complete the look is a floppy straw hat and some pruning shears and you could be my grandmother gardening."

Jacob ignores Vance's jab and climbs out of the bushes covered in scratches and dripping a steady stream of sweat. He wipes his forehead off with the back of his arm and takes a deep breath. "Christ," he murmurs. "I could've sworn the bag ended up over here, but I can't see a damn thing."

"Are you sure we're at the right mile marker? Could it maybe be the next one up?"

Jacob shakes his head firmly. "I'm positive this is the spot. Trust me, I paid careful attention. It was mile marker 77; the same year I was born. I'd have to have Alzheimer's to forget that."

Vance walks over to the neighboring brush, and joins in the search. It's nearly impossible to see anything beneath the dense foliage. The moon paints the outer leaves in mercurial streaks of silver that drape over the inner shadows like a shawl.

"Speaking of Alzheimer's," Vance whispers, shifting a thorny branch out of his way, to which a squirrel comes scampering out in a panic, casting an indignant glance over its shoulder for having the audacity to interrupt its slumber. "You just reminded me of a joke Clint told me last time I saw him. A man goes to see a doctor because he's concerned about his wife. She's been acting out of sorts lately. So the doctor runs some tests on her and comes back to the man with some bad news. He's narrowed the results of her affliction down to two possibilities: she either has HIV or Alzheimer's. The man is heartbroken. He asks the doctor what he should do. The doctor says, the way he sees it, there's only one option: Drop her off in the middle of the woods at night and take off. If she's able to find her way back home, don't fuck her."

Vance anticipates at least a chuckle from Jacob in response, but silence is all that greets him.

"Are you alright?" Vance questions. "Did you find the money?"

When Jacob approaches him, it's obvious that he's decidedly the opposite of alright. His expression is resolute and grim. His lips are pressed tightly together into a thin sharp scar, the anger radiating off him like the fallout from a nuclear explosion. Before Vance can even attempt to ask what's wrong, Jacob strikes him with a right hook to the jaw that causes him to lose his footing and gracelessly fall flat on his ass. Jacob then follows the punch with a kick to the gut that knocks the wind out of Vance, causing him to fetally curl in on himself, sputtering for air and floundering like a fish that's just been dropped on land for the first time, still too shocked to fully process the strange turn of events. Jacob stands above him, looking menacing in the dappled moonlight. His hands are clenched into fists at his sides, and his eyes are bright with a glow that seems to be lit from within, like the jack o' lanterns that are still perched on porches and in countless windows throughout the neighborhood; all gap-toothed and gutted, and starting to rot from the inside out.

"Did I find the money!?" Jacob spits out. "How can I find something that's already been taken?"

Vance shakily steps to his feet, like a drunken man climbing off a barstool, or a boxer starting the final round. The realization of Jacob's accusation hits him harder than any fist could ever manage. "What the fuck do you mean?"

"Do I have to spell it out for you? The bag of money is gone, and you conveniently had to leave earlier to pass a message on to an old friend. Don't try playing stupid with me. I know you took the money, and that's not going to fly. Now where is it, you fucking shitbag thief?"

Jacob steps up to Vance like a territorial animal. Vance doesn't back down. Instead, he leans in until their faces are within millimeters of each other. "Are you kidding me? I didn't take the fucking money!"

"Oh yeah, it was a wildfox, huh? Or, let me guess, one of those adopt-a-highway fucks took it? Is that what you're trying to tell me? You aren't going to win any awards with this act of naivety, cause I can see right through your bullshit. It's one thing trying to fuck with me, but this money is the only thing keeping my family from ending up in a fucking shelter. If the next words coming out of your mouth aren't telling me where the fucking money is there's going to be some serious blood! I can promise you that!"

"I'm the one playing an act, huh? Oh, that's rich." Vance has had enough. He shoves Jacob away with all the force he can muster. "You have the nerve to try and flip this around on me? Well, guess what? I'm not gullible, either. Quit with the reverse-psychology bullshit! You're the one that took the money when I left, but I'm not worried. I've got nothing to lose. You're the one with the liabilities! And in case you've forgotten, I know exactly where to find them!"

"You motherfuck!" Jacob yells, and charges at him like a bull seeing red. Vance manages to hit him in the jaw just before Jacob barrels them both over onto the ground. They roll around awkwardly in the dirt, cursing and trying to find leverage. Vance's shirt tears down the center as Jacob flips him down onto his back and grapples him into submission.

"You piece of shit," Vance gasps, as Jacob forces him into a headlock. "I should've known what you were up to when you threw the money out! Acting like you were worried the money was being tracked. What a crock of shit! I never should've let Trevor talk me into having you help with the heist! But karma's a bitch. You'll see."

Jacob waits until Vance goes limp, then releases him. He gets to his feet and points at Vance threateningly. "You're going to bring the money to me before tomorrow afternoon when Harvey comes back. You hear me? I won't accept any excuses. And if you make any more vague threats about my family again I'll burn everything you've ever loved to the ground and piss on the ashes. You say you've got nothing to lose? I'll make that lie a fucking reality!"

And with that, he wanders off into the night, leaving Vance to fend for himself.

30

Tobias and Maggie are fast asleep on the mildewed mattress in the living room with the quilt tangled between them, when a faint creaking causes them to awaken from the depths of their slumber. For a split second Tobias forgets where he's at: mistaking the squeaking sound for a mouse coming down from the rafters where he'd had his romp with Maggie. He can still taste her on his lips, can still see her hair spilling down in a waterfall to her breasts, which are creamy and delectable and just begging to be consumed. It takes a moment for him to deduce the sound for what it really is: the opening of a door.

Tobias sits up in bed, while Maggie rolls over and goes back to sleep. It's something he's always envied about her; the ability she had to shut things out and reach oblivion even without the aid of chemicals. He looks around but can't see anything in the darkness. It takes a moment for his eyes to adjust, but before they do, Vance extends the courtesy of announcing his presence.

"Hey, Tobias. Are you awake?"

Tobias feels around on the hardwood floor until his fingers make contact with his lighter. He then fumbles a candle from a sconce and ignites a flame that chases the darkness to the far corners of the room. Even in the dimness of the glow, Tobias can tell Vance is looking rough.

"Holy shit," he exclaims. "I'd normally tell you you look like shit, but this goes beyond that. I didn't know you could take your ugliness to a lower level. That's like finding a secret trapdoor in the lowest layer of hell. I'm impressed!"

Tobias untangles himself from the quilt with the difficulty of a spider's prey trying to disengage itself from a web, marvelling that his clumsy maneuvering doesn't cause Maggie to stir. He lifts his pointer finger in front of his lips as a directive for silence, grabbing the candle from the nighttime shrine, and motions for Vance to follow him into the kitchen. A few seconds later they stand beside the icebox with freshly cracked beers held between them. Condensation trickles down the side of the can, pooling in the palm of his hand, as Tobias tilts his can back and takes a swig. The beer has lost the crispness it had earlier, because the ice that kept it cool has met the same fate as the Titanic and has now been swallowed and lost and consumed by the water around it.

"So, how did you get those badges of honor?" Tobias asks, tracing an invisible circle in front of his face. "I'm guessing this had something to do with the dilemma you got into with Trevor?"

"I suppose there's no great point in trying to deny it," Vance admits. "Shit, it will be all over the news by tomorrow afternoon, and anyway, I'm planning on being long gone by the time the shit hits the fan."

"So, what happened? Clint told me you guys robbed a 7-Eleven a few months back, but I thought he was blowing smoke up my ass, because he has an elastic tongue and tells so many far-fetched tales he could put L. Ron Hubbard out of business. Was there truth to his story after all? Did you guys hold up a gas station?"

Vance shakes his head in annoyance. "I can't believe Trevor told Clint about that. He should've known better with the way Clint flaps off at the jaw worse than a little old lady at the hair parlour, but you know how Trev can get after swimming down the wrong end of a few too many bottles; but yes, it's true. We did hit up a few gas stations back in the day, but this time around our aim was higher."

"Let me guess, you guys held up a pharmacy and loaded up on painkillers and legal speed. Some Oxycodone, maybe? Where there's a pill there's a way."

"What do you take me and Trev for? We're not Oxymorons. You're on the right path and getting closer, but think bigger."

"Bigger?" Tobias asks, his eyes squinting together all cat-like and incredulous. "How much bigger are we talking? You guys wouldn't be crazy enough to hold up a bank, so what other middle ground does that leave?"

"When you're left with few choices, sometimes the least likely scenario is the right one."

"Wow, you guys have bigger balls than I ever would've given you credit for."

"Well, desperation can bring out the worst in people and make them behave in unexpected ways," Vance says, staring into the flame of the candle Tobias is holding with a naked hungriness as he speaks, as if the light provides comfort and sustenance; although he could be gazing through a wormhole into an alternate dimension if the distance in his eyes is any indication. "I thought we had everything planned to perfection for the heist. I stormed the front of the bank and handled the tellers, while Trevor was in charge of keeping an eye out from the rear to make sure nobody tried anything funny. We had a look-out waiting in the parking lot to let us know if anything suspicious was creeping up on the horizon. The plan was simple. If he noticed anything suspicious he was supposed to send us a message on his walkie to give us notice so things would go off without a hitch, but you know how simple plans have a way of unravelling."

"What went wrong? Was your lookout distracted?"

"Naw. It wasn't Jacob's fault. He did his part in trying to give us a heads-up, but we just weren't able to get out in time. Sometimes I swear, if we didn't have bad luck we'd have no luck at all!"

"You have to make your own luck in this world," Tobias interrupts. "If you wait for good luck to just come your way and fall into your lap without actively fighting to get what you deserve, you'll end up lying on your deathbed with regrets, dreaming about what could've been."

"Well, maybe that's true in the abstract sense, but making your own luck isn't of much practical use when you have a Dunbar rolling up on you all unexpected, with guards that are armed to the nines. It turned into a fucking bloodbath. One of the teller's rigged a bag of money with a dye pack that went off as soon as we left the bank, and Jacob started acting paranoid once we were on the road that they might have also planted us with a tracker, or at least, that was his excuse for tossing the money out while we were flying down the highway."

"He threw the fucking money out the window?" Tobias asks, his mouth hanging open in an O of surprise. "That seems pretty reckless and stupid!"

"Well, everything we did could be construed as stupid and reckless, but what seems like recklessness to one, could also be seen as calculation by another."

"You think he tossed the money out on purpose so he could have it all for himself?"

"I never trusted the cock sucker from the get-go. The only reason I let him in is because Trevor vouched for him. When we went to collect the money it wasn't there, and Jacob tried twisting it around on me, claiming I was the one that took it."

"Did you?"

Vance rolls his eyes in exasperation, flinging his arms out from his sides, a cascade of beer spilling in the process. "Would I be here right now bitching about it with you if I was the one who took the money?"

"I suppose not, unless you were trying to be clever by painting a picture of innocence around town."

"Like I said, shit went south. It's going to be front page news in no time. There's no reason for me to save face. I've got no face to save. I'm on a one-way ticket to shitsville and have no other option but to leave town. There's no reason for me to sugarcoat or try to stack my reputation. Come tomorrow, I've gotta make like the birds and go hibernate for the winter."

"So why haven't you gone back to his place and raised hell? If this is gonna blow up all over the local media as big as you're thinking, you can't afford to waste time. Does Jacob know you're here?"

"Oh, of course he knows. When I stopped by earlier to have you leave a message with Old Man Jones, that's when he took the money. He knew where I was going. I was walking on foot. Where else would I have gone?"

"So you're going to just let him take the money without doing anything about it?"

"Fuck no! He just caught me off guard. When we went to pick up the money at the drop spot I honestly thought it was going to be there. When he attacked me out of nowhere, trying to turn everything around on me, I wasn't expecting it. I told him that I knew how full of shit he is, and reminded him that he has more to lose in this scenario than I do, and he'd do well to remember that."

"You're not talking about that dumb cheating bitch that he's still been seeing since he got out, are you? I highly doubt he's going to give a flying fuck one way or the other about her. That's not exactly what I'd call leverage."

"You'd be surprised. Maybe she ruined his life, but she's still got her hooks in him deep. He wouldn't have taken her back in if she didn't mean anything to him. And don't forget, he was willing to take her back even though she'd had a baby with the asshole she'd been messing around with. He's raised that little girl like she was his own. No man would go through that kind of misery if there weren't deep attachments involved."

"So, what did you say to him?"

"I just told him how it was. If he thinks I'm just going to roll over and take it like a bitch, he's got another thing coming. He has his house to himself for the night, but he mentioned that Harvey was going to be coming back in the morning from her friend's house up the road, so I'd have to get lost. I pretty much told him that if the money didn't come back my way I was going to hit him where it hurt. That's when he saw red, and warned me never to make threats against his fucked up family again."

"So, are you a man of your word? Are you really going to hit him where it counts?"

"I'm going to get the upper hand," Vance says with a guttural chuckle. "You'd better believe it. I'm going to do whatever it takes to get back what's rightfully mine. He's a fucking moron if he thinks I'm going to just walk away with my tail tucked between my legs like a cowardly dog. I've got a gun and I can take him on any day of the week. Trevor once told me his aim is such shit he couldn't jump out of a boat and hit the water. I've got years of hunting under my belt. I'll make an example out of anyone that gets in my way."

"I admire that dedication, but if you came here tonight hoping to get me caught up in all this drama, I hate to be the bearer of bad news, but I'm not getting involved. You're going to have to do whatever you feel is necessary on your own. I'm comfortable with my situation and feel no need to create waves. I'm getting too old for that shit."

Vance chugs the last of his beer and sets it down on the counter. He grabs another from the icebox and cracks it open. As he's taking his first gulp, the distant rumblings of thunder can be heard approaching from the distance like a runaway train. "No need to worry. I didn't come here tonight trying to enlist you for help. I just needed a moment to regroup and plan out my next course of action. Truth be told, I was just hoping for some input. I figured if I vented to you, maybe you would have some suggestions on how best to deal with this, cause I'm at my wits end."

"I wish I could be of help, but I don't have any ideas that won't lead to more bloodshed. If this asshole is trying to hoard all your money for himself, he's probably not going to listen to reason. There's no use in being diplomatic."

"Then I guess there's no other option."

The thunder that's been rumbling is drowned out as a steady stream of rain starts falling in sheets, pattering against the windowpanes and pummeling the roof. Tobias finishes his beer and looks out the window into the darkness, admiring the way the rain shuts everything out. They continue talking well into the night, until there aren't any beers left to drink, as the thunder rumbles around them ominously, like a wrathful god freshly awoken and seeking vengeance. Once they've also run out of cigarettes, they decide to call it a night. Tobias sleeps like a baby, while Vance tosses and turns in anticipation of the day ahead and what must be done.

31

The rain continues falling throughout the night unabated, from bloated clouds that look so heavy it seems the sky should sag from under all the burden. The occasional flash of lightning brings light to the darkness, as the roar of thunder punctuates the hiss of the rain on grass and empty fields. If it had been a calm night, perhaps things would've played out differently. They might have heard the sound of breaking glass, and the whisper of footsteps along warped floorboards. But, as luck would have it, they slept in indifference to the intrusion, and it wasn't until the next morning that Tobias realized what had occurred. If it had been a calm night, perhaps there wouldn't have been a need for so much death in the day to come. But, unfortunately, it wasn't a calm night…

32

Tobias pulls up in Jacob's driveway shortly after noon the next day. Maggie is sitting beside him in the passenger seat, looking just as shocked as he feels. Tobias has been up for hours, ever since discovering the invasion, and the only thing keeping him fueled is the Adderall he swiped from the house on Arundel Street. He doesn't feel like the same man he was the night before. Hell, he doesn't even feel human. The break in has forced him to reassess everything. It's backed him into a corner, and forced him to make some tough decisions that he's afraid may come back to haunt him. He marvels at what a difference a few days can make in a person's life, and the audacity of the rollercoaster ride he's endured.

Maggie stays behind in the truck as Tobias climbs out, and before he even reaches the door of the house, Jacob is opening it. Apparently he's been expecting company.

"Jesus Christ," he says, looking pale and worried. His hair is in disarray. He's still wearing the same clothes from the night before. "Where the hell is he?"

Tobias doesn't even bother asking who he's referring to. "Vance is back at my place," he says. "He was gone all day, and when he came back he was acting strange. I was worried he might have already stopped over here. Shit, I was half expecting you to not even answer the door. Or be capable of answering it."

Jacob runs his hands through his hair in distress. "What the hell has he done with her?"

he asks.

Tobias is still walking toward Jacob when the question is asked, and freezes in his tracks. "Oh fuck," he mumbles. He can't look Jacob in the eyes. Staring at his shoes seems somehow more appropriate.

"What do you mean, 'oh fuck?' What aren't you telling me?" Jacob demands. His tone is bordering on frantic.

"That's why I came over here," Tobias explains. "Vance was saying some crazy things when he got back this morning that had me worried. He said you took what belonged to him. He said you had his money, and he'd done something to get your attention and make things even. He mentioned your daughter. He even said he had a gun."

Jacob's expression is grim. "If he did anything to harm her, I swear to God, I'll make him wish he was never fucking born!"

"How long has she been unaccounted for?" Tobias asks. He looks back at the truck and sees Maggie staring at him in concern. He waves dismissively at her, and turns back to Jacob.

The whites of Jacob's eyes are showing, and he reminds Tobias of a colt that's just been branded. It's the look of pain transfixing itself into lunacy. "I called her friend's house just before you got here. I was wondering what was taking her so long. Her friend said that she'd left a few hours earlier. I know Harvey well. She would have come straight home. I debated calling the police, but thought better of it. I didn't want to jump the gun for no reason! But, Christ, I was just on my way out the door when you pulled up. I was going to, ahhhh, I was going to…" His words dissolve into sobs.

Tobias pats him on the shoulder, not knowing how to respond.

"Oh God," he heaves. "How am I going to tell Tori what I've caused? That girl means everything to her. She means everything to *us*."

Tobias continues staring at Jacob's shoes. He can't bear to look him in the eye. "I wish we would've stopped by earlier. I didn't think he was serious when we were talking, but then, when he came back in a daze, I knew something was wrong. I'm so sorry, Jacob. I don't know what I can do to make this better. I wish I had the answers."

Jacob wipes the tears from his face with the back of his hand. "It's not your fault, man.

Whatever that crazy asshole has done he's about to atone for. I'll get the truth out of him. I'll make things right."

Jacob abruptly turns around and heads into the house. When he comes back outside a minute later he's clutching a double-barreled shotgun.

"What are you doing?" Tobias asks.

"Didn't you just hear me?" Jacob responds. "I'm going to make things right."

With that, he climbs into his vehicle, and peels out leaving a trail of rubber in his wake.

Tobias walks back to Maggie in the truck and leans into the open window. "Jacob's on a warpath," he explains. "He says he's going to make things right."

Maggie chuckles sarcastically, throwing herself back in the seat, causing her bangs to dangle in front of her eyes in a wild veil. "Well, he has his work cut out for him," she says through her smear of red lipstick. "Only he doesn't realize it yet..."

33

Vance is biking with Trevor through the dusty woods on his silver Diamondback, as the sun sets in the distance, casting everything in an amber glow of honeyed flame. The path they ride along is littered with leaves that crackle in protest under their tires as they head toward the train tracks. It's the end of fall. Vance can feel the chill of the changing season through his hoodie, and shivers as they reach the tracks. But the tracks are not their ultimate destination. Lake Winterfell is where they are heading. It is here where everybody meets up on the weekends. There is a hidden beach buried in the forest that features an impressive fire pit and a ramshackle shed that was used for fish-cleaning once upon a time, but has been commandeered and converted for teenage purposes and is now dubbed the Smoke Shack.

When they arrive at the site, Clint is tending the fire. There are a few teenagers swimming naked near the shore, playfully splashing. Joe Yorke is sitting on a boulder lazily strumming Santeria on his acoustic guitar, and asking for requests. Trevor suggests Heart Shaped Box as he dismounts from his bike. Clint throws another log on the fire, and the embers spark outward as the flames flicker up and lick enviously at the sky. Joe re-tunes his guitar, and then begins strumming the opening chords of the request as Trevor and Vance enter the shed.

Inside, the shed is sparsely furnished. There is an old burgundy couch that takes up the entire back wall. It replaced a huge metal table where the scaling used to take place, and if you look carefully enough you can still find remnants of the prior owner's craft; little iridescent flecks of fish scale that shimmer in the darkness like tempting jewels. Other than the couch, there isn't much. Just an old tin can of Folgers for the cigarette butts, and an end table that's cluttered with a deck of cards, a cribbage board, a couple empty cans of beer, and a notebook and pen that is meant for keeping score of various games; although more often than not, it's instead used to draw pictures of veiny erect penises ejaculating, and tits so enormous they would require a climbing expedition to explore.

Vance sits down on the couch and motions for Trevor to join him. He pulls out his pipe and takes a deep drag. He then hands it over to Trevor, who, only a few months earlier would have been hesitant about accepting, but has now taken to it like a fish taking to water: or a stoner taking to a fish shack, for that matter. Trevor takes a drag as well, and exhales. He stares complacently at the walls of the shed which are made of oak. Over the years a diverse collection of thoughts and opinions have been scrawled and engraved on the walls as evidence that not only was this once a place of great fish desecration, but also happened to be a spot where deeply stimulating adolescent contemplation occurred, with indispensable pearls of wisdom doled out, such as the inscription: SAVE THE WHALES… HARPOON A FAT CHICK; and of course, the ever-popular engraving: TELL YOUR MOM TO QUIT CHANGING HER SHADES OF LIPSTICK, CAUSE MY COCK IS STARTING TO LOOK LIKE A RAINBOW. Not to mention the usual affirmations of eternal love from couples that rarely outlast the summer, as is evidenced by the small etching that Vance himself engraved: V+S=4EVER.

"I can't believe she left me for that fucking nigger," Vance complains. That's all he's been doing all summer. Fixating and venting about Sasha, and how she left him for Jerome. Sure, he's slept with several other fixer-upper girls throughout the summer, but none of them have mattered or been worth much of anything to him, because Sasha had been a fully-developed woman in his mind, and the other girls were just sex object floozies of no consequence. Since she's left, he's been seeking mental oblivion like a bloodhound on the trail of a scent, moaning about how he'll never find another girl as amazing as Sasha again; and so it's really not much of a surprise that when Cowboy Billy shows up and joins them on the couch, offering an exciting new drug they aren't familiar with, that Vance accepts without the slightest bit of concern.

Cowboy Billy has always been a reliable friend and dealer. When Gerald from off Chesapeake Way had been overcharging them and loading their bags with an excessive amount of stems and beaners in their newbie days of weed-smokery, Cowboy Billy had been the one to let them know how Gerald was going around town laughing his ass off at all the new dipshit teens he was pulling the wool over; and since then, Cowboy Billy has taken them under his wing and always offered a fair price for a trustworthy product.

Vance takes the glass pipe and stares at it in confusion. He's never used a glass vaporizer before. He flicks the lighter and applies the flame under the bulb. The white crystals inside start to bubble and blacken.

"No, no," Cowboy Billy exclaims, noticing how Vance is handling the pipe. "You're doing it all wrong. You don't want the flame consuming the pipe like that. Pull back a little. You also don't want the flame lingering too long in one spot. Twist the pipe back and forth and spread it out. Don't forget to cover the choke, and don't hold the smoke in when you get a drag or you'll burn your lungs out!"

Vance corrects his mistakes and takes a huge hit. He expects the smoke to hit his lungs like a freight train and cause an apocalyptic coughing fit, but is pleasantly surprised by how smooth it goes down. It tastes like vaporized silk with an acidic edge.

"So, what do you think?" Cowboy Billy asks expectantly. He leans forward propping his elbows on his knees, as his cowboy boots tap in rhythm to the Nirvana song being played outside. "Crazy shit, huh?"

Vance takes a second drag and begins feeling pins and needles coursing through his arms. His head lightens and his thoughts gain clarity. "This is incredible! What is it?"

"Methamphetamine, my friend," Cowboy Billy replies.

"Holy shit," Vance says. "I've never felt more alert in my life! It's like inhaling the breath of God!"

Cowboy Billy laughs wholeheartedly. "I've never heard it put quite like that, but yes, it is something otherworldly, alright. This ain't no cheap hippie shit! That's for sure."

"Speaking of hippies, my dad used to live in a commune," Trevor chimes in. "He said all the hippies did drugs to transform their minds and the world. He never ended up changing much of anything, though. But I guess, how can you change the world when you don't even change your own clothes or your kid's diapers? All he gained from his experience is an army of head lice and a laundry list of venereal diseases. So much for turn on, tune in, and drop out, huh?"

Cowboy Billy bursts out laughing once again. "Sounds like your old man liked living on the edge, but hell, I don't blame him. You get your best views from the edge. It's the ones living on the edge that are the first to see the dangers on the horizon, because they have their fingers on the life pulse."

"Yeah, but it's also the ones living on the edge that die young, choking on the hearts beating in their throats," Trevor adds.

"Well, shit," Cowboy Billy says. "Things just got serious real quick up in here! Way to be a buzzkill! Just take this pipe and put your mouth to some good use! No need to overthink. Let's just live in the moment and have some fun!"

Trevor is reaching for the pipe when Vance stops him. "I don't think you should mess with this shit," he says, suddenly serious.

Cowboy Billy shakes his head in disbelief. "What the hell are you talking about, man? You just got done singing a chorus of praises about how amazing this shit is."

Vance looks Trevor in the eyes. "I don't know, man. I just suddenly got struck with a bad feeling about this. I think you should leave it alone."

Cowboy Billy chuckles. "C'mon now. He's a big boy and can make up his mind for himself. He don't need you holding his hand to cross roads. No need to get all dramatic all of a sudden."

Outside the shed Joe Yorke finishes strumming Heart Shaped Box and segueways into Paranoid Android to a smattering of applause and drunken hooting.

Vance's feeling of foreboding is suddenly amplified when a sleek black cat comes sauntering into the shed. His fur is lustrous and shimmers like oil. His tail is crooked and hangs like a question mark. His eyes are piercing and emerald green as he daintily steps forward and rubs against Vance's leg.

"Jesus Christ, Jasper," Vance exclaims. "What are you doing here?"

As he leans down to give Jasper a pet, he realizes that Jasper has something clenched between his pointy little teeth. It appears to be a dead bird. Jasper drops it at his feet, and looks up at him expectantly.

"We should probably le-leave, Trev," Vance stammers. "I don't think it's a good idea for you to mess around with that shit, and I don't think it's a good idea for us to be here right now. Something is wrong about all this."

Trevor turns to Vance, and nothing could prepare Vance for what he sees. Half of Trevor's face is missing. Where his eyes should be are just hollow sockets. His flesh is hanging loosely from his skull, like meat that's been left out in the sun to fester, and maggots wriggle and crawl out from beneath it, dropping and landing in his lap like squirming bits of rice that stink of rot.

Vance screams and jerks away from him, falling backward off the couch.

"What's the matter, buddy?" Trevor asks. "Is this becoming too *real* for you all of a sudden? Are you having trouble living in the fantasy?"

He climbs to his feet, towering over Vance. "I hate to be the bearer of bad news, but your fantasy is that you ever tried turning me away from meth in the first place. I didn't want to take it. Don't you remember? You kept pestering me and belittling me until I caved in. But it's always been that way with us, hasn't it? You've always been the one to lead us down avenues we shouldn't have gone exploring down, and look at where it got us? Strung out and desperate. The avenues led us down a dead end. *Dead* being the operative word, cause where do you think I am right now? I'm certainly not here with you in this shack. I'm lying on a cold shelf in the morgue right now. That's where I am. But I guess, who am I to complain? All paths lead in one direction. Death is unavoidable. Who am I to complain, when you'll see for yourself. You've been living in a fantasy dreamland, but reality is going to slap you in the face, man. You're going to wake up and see all the consequences of your actions. You're going to wake up... Wake up and see. *Wake up! Wake up, you cock sucker...*"

34

Vance opens his eyes in confusion, the sudden transition from sleep to wakefulness leaving him dizzy. He sees Trevor still standing above him, and his heart starts trigger-hammering in his chest even worse than it did when he was in sleep.

"Wake up you cocksucker," comes the voice from above, only it's not Trevor after all. Of course not. How could it be? It's Jacob. And Jacob means business, as is evidenced by the shotgun he's brandishing with a crazed grin reminiscent of Jack Nicholson in that infamous scene in *The Shining* when he's chopping through the door to gain access to his family, which he likewise aims to transform into kindling.

"Wh-what the fuck?" Vance manages to rustily croak as Jacob grabs him by the collar of his shirt and yanks him to his stumbling feet.

"Surprised to see me?" Jacob asks sarcastically.

Vance can only stare blankly. He realizes that his mouth is hanging open like an imbeciles, but there's nothing he can do to shut it. He feels detached from himself, like he's still swimming in the currents of a dream within a dream.

"Actions have consequences, my friend," Jacob explains. "And for your sake, let's just hope that you didn't exceed your boundaries."

Vance just continues standing with his mouth hanging agape, a lazy string of spittle dangling from his quivering chin.

"Can you hear me, numbnuts?" Jacob screams, and proceeds to slam Vance in the stomach with the butt of his shotgun.

Vance doubles over, and is met with a knee to his ribcage. Whatever remnants of his dream that still remained wash away as Jacob lifts the shotgun and places it against Vance's temple.

Instead of pausing to calculate and collect his thoughts and say the sensible thing one would expect someone to say when being held captive by a gun-wielding maniac with vengeance at the forefront of his mind, Vance lets his lesser motivations get the best of him and says the first thing that pops into his head. "You stole my motherfucking money, you piece of shit!" His tone drips with an indignance as poisonous as the strike of a viper.

"You're goddamn right, bitch," Jacob admits. "What did you expect? Did you think I was just going to play nice and forgive and forget your shady behavior? You should know me better than that. If you're gonna play with fire you're gonna get burnt, and I'm not the one who was caught with the matches in my hand. You brought this on yourself. And now you have the nerve to retaliate? When you're the one that set everything into motion in the first place?"

"I don't know what the fuck you're talking about," Vance exclaims, trying to pull out of Jacob's grasp, but his efforts are futile as Jacob tightens his grip pulling him in closer. Years of working out in a prison cell have their perks.

"You know *exactly* why I'm here. Where is Harvey? What did you do with her? Don't bullshit me!"

"Harvey!?" Vance asks, his eyes widening all owl-like as the puzzle pieces start aligning in his mind. "I have no idea where Harvey is! She could be out necking with some boy out by the overlook at the Miller's place for all I know. All I care about is getting my money back, so quit trying to divert the subject with these ridiculous made-up fantasies, and let's just cut to the chase."

Apparently Jacob doesn't find the visual being painted of the apple of his eye swapping spit too amusing, unless, of course, cracking Vance in the knee with the barrel of the shotgun is his strange way of showing appreciation.

"I think you're forgetting your place in this situation, so let me give you another subtle reminder," Jacob snarls through clenched teeth. He lifts the shotgun up high and slams it down on the crown of Vance's skull, causing a neon psychedelic swirl of fireworks to ignite and bloom across his field of vision. Vance weaves on his feet like an exhausted boxer, feeling the room lengthen and shorten around him to the beating of his heart, and sags in Jacob's arms like a wilted wildflower deprived of sunlight.

As the room fades away into dimness and obscurity, all he can do is hope that Trevor isn't waiting for him on the other side of the darkness once again; and this time, mercifully, his wish is granted and there are no more guilt-ridden dreams…

35

First National bank is in a flurry of activity when Tobias and Maggie find a spot in the parking lot. They've driven over from Jacob's place in mostly silence, only speaking once when Tobias turned on the radio. Normally Maggie would argue with him over who has jurisdiction over the station, but this time it was different. She didn't want to listen to anything. It's as if the sound of the music was too much for her to bear, amplifying the thoughts that were tearing into her mind with the ravish of a vampire on the prowl for blood. Thoughts of the dizzying shock of Tobias' revelation in the stairwell. Thoughts of the break in and the resulting aftermath of the choices that were made that spiralled into chaos, and the consequences of what those actions might imply. In the back of the truck there are several garbage bags filled with their possessions. Everything that they could manage to grab in the limited amount of time fate allotted them. Just the bare essentials; a hodgepodge assortment of clothing and personal hygiene products, and of course the source of all their misery and redemption, Just the essentials that were necessary to break free and try to rebuild their lives from the damage that arrived to consume them like a demon from the depths.

"Stay in the truck while I take care of what needs to be done," Tobias intones. He grabs the large jug of change he looted from the house on Arundel and climbs out of the truck. As he walks across the parking lot he's surprised by how hectic the environment is. He enters through the double doors, one of which is still shattered and has yet to be replaced, and bypasses the long line of people that are corralled in the grid of velvet ropes in front of the teller's station like livestock waiting for slaughter. He beehives over to the coin counting machine, waiting patiently for the woman in front of him to dump a paper bag full of change into the machine and collect her slip. Once it's his turn, it takes nearly ten minutes for him to do the same. The jug is heavy and hard to heft up, and lots of the change he feeds the machine ends up getting spit back out like the counter has a bad case of bulimia, forcing him to run it through a few more times until all that's left behind is a collection of coins that are either of foreign denomination or corroded with age to the point where they are beyond acceptance. When he pushes the button that spits out the receipt, he discovers that his haul is worth $2,227.12, which leaves him with a little over $2,000 after the 9.6% conversion fee the bank charges for not having an account with them. Taking his slip and the empty jug with him, he discovers part of the reason why business is booming as he waits in line. The drama from the day before has brought in two types of people. The first group is in line to close their bank accounts. They no longer feel safe at the Crookston branch.. They want to part ways and start anew in a better part of town. The second group is here to join the flock and glean any bits of gossip they can manage from the collective group. They talk to each other in hushed whispers, as if in reverence at mass, about the activities that transpired. Their talk resembles an adult version of telephone where the stories of what happened grow with embellishment and take on a life of their own. *Did you hear that Miranda is having a nervous breakdown? She told Shelly that one of the robbers jumped over the counter and forced his gun into her mouth. He was a big black guy, nearly six feet tall. John says he played basketball for Melrose U, and needed the money because he got one of the cheerleaders pregnant and couldn't afford to pay for the abortion. And not just any cheerleader, mind you, but Coach Richards daughter. He couldn't let Richards find out because Richards would've lynched him. Isn't that **just tragic**? I also heard from Greta that the bank tellers made a mistake during the robbery. Jeff told Randy that the bank has a security feature where they can click a button and lock the entryway doors, but they totally forgot to do it. If the doors had been locked they never would've made it out in time to escape. It also doesn't help that they let the security guard go without any notice last month. I wonder whatever happened with the basketball player's accomplice? You* *know. That burn victim? I heard from Kyle that he only agreed to help out with the robbery because he couldn't afford his skin grafting surgeries. It's a shame what these medical companies are charging and the situations they're forcing desperate people into. This would've never happened over in Europe.* And so on and so on the prattle continues in hushed reverence that barely conceals the enticement lurking just beneath the surface. It takes nearly 30 minutes for Tobias to get through the line. By the time he's handed over the slip and identification to the teller his patience is wearing out. Being handed a stack of twenties and hundreds, however, proves to be enough consolation to get his feet moving again.

When he gets back out to the truck, Maggie is exasperated. "Jesus Christ," she says, brushing her jagged bangs out from her line of vision. "You had me worried sick. It was taking so long, I thought something happened to you. What a fucking nightmare! I can't believe what you've done."

"What *I've* done?" Tobias asks, fanning the money in her face. "What!? Get you another two thousand dollars?"

"You know what I mean," she says all sullen.

Tobias snorts, casting daggers in her direction with his eyes. "What would you have had me do in your perfect little world? I didn't exactly have many options available at my disposal, princess. Would you rather I let her get to the house uninterrupted? We needed that window of opportunity. I can't help it that shit went south. How was I supposed to know she'd have a reaction? Luck can be a fairweather friend. They used to always talk about that in AA. You even said it yourself. I wasn't just going to sit back and watch our blessing become a curse. Murphy's Law, baby. Just like Old Man Jones always warned. I promised I'd never allow myself to be stranded on the wrong side of the shore if I could do something to change the tide. You should be happy! Things are lining up. We'll be on our way to making Frankie pay for his sins by weeks end. Lilly will be back in your arms like she never left. We'll get to do what so many couples always talk and dream about doing, but are too timid and somehow never get around to: we can rebuild our lives and start with a fresh slate."

Maggie throws her arms out defensively, as if warding off the animosity coming from Tobias' tone. "But at what cost? How are we supposed to feel good about everything when our happiness is at the expense of everyone else?"

"Jesus, Magpie, have you been living with blindfolds over your eyes your entire life, or are you just willfully ignorant? That's the way the world has always turned. Don't you remember hearing about what happened at the Miller's place a few years back? When they got hit by that terrible rainstorm? The one that knocked out the power from here all the way out to Albany. All the rain ran down the slope that overlooks their property flooding their land. All their pig pens were flooded. The only pigs that survived the night were the ones who were strong enough to climb atop the pile that huddled together in fear. The rest ended up drowning. The same principle applies to people. It's survival of the fittest. Float or drown."

"It sounds to me like you're just trying to justify your bad behavior. It's no different than a dealer who says they are only selling because if they didn't someone else would."

"Oh, fuck off Maggie. Who are you to be sitting in judgement of me? You don't seem to mind taking my money whenever I have any available, yet you have a problem with how I earned it?"

Maggie chuckles. "*Earned* seems like a bit of a stretch to me, Tobias, even by *your* questionable standards."

"I know what you're trying to do. You're just bitching for the sake of bitching, and I'm not in the mood to humor you."

Tobias reaches over to the radio and turns the volume up, effectively bringing their argument to an end. They don't speak to each other again as Tobias pulls out of the bank's parking lot and takes the exit onto 94.

36

When Vance comes to he's bathed in shadows. He gingerly reaches up to touch his head and winces. The throbbing coming from his temple feels like a rotten tooth that's been left to fester in diseased gums. He has no idea how long he's been out, but guesses that it hasn't been long. The scrapes along his arm from being dragged along the ground are still fresh, although he can't recall the experience itself. He opens his eyes to rafters which are far above, and realizes he's in the barn. Out of the corner of his eyes he can see Jacob standing with his back to him. Jacob is preoccupied gathering some objects over by the hayloft. Vance can hear the clink of metal on metal, and a deep uneasiness settles over him. He considers standing up, but the room is spinning. He knows he wouldn't manage to get far in the condition he's in. At the very least he has a concussion.

Vance can't figure out for the life of him what Jacob's intentions are. Jacob already admitted to stealing the fucking money after trying to play it off that he had nothing to do with it. What does he think he's going to accomplish by holding him prisoner in the barn?

Jacob turns around and the grin on his face is downright diabolical. "I see you're awake," he gloats. He approaches slowly. In his left hand he is holding a power drill. In his right hand he's holding rusty wire cutting pliers. "I suppose it's time to let the fun begin…"

37

There's a giant mural of a jazz quartet in the middle of a jam session on the side of the 4th Street Saloon that serves as a visual reminder as they cross into North Minneapolis. They follow West Broadway's meandering turns until they reach Penn Avenue, passing several buildings that are defaced with graffiti promoting various gangs fighting for turf. A cop exits the Penn Gas Stop just as Tobias pulls up.

"Shit," he mutters under his breath. He considers circling around the pumps and pulling out back onto the road, but doesn't want to risk drawing suspicion. Instead, he parks beside pump 7 and steps out of the truck, whispering to Maggie to keep her cool as he lifts the nozzle. A voice chimes in over the loudspeakers: "Pump 7, we require pre-pay, so use your credit card or come inside."

Tobias winces at causing the unwarranted attention, silently cursing himself for forgetting something so basic. Obviously they aren't going to allow people to pump gas before paying in this neighborhood. It's the same principle as going to a cheap whore house on the seedy side of town: you are treated guilty until proven innocent, and trust is the exception and not the norm. You take the money upfront.

Tobias walks up to the entrance of the gas station, where the cop is waiting for him. He feels a trickle of sweat run down his spine, and his heart skips a beat. Thankfully, his fear is unnecessary. The cop is only waiting to hold the door for him, reminding Tobias that despite the fact that it's hobbled and on life support, perhaps chivalry isn't completely dead after all.

"I haven't seen your face around here before," Tobias says. "Are you new?"

The cop nods his head in affirmation. He's carrying a cup of steaming hot coffee, which he carefully takes a sip of before responding. "Yes and no. I'm new to Precinct 4, yeah, but I've been on the force for quite a few years. They just transferred me here."

Tobias feigns laughter. "Sounds like a demotion to me, man. No offense."

"None taken. I don't mind it at all. I like keeping busy, and Lord knows there's more than enough to keep me occupied here. My wife swears I'm an adrenaline junkie, so it's a pretty good gig. It's better than trying to corral the college crowds back to their dorms on the East Bank after The Library lets out. Just a few weeks ago I had to break up a fight outside Burrito Loco over a game of beer pong after one guy had a few too many Blue Motherfuckers and accused the other guy of cheating,, but otherwise, it's more tedious than anything else. The only thing I miss about working at the U is Mesa. They had some phenomenal chicken alfredo pizza, and their slices of macaroni and cheese pizza were to kill for. And don't even get me started on a slice of their mashed potatoes and gravy."

"Sounds a little too experimental for my tastes."

"Well, to each their own," the cop replies. "Now you have yourself a wonderful day."

As the cop walks out into the parking lot, Tobias immediately feels a huge weight lifted off his chest. He gets in line and thanks his lucky stars that it wasn't one of the regular patrolmen on duty tonight, because they would've locked both him and his truck away faster than you can say repeat offender.

After a few minutes of waiting, Tobias grits his teeth with impatience. After spending over half an hour at the bank, he's reached his limits of having to wait in line. A shifty crackhead is buying smokes and a handful of scratch-offs with a mound of loose change interspersed with lint. Of course the Newports he's asking for are out, so the clerk has to go in the back to grab a fresh carton. While the clerk is dinking around in the back, the man proceeds to make good work on his scratch offs, and because God apparently gets off at taunting him at every available moment like any good bully would do, the crackhead ends up having several winners which he ends up exchanging with the clerk and trading for others.

By the time Tobias makes it to the front of the line, his annoyance has reached an explosive level on par with Chernobyl. The lady working behind the bullet-proof partition does nothing to alleviate his spirits. She's short and plump and covered in so much acne it looks like she's come out on the wrong end of an altercation with a beehive. Her hair is dyed a shade of purple so dark it verges on eggplant. You'd think that since it took so long to get the last customer through the line, she'd be especially diligent in trying her hardest to appease everyone else that's been patiently waiting, but alas, your assumptions would be wrong. She is so consumed in conversation with her coworker that Tobias has to clear his throat three times before she even bothers to glance in his direction. And when she finally does look his way, she has the audacity of rolling her eyes like a teenage primadonna.

"I'm sorry if I'm interrupting your stimulating conversation, sugar tits, but my time is just as important as yours in case you weren't aware, so how about you jiggle your chunky ass over to the Camels and grab me a pack of shorts."

Little Miss Eggplant's mouth drops open in shock. "Ex-*cuse* me!?" Her voice is the sonic equivalent of getting a root canal without novocaine. It makes fingernails scraping along chalkboard seem like Mozart playing *Don Giovanni* at his prime.

"I'm pretty sure you heard me clearly, darlin," Tobias responds. "But on the off chance that you were too busy fantasizing about diddling yourself with your Eager Beaver 5000 to pay attention, I'll repeat myself one last time. I said jiggle your lumpy cottage cheese ass over and grab me a pack of Camels. I haven't got all fucking day, and you've already gotten on my very last nerve."

The woman, whose name tag reveals to be Angela, flushes a dangerous shade of crimson- the same ruddy glow of a volcano on the verge of eruption. "Fuck you, you misogynistic twat!"

"Fuck *you*!? I wouldn't touch you with a ten foot pole, let alone fuck you: nor would any man that has an ounce of self respect or functioning vision. So how about you just get me my smokes and put twenty dollars on pump 7. You've wasted enough of my day as it is!"

"You can stick that twenty up your ass for all I care. I'm not doing shit for a mean-spirited old crackhead like you!"

Just then, when things seem like they can't get any more annoying, the door to the gas station swings open and Mr. Precinct 4 steps in. "Is there a problem here?" he asks.

Before Tobias can even try to neutralize the situation by responding, Little Miss Eggplant chimes in: "This guy is harassing me, Paul. He's being crude and sexist."

Precinct 4 turns to Tobias, and the friendliness he was displaying only moments earlier is gone. His expression is determined and nothing but business. "Is this true?" he asks. His gaze could pierce body armor.

"She's blowing this way out of proportion," Tobias nervously responds. Out of the corner of his eye he can see Maggie climbing out of the truck with a worried expression on her face. He motions for her to get back in the vehicle, and Precinct 4 follows his gaze.

"I'm not blowing anything out of proportion!" Eggplant squeals. "If anything, I'm understating. He told me I have a jiggly ass and started talking about sex toys! I've seen him around before. He's a bitter old crackhead who's always getting in trouble! He was at an AA meeting one time when I was going to support my sister. I'd be surprised if he has a current license. Either way, he certainly shouldn't be driving. Just look at him! If he's not in the middle of a three day bender, then I've been shacking up with Johnny Depp in a Paris love nest in my off time!"

"Now wait just a damn minute!" Tobias protests, hating the nervous tremor invading his tone. "I was just frustrated because Angela here is slower than molasses and had me waiting in line forever! She doesn't know how to do her job. Somebody needed to give her a wake-up call, and I figured that that somebody might as well be me!"

Precinct 4 gives Tobias a full one-over, assessing his body language as much as his response. Apparently what he sees leaves much to be desired.

"Alright," he tells Angela reluctantly. "Just take the higher road and ring him up real quick. I'll take care of the rest."

Tobias notices to his dismay that Precinct 4 turns back in the direction of his vehicle as he says this last bit, no doubt intending to run his plates.

Angela grudgingly rings up the smokes and gas, giving Tobias a subtle finger as she hands him his change. Precinct 4 is already out in his car by the time they finally finish their transaction. As Tobias walks out to his truck, he notices Precinct 4 leaning into his car and clicking away at his laptop. It doesn't take a rocket scientist to figure out what he's up to.

"Damn, Tobias," Maggie says, as he steps up to the pump and begins getting gas. "You had me nervous as fuck! What took you so long in there?"

The gas begins slowing to a glacial crawl as the meter nears its stopping point. Tobias glances over his shoulder in paranoia, ignoring Maggie's question. Much to his chagrin, he notices that Precinct 4 has finished tinkering on his laptop, and is approaching the truck in mid-stride with a grim look on his face… the look of a doctor about to tell a patient of news about a terminal diagnosis.

"Lock your door, Maggie, and roll up your window now," Tobias orders in a whispered rush. He expects Maggie to talk back, as is her usual custom, but the desperation and intensity in his voice must be apparent, because she instantly complies.

Precinct 4 calls to Tobias. Tobias chooses to ignore him, and proceeds to put the gas dispenser back on the nozzle and screws the cap back on his gas tank. As the cop nears, his right hand hovers between his gun and billy club like an indecisive bee unsure of which flower to pollinate first. Tobias attempts walking to his driver side door, but Precinct 4 circles around the opposite way and intercepts him.

"I'm afraid I can't let you leave just yet," he explains, with a shamefaced expression. "It's nothing personal. I just happened to notice you have whiskey plates. Can I see your license and proof of insurance?"

"This is unwarranted," Tobias protests. "You need probable cause."

Precinct 4 is incredulous. "Are you kidding me? You just got into a heated verbal altercation with a cashier looking three sheets to the wind, and this truck has whiskey plates to boot. Unless you're covered in blood and waving a firearm, it doesn't get much more probable than that."

"Fine," Tobias concedes. "I suppose you've got me dead to rights. Hold on for a second, and I'll get you everything you're asking for."

Tobias opens the driver side door, and leans in as Precinct 4 lurks behind him patiently like death in a hospice.

"Could you open the glove box, sweetie?" Tobias asks Maggie. She is looking at him as if he's lost his mind, which is appropriate enough considering he obviously doesn't have any of the documents the officer is asking for, and sweetie is probably the very last descriptive term he'd pick to describe her if handed a dictionary and prompted to do so.

Maggie opens the glove box and pretends to search within. After waiting an appropriate moment of delay, Tobias leans in and pretends to help her. He digs around until his fingers grope what he is looking for, and before Precinct 4 even begins realizing something astray, he whips around and cracks him in the jaw with the flashlight he's white-knuckling in a deathgrip.

Luckily for Tobias, the element of surprise is still on his side. Precinct 4 staggers backward, and before he can even attempt to try and draw his billy club or gun, Tobias is on him. He awkwardly scrambles forward from his reclined position in the truck bed, and locks his arms around the officer's waist with the strength of a Boa Constrictor tightening around its prey.

He pushes off with his legs, twisting sideways with the full force of his body weight, tumbling them both out onto the pavement in a mess of sweat and tangled limbs.

Precinct 4 finally regains his senses enough to reach for his gun, but Tobias is once again far too quick for him. He knees him in the groin, and as Precinct 4 starts to double over in pain, he swings down with his flashlight and pummels him across his nose, snapping it like a twig. A geyser of blood sprays out from his mangled nose, sprinkling Tobias' shirt in a fine mist.

"It's nothing personal," Tobias says as he delivers the final blow that separates Precinct 4 from his consciousness as cleanly as the soul leaving the body in death.

Tobias drunkenly weaves to his feet, feeling a wave of dizziness wash over him. As he starts the truck he can hear a flurry of whispers coming from a group of people who have gathered by the entryway of the gas station, no doubt drawn by all the chaos.

"Here. Take this," Tobias says, handing Maggie the bloodied flashlight. Her hands tremble as she accepts it. Her eyes are opened so wide she looks like she's just witnessed the second coming of Christ.

"What?" Tobias asks defensively. "He said he lives for excitement. I was just giving him what he wanted. Be careful what you wish for."

They pull back onto Penn Avenue and follow it until they reach Dowling. The street itself is surprisingly empty for this time of day, but many people can be found milling about on the corners and conversing on their porches. Tobias spots a woman passing a flask of liquor to an elderly man as they drive past a bus stop. The man reaches for the flask with gnarled weather-beaten fingers and a hungry look in his eyes that Tobias knows all too well. It doesn't take long until they are on Fremont and reach the next location of their scavenger hunt. After all, what's a long road trip without drugs?

38

Vance is hogtied on his side with a coil of rope. He'd tried escaping when Jacob came towards him with his instruments of torture. Instinct had kicked in and he'd leapt to his feet, but the spinning of the room had overpowered him, and he'd lost his balance. After falling to the ground like dead weight, Jacob had decided to use the opportunity to truss him up tight.

"How are those ropes treating you?" Jacob taunts.

Vance isn't in the mood to give him any satisfaction. "Fuck you, you demented piece of shit!"

Jacob doesn't like being called names. He kicks Vance in the gut, knocking the wind out of him. "Your hands and feet are starting to turn purple," Jacob observes. "I'm guessing you have no feeling in them by now. Pretty soon you're going to be wishing you had no feeling anywhere else." With the threat still lingering in the air, Jacob pushes the trigger on the power tool. It rustily groans to life. He lowers the point of the spinning drill in front of Vance's eyes. Vance squirms, but can do nothing to avoid it.

"Tell me where my daughter is," Jacob calmly responds. "I'm not playing games with you. I'll use this if I have to."

Vance can tell by his tone that he means exactly what he's saying. "Why do you think I have your daughter?" he asks. "I don't have a clue what you're talking about."

Jacob smiles, but his smile doesn't reach his eyes. They are cold and clinical, like the eyes of a mortician at the morgue getting ready for a dissection. "Oh, you know a lot more than you're letting on. I talked to Tobias a little bit ago. He was concerned. He said you came to him acting like a crazy man. He said you knew I took the money and had plans to retaliate."

"I didn't really mean it!" Vance cries.

"Oh, I'm sure you didn't mean a damn thing," Jacob teases, clicking the trigger on the drill once again. "Just like you didn't mean it when the money went missing and you said you'd come after my family! Now talk!"

"I don't know a fucking thing!" Vance insists.

"How convenient," Jacob whispers. Apparently the time for playing games has reached its expiration point. Jacob cuts open Vance's shirt with the rusty pliers and lowers the drill down to his ribcage. The squeal of the drill grinding into Vance's ribs is unpleasant, to say the least. But the squeal from Vance's lips is even more unbearable. Jacob pierces through the flesh, and drills into the bone until it snaps. A film of blood covers his hands, and Vance's shirt is drowned in crimson. As Jacob continues drilling, the smile on his face never wavers.

39

"Well, if it isn't the man, the myth, the legend," Tobias says as he walks up on an old man who is hard at work mowing his front lawn. The man is dressed in faded blue overalls covering a stained wife-beater, and looks more like a farmer from a small hick town on the verge of retirement than the dealer he is.

"Well, hot damn," Old Man Jones says, offering Tobias his fingerly-challenged hand in greeting. "I haven't seen you in a dog's age. What brings you around my palace?"

"I think we both know the answer to that," Tobias says.

"Well, aren't you looking pretty as a peach," Old Man Jones says, embracing Maggie. He cuts the engine on the mower and pulls a red bandana from his side pocket. He dabs at the perspiration on his brow absentmindedly. "How bout you guys follow me to my office? You know I don't conduct business in daylight. I'm like a vampire in that way. The sun doesn't suit my purposes."

His office ends up being a one-car garage that could be taken straight from an episode of Hoarders. They have to walk through a maze of hoses, yard supplies, tires, power tools, and what appears to be components for explosives that are in various stages of completion.

Old Man Jones steers them through the mess across the oil-stained concrete to the far northwestern corner of the garage, where a workman's station is set up. He opens a small oak chest that sits beside scaling apparatus, and pulls out a few ziploc baggies filled with cloudy white fragments that glisten like ice that's grown dangerously thin from the thaw of spring.

"How much are you looking to score?" he asks. His lips spread in a devious grin as he holds two baggies up to the light..

"Give me a couple bags of your best Heisenberg," Tobias jokes.

Ever since the cult success of the cable drama *Breaking Bad*, which is about the rise and fall of a drug kingpin, small time dealers have started dyeing their products to make them more marketable. Apparently their clientele equates the potency of the drugs as having a direct correlation with the hue associated with them. Unsurprisingly, sky blue is the favorite color of choice, as it was the color popularized in the show by Walter White and his alter ego Heisenberg. Clint once suggested to Old Man Jones that he might want to consider capitalizing on all the hype, but Old Man Jones had been quick to shoot that idea down. He reminded Clint about Travis King. Travis had been a moderately successful dealer who started staining his product gold as a trademark, but the problem about a trademark is what makes it a blessing can also become its curse. Sure, having a product that stands out from the rest can draw in new crowds through word of mouth, but on the flip side, the ease with which it's identifiable can also make it an easy target to trace back to its source. Only four months after flooding St. Paul's East Side with golden Royal Crown to sales that skyrocketed, Travis decided to put another product on the streets. It was dyed lavender, and extremely potent. They decided to nickname it Purple Reign after the Twin Cities' most famous resident. Unfortunately for King, his empire was about to collapse, and he didn't even have a clue. One of his new dealers he'd enlisted to push his new product was in a bind. The dealer was looking at serious time for violating his probation following an armed robbery stint, and turned on King by collaborating with the police as an informant. The police were able to link all of King's products right back to his doorstep, and now, instead of slanging dope to survive and thrive, he was behind bars bartering for cigarettes while trying to maintain the sanctity of his backdoor virginity, and unlike the informant who snitched him out, there would be no chance for parole in his future. True, the informant ended up disappearing under mysterious circumstances, only to be found months later fertilizing a ditch near Elk River, but at the end of the day King's revenge was a wash, at best, because the informant's suffering, while intense, had been relatively brief, and King's suffering was still hovering before his eyes and taunting like a mirage in the desert, where the sands represent an endless sea of years, and the oasis was a freedom he'd never achieve. Ever since hearing about Travis King's downfall, it had turned into a running inside joke between Tobias and Old Man Jones.

"You know I don't sell that gimmicky bullshit," he cackles. "I'll be damned if I end up in the slammer with King as my cellmate bum chum."

A hint of a smile reaches Maggie's lips. It's the first sincere smile he's seen from her since the break-in and subsequent damage control, and he finds it as refreshing as the first revelation of green grass after a long bitter winter.

"Bum chum?" she asks.

"It's the expression they use for butt buddy across the pond," Old Man Jones explains.

"Across the pond?" Tobias asks with a smirk.

"Christ, haven't you numb nuts learned anything since cradle school?" Old Man Jones asks in exaggerated exasperation.

"I'm sorry we don't have all your worldly wisdom," Tobias responds, "but in our defense, we haven't had the same advantage of being alive since before the Middle Ages. My memory is foggy. Could you remind us again what it was like being a waiter at the Last Supper?"

"You're no George Carlin," Old Man Jones grumbles. "I'd tell you to keep your day job, but you and I both know your ass is too lazy to maintain a nine-to-five like the average Joe Dirt. Now, how about we get back to brass tacks. How much are you looking to score again? Half a gram?"

Tobias reaches into his pocket and pulls out a wad of twenties that he teasingly waves in front of his face like a fan. "How much do you suppose I could get for this tidy sum?"

"Shit!" Old Man Jones says, his eyes opening wide in surprise. "For that kinda money I can get you enough dope to resurrect Amy Winehouse and kill her with an overdose again!"

Tobias laughs. "A couple of 8 balls should do the trick."

Old Man Jones looks at Tobias suspiciously as he begins weighing out his product.

"What are you guys up to? Prepping for doomsday? Or is there a drug drought on the horizon I should be made aware of?"

"It's complicated," Tobias says defensively. "Let's just say that I have some out of state unfinished business to take care of for Maggie and leave it at that."

"Okay. No need to get your panties all in a bunch. I was just curious, that's all. I get my kicks by blowing things to hell. Who am I to judge?"

Old Man Jones finishes weighing the product and Tobias gives him the required cash. As he grabs the meth, he decides it's time to *really* get down to brass tacks. "Speaking of blowing things all to hell, did you hear about that explosion at *The Hungry Mind* yesterday, and the bank robbery in Crookston?"

Old Man Jones tilts his head back and cackles once again. His explosive laughter could make a hyena cringe. "Did I hear about it? *Of course I heard about it! How couldn't I have heard about it!?* They keep replaying it on the news like it was the fucking Kennedy assassination! The interior of that bookstore was eradicated! Fucking ashes to ashes and dust to dust!"

"It was something else, alright," Tobias agrees. He pauses for a second, not quite sure how to broach the elephant in the room.

It turns out he doesn't have to worry. Old Man Jones does the job for him.

"You're goddamn right!" he replies. "Truth be told, I couldn't watch the footage without getting that familiar itch. It reminded me of something I would've done!"

Tobias takes a deep breath before proceeding. "In a sense, your handiwork was very much present."

Old Man Jones narrows his eyes at Tobias in confusion. "How do you mean?"

Tobias hesitates again.

"Just spit it out!" Old Man Jones says with impatience.

"Well, here's the deal. I'm not quite sure how to tell you this, but your son was involved in the robbery. Did you hear about the man disguised as a burn victim?"

The look on the old man's face tells Tobias all he needs to know. "I'm sorry to be the bearer of bad news, but Trevor was the one they talked about in the news who died in the robbery."

Old Man Jones is at a loss for words. He opens his mouth, but nothing comes out. Instead, he starts breathing rapidly and gasping as if he's choking on the air.

"Are you alright?" Maggie asks in concern. Old Man Jones slides down to his knees, with his back propped against the workmans station.

"Why would you say that?" he gasps. "They haven't released any names on who was involved. How in the fuck could you know?"

"Let's just say I have an inside source," Tobias says.

It doesn't take long for Old Man Jones to deduce who that inside source must be. "Vance Fisher," he groans. "Trevor never went anywhere without that sack of shit!"

"If it's any consolation," Tobias begins, but Old Man Jones cuts him off.

"Consolation my ass!" he rasps.

Tobias continues his train of thought, unperturbed: "Vance just wanted me to let you know that he feels terrible for what happened. He says he understands he's completely responsible. Trevor never wanted to hit up the bank. Vance talked him into it, and he'll feel forever guilty for how things played out. He thought of you as a second dad."

"He's no child of mine!" Old Man Jones spits. "Because of him I have no child!"

His words disintegrate into tears as the realization of what he just said fully sinks in. He starts hyperventilating again, and brings his mangled hand up to his chest.

"Oh, Christ," he wheezes. "My heart! My fucking heart! Can you get my cell phone? It's in the kitchen!"

Tobias stays with Old Man Jones as Maggie scurries off to call an ambulance.

"I'm really sorry, man," Tobias says.

Old Man Jones is sweating like he's in a sauna. His skin is starting to pale. "But not sorry enough to tell me the truth before getting what you needed," he wheezes. "Acting like everything was just fine so you could get your dope."

Tobias doesn't know how to respond, so he chooses not to. He just pats Old Man Jones on the shoulder and walks back out to his truck. There's really nothing left to say. He's kept his word to Vance, and as far as he's concerned his obligations have been met.

Maggie joins him in the truck a minute later. 'Is he going to be alright?" she asks.

Tobias shrugs. "How would I know? But that's none of our concern. We've got what we came for. All that matters is we're long gone before help arrives."

Maggie looks at Tobias expectantly. "Are we ready to head to Vegas?"

"Almost," Tobias says. "There's just one last stop we need to make. Just one last bit of unfinished business. Then the real fun can begin…"

40

Vance awakens to a world of soul numbing torment. He's still in the barn. Jacob still hovers over him. The bloody power tool has been set aside. For the moment, at least. Vance passed out from the crippling pain after Jacob fractured his third rib. Jacob never even bothered to stop and continue the interrogation. It's like he got a high from the pain he was inflicting, and Vance discovers a bitter truth.

"You have no intention of letting me leave here alive," he says. His voice is barely above a whimper.

"Well, look who joined the party again," Jacob replies. It's obvious he's having a good time. The sadistic fuck. "Tell me what you did with Harvey and I'll make up my mind on what to do next."

Vance notices that Jacob has wrapped a tarp tightly around his midsection to staunch the bleeding. Vance tries to respond, but the pain of even speaking causes him to stop.

"What were you going to say?" Jacob asks. "Have you had enough? Have I convinced you that I don't mean business?"

Vance gags, tasting blood on his tongue. "I'm the final link," he gasps, realization fully striking home. "With Trevor already dead and about to be identified, it won't take long until they trace him back to me. If I'm dead, you won't have to worry about getting implicated."

Jacob chuckles. "I'd be lying if I didn't say that hasn't crossed my mind," he says. "But I don't want to hurt you anymore than you want to be hurt. I just want to have my baby girl back. If you tell me where she is, and she isn't hurt, this won't have to get any more messy than it already has. I swear it! Just tell me where my baby girl is."

Vance coughs, spattering his chin with blood. "I'll tell you," he finally relents. "Come closer, it's hard to speak." His voice is so soft Jacob can barely hear it. He leans in to discover Vance's revelation, and when his ear is close to Vance's mouth Vance strikes. He lunges forward and tears into Jacob's ear with his teeth. Jacob yanks away in a panic, and his earlobe is torn off. Vance spits it at him and screams: *"Fuck your baby girl! She's probably sucking Satan's cock in hell!"*

Jacob is so surprised by the sudden turn of events that it takes him a few seconds to recuperate. "I was hoping it wouldn't have to come to this," he replies. His voice is trembling with anger. "But you've left me no choice, motherfucker. What I'm about to do is going to make what I did to your ribs look like child's play." He leans in close with the pliers.

41

The bell jingles as Tobias enters Casey's Hardware. He knows that he shouldn't have bothered wasting his time. He knows that it's incredibly petty and reckless of him to come here, given the situation. Yet, he couldn't resist himself. A promise is a promise, after all.

Thankfully, Jackson is behind the counter again this afternoon. He's not unloading supplies this time, however. Instead, he's sitting by the cash register leisurely flipping through a copy of *Time* magazine. He's so absorbed in his reading material that he doesn't even bother looking up to see who came in.

"Well, hello there Jackson," Tobias says.

Jackson jerks his head up so fast that his double-chin jiggles. He looks like he's just been busted reading a copy of *Hustler* instead of *Time*. It's the classic deer in a headlight expression that reminds Tobias why this pitstop was so worth it.

"What do you want?" Jackson barks. "I already made up my mind! I told you yesterday that I can't be handing out loans like Halloween candy. My old man won't stand for it!"

"Oh, I don't need a loan now," Tobias replies, as he cockily pulls a handful of money out from his pockets. "I guess you could say I came into some good fortune."

Jackson relaxes a bit, but still looks a little on edge. It's amazing how much of a difference the promise of potential money can make in a person. "W-well, I'm glad to hear that," he awkwardly stammers. "Now what kind of propane heater did you come here looking for again? One of those portable ones, right?"

"I didn't come here to buy a propane heater, you damn fool," Tobias laughs. "Don't you remember what I said to you last time before I left?"

Jackson is looking like he wishes they had a security system with a panic button installed that he could push, and frankly Tobias doesn't blame him in the slightest. "Um, uh-uh…" His stammering is growing tedious to listen to. Tobias cuts him off, answering for him: "I told you that you better pray to your God that next time I come back here you're not working, or you'd be in for a surprise. Did you pray?"

"Uh, I-I-uh-always pray," comes Jackson's hesitant response.

"Well, apparently your God wasn't listening," Tobias laughs. "Now imagine that?"

Tobias leans over the counter and starts pummeling Jackson with his fists. With each strike he feels more powerful. Maggie can hear the frantic screams from outside in the truck. As Tobias heads out of Casey's Hardware he feels like a man with a new lease on life.

"Can you spare some change," comes a voice as he settles behind the driver's seat. Lo and behold, Tobias discovers his day has gotten even better than he could've imagined. It's the same homeless guy who annoyed the living shit out of him last time he was in the Cities. Only this time, there's a remarkable change. The homeless man reeks of hard liquor, and sways on his feet like a ship tossed at sea. In fact, he's so delirious from drink that he doesn't even seem to remember who Tobias is.

"You thought you were all high and mighty," Tobias chuckles. "Well, welcome down to the basement where everybody else lives. Couldn't resist that cake tempting you from the windowsill, could ya?"

The homeless man just stands there as if he's deaf and mute. "Could you spare some change?" he asks once again, as if he hasn't heard a word Tobias just said. His eyes are shiny and blank.

Tobias pulls out a twenty and hands it to the old veteran. "Now that you've got your head out of the clouds and out of your ass I'd be more than happy to help you find some real relief."

"God bless," comes the reply, as he pulls away from the curb leaving the homeless man behind in the fumes of his exhaust…

42

Vance struggles as Jacob pulls his pants and boxers down around his ankles. As Jacob brings the rusted wire cutting pliers down to his penis, his testicles constrict to the size of grapes, as if trying to find a way to burrow back within his body.

"You brought this on yourself," Jacob says as he opens the pliers, applying the tips of the rusty blades to the base of Vance's limp penis. "Everything could've been alright if you didn't let your greed get the best of you. But you had to deceive me and steal the money my family so desperately needed."

Vance's eyes open wide in confusion. He tries screaming his innocence, but ends up gargling on blood instead.

"You twisted fuck!" Jacob yells, applying pressure on the blades. "Why did you steal the money? Did you really think I wouldn't follow you back to where you were keeping it? We could've split it down the middle, but you just had to keep it all for yourself! I broke into the house and found where you hid it. And let me say, you did a half-assed job putting it in that crawl space by the stairwell. Shit, you might as well have had a neon sign announcing where it was. And then you have the nerve to retaliate when I go to get what was rightfully mine!? Luckily, Tobias let me know what you were up to this morning! If it hadn't been for him telling me about your threats I wouldn't have you right now!"

Vance continues choking on his blood. Splotches of red have soaked through the tarp covering his ribs, and he can feel the world around him fading in and out of focus. He tries speaking again, but his lungs are completely submerged, and the only sound that comes forth is a raw bubbling.

"Did you really think I wasn't going to kill you when I found out what you'd done!?" Jacob screams. "It's a dog eat dog world, and if I wasn't here to finish the job now, God only knows you'd be coming back to reclaim the money later! And I can't let that happen. Tori is going to be back soon, and I can't let anything happen to her! You've already taken enough from us. Now I'll give you one last chance so you can at least go to your grave with a clean conscience. Tell me what you've done with Harvey and this madness can stop! You don't have to suffer any longer!"

The raspy bubbling is Vance's only response.

"Suit yourself, you racist piece of shit! Have fun in Hell. Send Trevor my regards."

The wire clipper has trouble tearing through his flesh, and the dance with death he'd managed to narrowly evade outside the bank has come back to haunt him with a vengeance. While everyday can be a potential miracle, it can also be a curse. The clipper becomes slippery with blood as Jacob slices through a bulbous vein in Vance's cock. He has to snip five times through the spongy mess of tissue before he's able to sever it, and by the time he's finished, Vance's eyes have rollen back in their sockets, and darkness is the only thing he sees as it blankets him like an old friend and swallows him whole...

Part 5

All's Hell That Ends Well?

43

The early afternoon of November 9th finds Tobias and Maggie in a motel on the outskirts of Sante Fe, New Mexico. Maggie stands before the chipped formica countertop in the kitchenette staring through a window at a vast expanse of desert that stretches before her like a shimmering dream. She is wrapped from head to toe in a faded pink shawl they found at a thrift shop, but the chill in the room is still finding ways to permeate despite her precautions. There's just no escaping the cold now that the room's heater suddenly went on the fritz, and she doesn't fail to miss the irony of the situation: now that they have all the money they could have ever hoped for, they are still in the same terrible predicament they were struggling to avoid only 9 days earlier. True, winter isn't nearly as terrible here in the southwest as it is back in Minnesota, but it's still disconcerting nonetheless. She'd been envisioning damn near tropical weather when they'd hit the road for Vegas. Now she feels like the cold climate has followed them like a bad boyfriend who couldn't give a shit less about a restraining order.

Maggie is starting the coffeemaker up when Tobias exits the bathroom. He looks remarkably different than he did when they embarked on the trip only a week earlier. For one thing, he's shaved not only his head, but all of his remaining facial hair. He's wearing a freshly ripped pair of jeans, as well as a faded leather jacket that could've been ripped straight from the set of *Happy Days*. He's also put on a good ten pounds, as will happen when going on a long road trip and having the finances to stop at whatever fast food joint that catches the eye. Now, instead of looking like an emaciated Santa Claus, he merely looks like a Hell's Angel or neo-nazi that's fallen on hard times.

Maggie, likewise, has taken pains to change her physical appearance as well. She's shaved the undersides of her scalp and streaked her hair pink. She's bought a nice fur jacket and a pair of dangly gold earrings that look like a helix. She's also updated her wardrobe to include several lingerie slips in various animal prints, and accumulated a large collection of Mary Janes that Tobias is mysteriously drawn to and keeps tripping over as if they're magnetic.

Ah, the joys of finally having money.

Living in the motel has been an eye opening experience. That old saying about how you don't know what you got til it's gone also works in reverse. You don't appreciate what you've been missing until it finds its way back. She relishes the little details of life she's been lacking, like the opportunity of being able to bathe whenever she feels the urge. Likewise, having access to electricity again has been incredibly liberating. Tobias complains about the motel bed not being firm enough. He says it hurts his back, so he keeps sleeping on the ground instead, but otherwise, they've slipped back into the routine of modern living with few qualms.

Now, if they could just get rid of the damn chill that keeps lingering, maybe her sense of unease would fade.

"Care for a cup of coffee?" Maggie asks as the Keurig gurgles to life. She finds something about the hiss and spatter of the coffee filling the cup strangely comforting. It's just another domestic perk that most people take for granted on their monotonous drive to work, but as far as Maggie is concerned it doesn't get much more heavenly than a cup of coffee paired with a fresh cigarette in the morning. Between that and a book, there isn't a better paradise to be found when down and out.

"No thanks," Tobias says. "It'll make me piss like a racehorse. I just finished smoking all the energy I'll need for the morning. I don't need any damn drink to give me wings. I'm already higher than any wings could ever take me."

Maggie shrugs dismissively, playfully taking a sip from her freshly filled cup of coffee with her pinky finger daintily pointing outward; the way her grandmother taught her during tea time as a child. "Suit yourself, but don't come crying to me when you start fading. Caffeine and nicotine make the world go round, Tobi. You need to get with the times."

Tobias crosses the kitchenette and takes a seat on the red polyester pull-out couch by the television. He motions at the opened zipper bags brimming with money on the coffee table before him.

"I don't need to get with the times, Magpie," he says with a smirk and a wink. "I've seen the future and I know what makes it tick. It's the same thing that's always governed over everything: the almighty dollar. And now, finally, thanks to our ambition, for once we've got a stake in our own destiny. The drought is over."

Maggie opens her mouth to respond, but Tobias cuts her off instantly, as if reading her thoughts: "And don't even try feeding me that bullshit 'but at what cost' line again. I did what was necessary, and you clearly don't mind spending the fruits of my labor."

Maggie wisely decides to keep her mouth shut. She's not in the mood for an argument. It's too fucking early to start with the verbal warfare, and besides, their talks would only lead to gridlock anyway. Maggie has already resigned herself to carrying all the guilt for the both of them. She wishes she had the same mental capacity that most men are innately born with; the ability to compartmentalize her emotions. But she's just a bleeding wound and there's nothing that can be done about it. She can try to numb her rawest edges, but they'll always be waiting around a corner like a mugger in the dark for the right moment to catch her off guard. It's best she just bite her tongue and let it bleed.

Although he'd be loathe to admit it, Tobias is equally just as befuddled as Maggie is by the sudden curious turn of events, although he doesn't want to dwell on what can't be changed. He's learned it's easier moving forward when your eyes aren't drawn to the ground. But, despite his best intentions to ignore the looming elephants in the room, once in awhile, usually in the dead hours of night when sleep is evasive, he can't help but mentally circle over the bits of drama like a vulture trailing carrion.

It seems as if it was only yesterday that he went down to Minneapolis on his excursion to score a propane heater and make some profits. It had felt like everyone was conspiring against him on that day, and sadly enough, he didn't know what bothered him more in retrospect: the contempt he'd experienced with Jackson and the homeless man, or the alienation he'd felt from being surrounded by so many people blindly cloaked in happiness and oblivious to the pain that crawled around them.

Hitting up the house on Arundel Street had been the turning point he'd so desperately needed. All the minor annoyances and petty grievances were rectified when he got ahold of that Culligan jug filled with glimmering coins and hit the highway for home. He'd felt a strange exhilaration pumping through his veins that was better than any drug could provide, and he'd remembered having a wild moment of clarity that struck him like an anvil, a random epiphany that didn't seem to come from his own thoughts, strangely enough, but beamed in from somewhere alien and far greater: the comforting realization that with or without the money, things were going to end up the way they were meant to.

He watched the road unravel before him through eyes that belonged to someone else. He noticed the perfect symmetry of the pine trees blazing in the distance, and heard the calls of migrating geese overhead through ears that weren't his own. As he lifted his pipe to his lips with the trembling fingers of a stranger and took a drag, he felt the silky smoke invade his lungs, and when he exhaled, he felt the weight of the earthly world wash away, and with it, the last whispers of his weariness and self doubt. The road around him became like a shimmering mirage, the sky a melting watercolor painted by hands that were beyond human. He could feel down to his very bones the sense that he wasn't alone. That a passenger rode along with him that would never leave because they were fused at the root. And this passenger reassured him that there was no need for regrets. That the road that unravelled before him was nothing but a stage, and his bit part in the play had been written as was intended. This force guided him as smoothly as a planchette along a ouija board, and he realized why he'd always felt such unease around the people that populated his life; whether friends, family, lovers, or strangers. They were all a part of the symmetry that surrounded him. They were part of the balance that kept life afloat, while he was a source of chaos that came from somewhere darker and deeper and more primitive. Somewhere more honest. Where others were meant to be subservient and play by the rules, he was meant to carve a path that didn't follow any guidelines. The people in his life created things in their own image, symmetrical and boringly predictable. They didn't possess the bravery he had to throw all caution to the wind and breed with destruction. He may have been born of flesh and bone like every other bland creation, but he'd had intercourse with chaos, and while others were slaves to the trappings around them, he'd gone against the grain and now his sand could build a sea. It was all as was intended.

And then, as if in affirmation to his sudden epiphany, the vehicle he's been following jerks to the right- as if the driver has nodded out after too many miles behind the wheel, or maybe too many cocktails. But this isn't just a case of typical highway hypnosis or a drunken stupor. The driver and passenger in the car seem to be in the middle of some sort of heated altercation. The driver is flailing his arms about, and the vehicle is slowing to a crawl. The passenger window is being rolled down, and a small bag is tossed out and tumbles down the embankment like a runaway train. A few seconds later, it is followed by another bag that ends up meeting the same fate as its predecessor. The car continues driving along as if nothing out of the ordinary has happened. As if the driver considers it part of his patriotic duty to smite all tree hugging hippies and environmentalists that are turning society into a bunch of whining pansies by converting every highway into his own personal dumping ground.

Tobias pulled his truck over to the shoulder of the highway, leaving the engine idling as he climbed out. He slammed the door behind him with a hollow thud, all the while his imagination running wild with the limitless possibilities of what the bags may contain. He knows from random pilfering expeditions they will more likely than not be empty or filled with dirty running pants or sweatshirts hastily discarded from a post-gym workout, but still his mind stubbornly reels with hopeful visions of jeans carelessly forgotten with debit and credit cards still safely stowed away in pocket, or knock-off second rate purses loaded with bottle after bottle of pharmaceutical bliss, like a genie in pill form awaiting his every personal desire. Hell, he'd even settle for a half empty pack of Pall Malls or a skin mag featuring trannies. Beggars can't be choosers, as the saying goes.

As Tobias neared the spot where the first bag was tossed, a black cat jumped out from the undergrowth startling him. It scampered up the embankment, casting an annoyed glance over its shoulder, before plopping down in the grass to daintily start licking at its paws. Tobias lowered himself down onto his hands and knees, tentatively maneuvering the branches of the primrose bush so the sunlight could filter in. He noticed the duffel bag lodged sideways against the roots of the primrose bush, and could tell that his first assumption was clearly wrong. The bag wasn't empty. In fact, it was bloated and bulging like the belly of a mosquito after an extreme blood binge. And after managing to pull it out from the hellish thorns of the primrose to reveal what it was hiding, the whole world seemed to pause and tilt on its axis. He'd never seen so much money gathered together in one place in his entire life. It was surreal. All the crisp bundles cast such a spell on him that he had to remind himself to keep breathing.

Tobias glanced over his shoulder for someone on the horizon, his mind screaming that there had to be a catch. He expected to see a drug dealer with a semiautomatic coming to pick up the drop, or an undercover informant dressed in a dapper suit set to intercept, but none of the phantoms from his vivid imagination materialized. It seemed too good to be true. Things like this never happened to people like him, at least, not outside of the movies or a novel. He had to act fast.

Tobias clutched the bag of money tightly against his chest, and ran back to his truck with the single-minded determination of a running back intent on avoiding a fumble with the end zone in reach. His paranoia of time constraint almost propelled him to take off without even bothering to gather the other bag, but ultimately his greed ended up outweighing his paranoia. This was a once in a lifetime opportunity, and he'd be damned if he was going to be short changed. After all, while one bag of money is undoubtedly wonderful in and of itself, he was a gambling man at heart, and when given the opportunity of doubling down, only a sucker or coward will back down. The age old Vegas adage says it best: go big or go home. And he'd been staying at home for far too many years- long after everyone else had had the sense to move on; whether through death and senility, like his father and mother, or through good old-fashioned motivation and willpower like his sister Krissi. He was ready to be free from the self-imposed shackles of his youth. He was ready to shed the skin of his former life, and this money would be a perfect way to celebrate and usher in a glorious rebirth.

When Tobias reached the second bag of money, he noticed it was sopping wet with what, at first glance, appeared to be bloodstains, which, needless to say, did little to alleviate his paranoia. He chose to grab it anyway. He was all in as it was. There was no turning back now.

Once safely back in his truck, Tobias realized that the stain wasn't blood after all. It was clearly some sort of ink or dye, like the type that are used by banks to catch a criminal. At least what happened was no longer in dispute. Somehow, the bank heist scenario made him feel less worried. It's better the devil you know than the devil you don't know, after all.

Tobias brought the money back to the farm, feeling like he was being watched the entire drive. Luckily, Maggie was nowhere to be found when he arrived. Despite not seeing anyone tag him on the ride back, he still couldn't shake the persistent nagging thoughts that someone was watching him. The feeling reminded him of one time when he was a child and saw a Monster Movie Marathon shortly before Halloween. For the next few weeks he couldn't sleep without fears of what was patiently waiting under the bed to pull him in. Even surrounding himself with a semi-circle of protective stuffed animals did little to alleviate his fears. After all, what match are flimsy animals filled with stuffing compared to the rusty steel blades of a maniacal child murderer that attacks you from beyond the grave in your dreams? And likewise, what was paranoia if not a survival instinct?

Tobias originally decided to hide the money in the hayloft after repetitively counting it. He felt a wave of dizziness wash over him, and expected to wake up at any moment. He couldn't comprehend what his eyes and his repetitive re-counts were telling him. There was no way that the bulging duffel bag contained over eighty thousand dollars. It wasn't possible that the stained bag contained well over twenty. It was inconceivable.

He buried the bags under a bundle of hay and climbed down the rickety ladder. He was halfway back to the farm when self-doubt made him turn around and climb back up the loft again. He unearthed the bags expecting them to be empty. He still couldn't shake the feeling that this was all just a vicious dream. The money was still there, of course, but he realized that he wouldn't be able to sleep knowing it was so far away. He had to bring it back to the farm. But where could he store it without feeling like the narrator in the Tell-Tale Heart? It would have to be somewhere in close proximity to his mattress. It's then that he thought of the stairwell. There'd been some loose and missing boards in the woodwork for quite some time. Maybe he could convince Maggie that he was just trying to keep the windchill to a minimum by working on it, at least until he had time to properly wrap his mind around the sudden turn of fortune and figure out what to do next.

Tobias went back into the farm to find Maggie taking a nap in the living room on their stained mattress. He cautiously removed enough boards to stow the money away, nervous that it would wake Maggie up and he'd have to explain himself. Every creak felt like a spike being driven into his skull. But somehow, despite his intense focus and tunnel-vision determination, all his efforts at discretion ended up being to no avail, because Maggie ended up catching him off guard anyway. Luckily, he'd already hidden the zipper bags and Culligan jug behind the partition, but when he'd attempted explaining his reasoning behind why he was tinkering around near the entryway, Maggie had been noticeably suspicious. She knew that Tobias wasn't a handyman, and fixing things was about as appealing to him as attaining sobriety.

Tobias made a mental note to move the money at his earliest convenience, but unfortunately what seemed incredibly simplistic as an objective proved to be a lot easier in theory than it was in practice. Maggie ended up following him around like a hemorrhoid. Every time he attempted breaking away from her, she'd cling to him like a sex addict at the club looking for their next orgasm. It was as if she knew what his intentions were. Something was certainly out of the norm, because she was never the type to be clingy. That was what had attracted him to her in the first place, after all: her not give a fuck strain of fierce independence. Needless to say, Tobias was getting thoroughly annoyed by her shenanigans. When she asked him if he'd scored any meth well down in the cities he claimed he was all out, having no interest in listening to her manic ravings. He talked her into going upstairs to get some gutter weed instead, thinking that might buy him enough time to move the money, but of course, his attempt was short lived. She went flying up the stairs like a bat out of hell, and he barely had a chance to take a puff off his pipe before she was back in his face and giving him an interrogation, claiming he was holding out on her. Of course, that was the truth, but trying to reason with Maggie about his reasons behind why he was holding out was as hopeless as a chihuahua being pitted against a pitbull in a dog fight. He was never going to win.

Luckily, Tobias was saved the futility of defending his actions by a knock on the door. And boy, what a knock it was. The door trembled in its frame like it was in the grip of a grand mal seizure. Tobias assumed it would either be the police or a Jehovah's Witness, seeing as how they so rarely had visitors. The paranoid voice in his head chimed in that the gig was up. Obviously, the money had been planted with a tracking device. It would be all too fitting for his dreams of flight to be derailed before he even had a chance of leaving the runway. He expected nothing less than Murphy's mother fucking Law at its mother fucking finest, and all that jazz. Therefore, when the door thundered open, and Vance was waiting on the other side of it instead of imminent disaster, he was utterly flabbergasted. It had been a couple years since he last saw the stubborn son of a bitch, and had somebody told him earlier that day how excited he'd be to be reunited and see Vance's ugly drug-addled mug again, he'd have told them which end they were talking out of; and it wasn't the end you kissed your mother with.

Vance was an absolute fucking hot mess. In other words, he looked pretty much exactly the same way Tobias remembered him to be, open sores and all. It became clear by the look on Vance's face that wasn't just visiting for a social call. He was noticeably distracted and bothered by something, and Tobias had a sneaking suspicion that the roots of what was troubling him could probably be traced back to what he'd hidden in the partition only hours earlier.

Vance asked if they could go outside to talk, and Tobias had been more than happy to accommodate his unexpected guest. Once outside, Vance started acting oddly poetic and reflective. After barely any prodding, he admitted that Trevor had died at his expense, and wanted to know if a message could be passed on to Old Man Jones on his behalf. Tobias asked him why he couldn't pass the message on himself, secretly relishing the opportunity of playing devil's advocate, but Vance had been purposefully vague in his response. He steered the conversation back to the tribulations of dealing with survivor's guilt. He made Tobias promise to follow through and relay the remorse he felt to Old Man Jones. Tobias convinced Vance that there was no need to fret. If he'd been a man of a weaker disposition, he would've felt a twinge of guilt over the windfall of money he'd gained at the expense of his childhood friend. But, if there's one thing he'd taken away from all the collective years of dealing with bio-dad, it was the irrefutable fact that it was a dog-eat-dog world out there, and if he didn't tear out the throat of his opponent first, then surely they'd tear out his. If the roles were reversed, Vance wouldn't hesitate to bare his fangs and go for the jugular, so why should he waste even an ounce of emotion on something as useless and counterproductive as regret for the sake of regret? It was a no-brainer.

Tobias led Vance back to the house, and it was there that they were met by Maggie, who was standing in the entryway with her hands on her hips like a warden assessing the aftermath of a prison riot. He tried talking to her civilly, but she was unusually chilly in her response. She was hinting at something bothering her, and he knew in his gut that he had every reason to panic. He cursed himself for being so naive to leave her in the house unattended after the suspicious way she'd been acting after finding him in the stairwell. When she admitted that she knew he'd been lying to her and revealed that she knew about the money, his breath caught in his throat. For her to drag everything out into the light of day in front of Vance was his worst nightmare come to fruition. He was about to try and defend himself, knowing that in all likelihood he'd probably just end up digging his hole deeper, when the pressure from his gut was lifted after she made it clear that she was just talking about the change from the Culligan jar. He tried explaining why he'd held back on telling her, but she wasn't in the mood to humor him. Hell, she'd even turned down a peace offering of dope. He didn't need to be a neurosurgeon to know that his odds of winning this argument were stacked. Apparently Vance seemed to catch the drift that this argument wouldn't be settled anytime soon because he made an excuse to leave, which was more than fine with Tobias.

After the argument, the rest of the evening was relatively uneventful. Then again, anything would pale in comparison to the amazing morning he'd experienced. Maggie spent a lot of time curled up on the mattress reading *Full Dark, No Stars*, and Tobias spent a lot of time being drawn to the cooler like a victim in a science fiction novel being pulled against their will aboard a spaceship. Tobias tried engaging Maggie in conversation, but of course she was cold and dismissive. He asked her what was wrong, and she denied that anything was amiss, insisting that she was just fine, and would be even better if he'd just stop pestering her for a minute, so he decided to follow her advice and head out to the outhouse to recycle a few beers. While he was on the shitter he wondered if he should just come forward with the truth. He hated it when Maggie was distant and sulky. It was obvious she was still pissed that he left her out of the loop about the money he'd scored from the GPS heist. A part of him strongly wanted to be upfront and tell her about the *real* extent of his gains, but he knew from experience what a crapshoot that could end up being. There was a possibility that she'd be head over heels with elation, and it could seal the deal in gaining her unwavering trust. But there was also an equally distinct possibility that she'd just take off in the middle of the night and leave him high and dry. God knows, it wouldn't be the first time he'd travelled down that dreary road. I mean, sure, he'd been there for her in her time of need and provided a temporary roof over her head, not to mention an endless all-you-can-smoke buffet of dope, but gratitude was notorious for being fickle, and loyalty could be even worse when it came to being a fleeting whore.

Telling Maggie would be a risky proposition, There was no doubt about it. And was he willing to wager over $100,000 to find out if they had what it takes to weather any storm? He'd already been burnt once by Emily. He'd worked his ass off at the manufacturing plant putting in overtime as a solder wave machine operator. It had been monotonous as hell, but he'd done it anyway to bring in enough money to curb her nagging. But the money he brought home was never enough, She kept complaining about how her best friend was able to get whatever she wanted without having to feel like she was applying for a loan, and implied that maybe her father had been right after all. Maybe she should've stayed with Duncan. He'd recently passed the bar, and was litigating with a powerhouse firm that regularly aired commercials during primetime. But she'd let her adolescent hormones get the best of her and allowed herself to fall into the age old trap of falling for a guy just because he was a free spirited bad boy that didn't take shit from anybody and played by his own set of rules. She thought she could mold him like clay and iron out all his wrinkles, and look where that had gotten her. He was just as reckless as he'd been in his teens, if not worse. And while she'd found it exciting in the early days, when it was just wild sex and endless parties, now that her thirties had gone from being a blasphemous rumor whispered of from far away lands to a painful reality that was as unavoidable her shadow in a brightly lit room, the charm had quickly worn thin, and Emily had reached her limits. When Tobias took out his frustrations on her by fucking her flirtatious friend, it was the last straw. Emily left everything behind without so much as a backward glance, and it didn't take long for Tobias to self-destruct on an even grander scale. He'd attempted living the straight and narrow for her, but, when the shit hit the fan, like any addiction run wild, the farm had pulled him back in like quicksand, with a gravitational force that was simply too irresistible, and provided a haven and fortress from the outside world that had rejected and spit him out like a wad of disposable human snuff.

He'd felt like he was just going through the motions of living without feeling a real pulse until Maggie entered his life. And if he lost her, well, he knew there would be no rebounding this time. He'd be jumping from an airplane without a parachute. And he'd make Nicolas Cage's suicide pact of drinking himself to death in *Leaving Las Vegas* look like child's play. There'd be no limits to the depths he'd plunge.

Maggie was curled up on the mattress still reading her Stephen King novel when Tobias came back in from the outhouse. He was still wavering between coming clean or continuing with his deception, when Maggie did him the favor of making up his mind for him. She admitted to him why trust was so important to her, retreading the experiences she'd had at The Meat Market. He'd heard her talk about what a living hell it was so many times over the past few years that he could quote it in his sleep. Only, this time, she elaborated with some details she'd neglected to mention in the past. And not just *little* details, either, but *fucking Chernobyl* details. Obviously, it was no secret that Frankie had been abusive and dehumanizing. After all, it took a special kinda asshole with questionable morals to run an establishment as colorful as his in the first place. But Tobias had underestimated how dark and twisted his perversions really ran. Not only was he abusive mentally and physically, but he also had no qualms with making people that tried to stand against him disappear. He ran his fetish joint with the iron fist of a dictator towering over a struggling nation. Whatever girls he wanted to sample were his for the taking. He kept them satiated with a steady diet of sex, drugs, and alcohol, and expected their full obedience and a life of servitude in return. Maggie had been his main concubine, and he'd unwillingly fathered a kid with her that she wasn't allowed to see. He'd cut her off from all her worldly ties, and paralyzed her with threats and consequences toward the ones she'd left behind. All Maggie knew of her daughter was that her name was Lily, and that she was being brought up at his main residence in California by hired hands that also took care of the other babies he'd raped into this world. She admitted that Frankie and his men were probably still looking for her, and coming to Minnesota had been her way of trying to get away from it all. Living off the grid hadn't been ideal, but it was a lot better than dealing with constant paranoia and fear. So, in a way, she'd used Tobias every bit as much as Emily had in the past, but unlike Emily, her intentions had been in the right place. She'd grown to not only like her unorthodox lifestyle, but learned to embrace the relationship she'd stumbled into. She didn't have any intentions of ever leaving. In fact, her ideal dream was to get Lily back so they could start a family of their own. But the looming threat of knowing that Frankie was still out there kept her up for many sleepless nights, and she was worried that her dreams could never become a reality.

On a day that had been ripe with epiphanies, this one took the cake. And what better day for epiphanies than on Halloween? It was a day meant for transformations, after all, and thanks to Maggie's revelations, Tobias felt, for the first time in his seemingly endless life, like he finally had a rough blueprint of what his future might hold. And he knew that a future without Maggie in it would be no future at all. So, without hesitation, or any second-guessing, Tobias came clean about the riches he'd came into, and not only that, he also promised to solve the Frankie problem as well. After all, the odds were finally on his side. He'd already proven himself to be adept at finding things, and he had a sneaking suspicion that if Frankie could handle it, than he could be just as equally good at making them disappear.

Maggie was overjoyed, to put it mildly. They consummated their happiness in the hayloft, and Tobias couldn't remember the last time he'd felt more alive. Therefore, when he woke up later that night to find Vance had returned again, his dismay felt amplified. It was obvious that Vance had gotten the shit beat out of him, and it was hard for Tobias to mimic surprise when Vance told him the reason why. He'd gone back to collect the money and it had up and disappeared like a fart in the wind. He knew that his partner in crime was responsible, and he had no idea what to do about it. Tobias prodded him about where the money came from, and Vance admitted he'd robbed a bank. He explained that it would be all over the news come tomorrow morning, and it wouldn't be long before law enforcement identified Trevor as one of the robbers and be able to trace the crime back to him. He was pissed because he'd been double-crossed by his other accomplice, and he no longer gave a fuck. He proved just how little of a fuck he gave by calling out his third conspirator by name. It was their childhood friend Jacob. Jacob fucking Black. While Vance had stopped by the farm to have Tobias pass his message along to Old Man Jones, Jacob had had the fucking no good dirty rotten nerve to steal his share of money right out from under his nose. And then the motherfucker played stupid on top of it, as if he thought Vance was a complete imbecile and wouldn't see through the bullshit. It had led to a fight, and Jacob threatened that Vance had better bring the money back before Harvey returned from her sleepover or else there would be grave consequences. Vance wasn't having it, though. He'd threatened Jacob and his family. Now he was just waiting for Jacob to make the next move. Tobias asked if Vance really meant what he was saying, and Vance hadn't shied away. He said he had a gun and would use it if he was left with no other resort. His life was over anyway once the news came out. He had nothing left to lose, so why not make Jacob feel some of his pain?

    Tobias told Vance to sleep on it, and maybe they could find some way of avoiding resorting to violence in the morning when they could think more clearly. After all, he wasn't in any danger of losing track of Jacob. He knew right where he lived. He also had leverage because he could bring Jacob down with him if he didn't come to reason. Vance agreed. He was still thoroughly disturbed, but he knew that some rest would do him good. So that's just what they ended up doing. Before Tobias closed his eyes and let sleep overcome him, he made a vow that he'd take the money and leave with Maggie in the morning, and let the chips fall as they may.

44

But the morning had other plans in store for them. Tobias awoke from a loud rumble of thunder. The storm was tapering off, but even in the hazy morning light he could instantly tell that something was amiss. For one thing, it was cold. Obviously, that was nothing new for this hell hole, but it wasn't just cold. It was *fucking freezing*. His arm that had came loose from the blanket in the middle of the night felt like it had been submerged in ice water. Tobias climbed out of the bed and could feel a draft coming in from by the entryway. He walked towards the source of the chill and froze in his tracks. He could see a fan of broken glass fragments glimmering along the floor near the far wall. And all that was left of the window above it was a maw of jagged glass that resembled teeth in a rotten mouth.

Tobias knew before he even checked that the money would be missing. And his intuition didn't lead him astray. It took everything inside himself not to scream out in frustration. He ran up the steps in desperation, expecting Vance to be long gone, but Vance was safe and sound, curled up in the depths of a deep sleep that Tobias knew all too well. It was the crashing aftermath of a drug frenzy, and judging by the expressions on his face, Vance's dreams were anything but pleasant.

Tobias went back downstairs and woke up Maggie. He brought her into the kitchen, and relayed all the information Vance had provided him with the night before. Maggie listened intently, and when he was done telling her all the latest developments, she came to the same conclusion that he'd been thinking. Jacob must have been behind the break in. There was no way that he would just let Vance walk away from the drop off location alone if he thought Vance had the money. Surely Jacob must have followed him back to the farm, assuming that Vance must have left the money someplace nearby. He probably did a thorough search of the property, and after coming up empty handed, decided that Vance must have hidden the money somewhere inside the house. It was so ridiculously obvious that Tobias had to fight against the delirious laughter that was rising in his throat. He'd found the money, sure enough, but ironically, he was none the wiser about how it came to be at its final resting spot. Now the money was likely to be back at his house, and Jacob's paranoia would be on full alert. He'd be waiting for Vance to try and retaliate. Especially considering the cryptic threats Vance had directed towards his family...

It was then, just when Tobias was at his peak of despair thinking about how terribly his odds were stacked, that a solution to reclaiming the money presented itself with the force of a brick hitting him upside the head. How do you stop somebody who is alert and driven by fear? It was simple, you had to turn their fear against them and use it in your favor. You had to flip the expectations. Jacob was worried that Vance was going to retaliate, so all Tobias had to do was make that retaliation a reality and confirm his fears. If he could distract Jacob with a diversion, it would give them just the window of opportunity they needed to get the money back again. All they needed was the perfect weapon, and when it comes down to it, what could be a better weapon to use against someone than their child?

Jacob's daughter was just the bargaining chip they needed.

After considering the options at his disposal, Tobias came up with an idea. He told Maggie his proposition.

Maggie wasn't completely convinced, however. She was still worried about the aftermath of how things might play out. But Tobias reminded her, they really didn't have any choice. If they wanted to set off to Las Vegas and California it would require some serious funding, and they'd never be able to make due with a child if they didn't follow through with this. Besides, living life on the lamb was nothing new to either of them, obviously, and this time they'd be doing it on their own terms, and with resources they weren't used to. Considering they'd managed to do just fine with next to nothing, imagine what they could achieve with $100,000? The possibilities were limitless. She just had to look at the greater good. And besides, he reminded her, with a smartass smirk, God had a plan for everyone. She'd said so herself the night before. There was no need to worry about taking ownership for their actions. Worst case scenario, if shit blew up, they could repent on their deathbeds or go to confession and all would be absolved and forgiven.

Maggie grudgingly agreed to help Tobias out, after realizing the implications of all that was at stake. She snuffed out the candles beside the mattress, as Tobias went into the kitchen and grabbed a can of Coke from the icebox. He threw it in a plastic baggie along with the last of his meth and drug paraphernalia. He was walking out to the truck, eager to get the show on the road, when Maggie reminded him that he forgot something in the house. Something that was crucial to their plan. He went back inside, chastising himself the entire way. Apparently his memory was faltering at a higher rate than he realized. That chemical persuasion was having an effect, after all, whether he'd like to admit it or not, although, God knows, he had no intention of slowing down. He could've sworn he'd left what they needed in the glovebox. They couldn't afford to make stupid mistakes like this when they were on such unpredictable time constraints. Jacob's daughter could be coming back from her friend's sleepover at any moment, and if they missed their window of opportunity now, the odds of getting the money back without resorting to violence and bloodshed would be slim to none.

They got in the truck, and took off at a casual pace, defying every instinct Tobias had to put the pedal to the metal. The last thing Tobias wanted was to draw undue attention. They parked the Ford near the intersection of Armstrong and Orchard Lane, a block up from Jacob's house, and began their stakeout. It was painstakingly tedious. They kept their eyes peeled, but no one was out walking. Since Jacob's house was at the end of a cul de sac, his daughter should have been easy to spot, but there were no signs of life.

Maggie was getting antsy. Tobias was wishing they'd stopped to get something to snack on to pass the time. It was no wonder so many cops ended up getting so heavy set. When you were stuck for long periods of time in a vehicle with nothing to do, it was only natural to want to activate your pleasure centers when caught in the merciless grip of boredom. Tobias reached for the can of Coke, but Maggie slapped his hand away. Instead, she offered him his pipe.

They were in the middle of smoking the last of his meth when a group of teenagers finally appeared. There were two boys and two girls. The boys were riding on skateboards, shaggy hair blowing carefree in the breeze as they chattered incessantly about the Vikings and their new billion dollar taxpayer-funded stadium. The taller boy had a beanpole figure that wouldn't look out of place in Ethiopia. Everytime he did a trick, he tossed a quick glance over his shoulder at a blonde girl with incredibly huge boobs. He was looking for approval, but apparently his alley oops couldn't hold a flame to the power of Snapchat, because each time he passes a glance at her, she leaves him invariably disappointed, as she is lost in a more important world all her own, absorbed within the screen of her cell phone.

Tobias quickly lowered his pipe, and exhaled a cloud of smoke that shimmered in the early morning sunlight like a mirage. He rolled down the window of the truck and called out to the kids. They looked over at him uneasily, and their faces were a collective reminder of how far down the rabbit hole he must appear. He probably reminded them of the type of guy they were warned about in horror stories when they were little. All he needed was a handful of Jelly Bellies and a rusty old rape-van with impenetrably dark window tint, and the picture would be complete.

Tobias glanced at the girl that was straggling behind the group. She had brunette hair and pretty eyes and was wearing a *Silversun Pickups* t-shirt. He asked if she was Jacob's daughter. The girl adamantly shook her head no. The shorter boy with the mop top chimed in that Harvey was up the road at crazy Miranda's house. Tobias asked for further clarification as to where this alleged mentally incompetent girl lived, noting that the road was littered with random houses filled with people of questionable mental status. Silversun fanned her hair out with her left hand, pointing at a streak of lavender. She explained that Crazy Miranda's dad was a huge Prince fan, and his house was painted accordingly. Mop top agreed. He said that her dad must have played *Let's Go Crazy* one too many times while she was still in the womb, because he couldn't think of any other logical explanation for how batshit nutty Miranda ended up. Tobias thanked the teens for being helpful, and started pulling away when Little Miss Hugetits stopped him in his tracks. She wanted to know why they were looking for Harvey. Thankfully, Tobias was able to improvise quickly. He said they were coworkers of her father, and that something bad had happened at the worksite. Silversun looked skeptical. She asked what went wrong. Tobias silently cursed her. He had no fucking idea what Jacob did for a living. He decided it would be safest to just remain as vague as possible. He explained that Jacob was injured on the job, and they had to pick up Harvey quickly because things were looking critical. Silversun wasn't convinced. She wondered how he could manage to get hurt so badly considering he worked in a tollbooth. So much for maintaining a forgettable profile. Oh well. Fuck it. They wouldn't be in town for very much longer, anyway, and he'd gotten all the information he needed, so what did it really matter?

    Tobias shifted the truck back into drive, and left the teens behind in a cloud of dust and confusion. He found the lavender house two blocks down the road, just as promised, on the intersection of Armstrong and Northview, and betcha by golly wow were they serious about Miranda's dad being a huge Prince fan. He'd expected the house to be a nondescript lavender stucco, maybe two stories, with paisley drapes as a subtle nod to his musical inspiration. Some kind of cool tribute, albeit easily forgettable, but this place looked like it had been beamed down from outer space. It was painted lavender, just as they'd said it would be, but they'd failed to mention the incredibly massive decals emblazoned across the double car garage featuring the Love Symbol that Prince changed his name to when he got into a dispute with his record label, alongside a gigantic hallucinogenic dove floating on a wispy pool of metallic amethyst tears. But the real kicker was in the alcove by the front door. After walking along a Wonka-esque looping cobblestone path that cut through an ocean of what would undoubtedly be violets, had blooming season not already come to an end, Tobias stopped beside a stone statue of the Purple Jesus Himself. It was imposing at nearly seven feet in height, which was ironic considering his natural stature in real life, and the level of detail was incredible. It captured Prince in all his glorious purple splendor. He was decked out in his iconic suede jacket with the medieval dress shirt underneath, replete with flowing white ruffles and sweeping sleeves. Tobias was still marvelling at the level of detail in the statue when the door opened abruptly, and he was greeted by a short man with a balding scalp that vaguely resembled Danny Devito. The man inquired how he could be of help. Tobias complimented him on his incredible statue and choice of landscaping, and then explained how he was a co-worker of Jacob's, and how he needed to pick up Harvey because there'd been an accident at the worksite. The man seemed a little taken aback, but said he'd get Harvey and offered his condolences, adding, almost as an afterthought, that Jacob would be in his prayers.

When Harvey came to the door, Tobias was awestruck by her overwhelming beauty. She had long raven black hair which she wore in braids down to her shoulders, and an olive complexion that hinted at an ancestral heritage that could probably trace its roots to someplace near the Mediterranean. Tobias had heard the expression before claiming how the eyes are the windows to the soul, but Harvey took it to another level. Her eyes were large and almond-shaped. They were a beautiful hue of hazel and showed no signs of mistrust as Tobias explained what had happened to her mother's boyfriend. She just grabbed her overnight bag and followed Tobias out to his truck as blindly and purposefully as one of the children in the old fable about the Pied Piper being led by enchanted music to their inevitable demise. Tobias missed being that naive. He missed the comfort that came from having faith that things had a purpose and happened for a reason.

Maggie was waiting in the truck, and she let Harvey scoot past her to sit in the middle. Harvey was worried. She asked if her mother knew what was going on, and whether or not she was already on her way to the hospital. Tobias assured her that she would be waiting at the hospital for them, and not to worry. It was almost sad how easily she could be deceived. It amazed Tobias how trustworthy she was considering the instability of her upbringing. He wondered if she was aware that her real father was locked up in prison. Then again, she lived in a small town, and Lord knows small towns were synonymous with tongue-wagging gossip, so she shouldn't be completely naive.

Harvey asked how far away the hospital was. Tobias reassured her that they'd be arriving soon. As he merged onto 94, Maggie offered her the Coke that Tobias had tried sampling earlier, and Harvey politely accepted. Apparently her trustworthiness knew no limits. She had no qualms that the Coke was already open and being offered by a stranger. She just tilted the can back without so much as the slightest hesitation and took a big gulp. She grimaced and commented how the drink tasted funny, but that didn't stop her from chugging some more. She trusted that they were on the way to the hospital. She wasn't worried about getting in a vehicle with strangers, because in her little world people actually said what they meant and meant what they said. In her world adults were trustworthy and she'd never heard the horror stories of drinks being spiked with mild drugs, let alone a stronger painkiller like Tramadol.

Maggie switched the radio on. Apparently the awkward silence was getting to be too much for her to handle, although the chipper banter from the dj wasn't much better. She kept glancing at Harvey in the rearview mirror with the curiosity of a scientist watching a lab rat scurrying safely beneath glass. It didn't take long before the science experiment hit a rough patch and Maggie's eyes filled with alarm. Harvey had started to nod out in the backseat, which had been their intention, but her arms were breaking out in angry patches of vivid red hives. It was clear she was having an allergic reaction of some kind.

Tobias took a sharp left onto Chippewa. He was trying to bide time for the sedative to kick into full gear and render Harvey unconscious. They were no longer heading in the direction of the hospital, but Harvey was no longer in the right state of mind to notice. She had bigger fish to fry. Instead of falling peacefully to sleep like they'd so naively envisioned, she had instead started to hyperventilate. Her breathing was labored and had the same type of raspy hitch that brought Tobias back to the last time he'd visited his mother in the nursing home when she was on her deathbed. She'd been a pale imitation of the woman he'd remembered, a caricature at best, with a mess of tubes snaking around her in a mad nest. While once she'd worn her hair elegantly in a bob that had been all the rage when Onassis became the first lady, all that was left were random patches of fluff that came out when a brush passed through. While once she'd prided herself on her smile, more often than not she spent most of her time in the nursing home neglecting to keep her dentures in, so her lips were perpetually puckered like she'd tasted something sour that she disagreed with. Her skin had turned nearly translucent, aside for a patchwork mess of liver spots, and a network of veins could be seen struggling to keep the blood flowing to her faltering heart beneath. On the day they'd buried her, the last time he'd seen his sister Kristi, she'd looked nearly sexless in her casket, with her hands, which looked more like skeletal claws, crossed before her chest. They'd displayed her in a string of pearls and the type of silk dress that she'd never been able to afford while she was alive. Nothing wrong with a little false advertising when it came to the afterlife.

Tobias pulled the truck over on the shoulder of the road. He asked Harvey to tell him how she was feeling, but of course she didn't respond. Her eyes were squeezed tightly shut as if in pain, and her arms had started to twitch slightly, as if a small electrical current was being applied. He opened her mouth and checked to make sure there were no obstructions, but her airway was clear. Thankfully, she hadn't swallowed her tongue.

Maggie asked what she should do to help, but Tobias had been at a total loss. He just told her to remain calm while things ran their course, which, of course, was easier said than done when the phrase is used as a distancing mechanism for what could amount to potential death. Maggie tentatively suggested that maybe they should bring Harvey to the hospital after all, but Tobias made it crystal clear that that wouldn't be happening anytime soon.

Five minutes went by and Maggie just watched helplessly as the tremors Harvey was experiencing went from a mild spasm to full fledged teeth chattering seizures. She tried to hold Harvey steady, but Harvey was shaking so badly it was as if she were in the throes of an exorcism. Her little polka-dot dress had hitched up to her thighs, and her ponytail had come undone from its rubber band and lay in a silken sheet beneath her head, which whipped back and forth. A skim of froth had escaped from between her lips like a rabid animal, and for some ludicrous reason it reminded Tobias of the venti vanilla latte Maggie sometimes liked to order from Starbucks when they had a little extra spending money to piss away, which was next to never. Just when it seemed like it would never end, Harvey's seizures started to taper off, and Tobias was cautiously optimistic that everything might end up being alright after all.

By the time they pulled back up to the farm it became clear that Harvey's seizures stopping had just been a red herring, because her breathing had slowed to a crawl, and her pulse was likewise practically nonexistent. They tried talking to her again, but she was still unresponsive. They carried her into the house and laid her down on the mattress. Her skin was sickly pale.

Tobias ran into the kitchen and grabbed an ice cold can of beer out of the cooler to calm his nerves which were on edge. He had just finished chugging it in a quick succession of monstrous gulps when Maggie called out to him from the living room in unmistakeable panic. He rushed to find her propped over Harvey on the mattress desperately trying to perform resuscitation. Tobias joined them on the mattress. He lifted Harvey's arm up to check for a pulse, but there was none. He lowered his head to her chest, just to make doubly sure, and his suspicions were confirmed: her heartbeat was equally nonexistent.

Maggie was beside herself. She started pacing and crying and listing the various ways they were legally fucked. Tobias tried to explain that none of this would come back to haunt them, as long as they acted quickly to avert the avalanche of shit that was developing, but getting through to Maggie was as futile as trying to shout through to someone caught in the eye of a tornado. She'd reached her limits when it came to death and destruction, and couldn't handle this surplus of pain. She collapsed next to Harvey on the mattress and started sobbing uncontrollably. It was shocking to watch her hard exterior come crumbling down. Had the hand of God came crashing in through the ceiling at that moment to crush them like the insects they were, it wouldn't have been anymore unexpected or jarring to witness.

Tobias tried to coax Maggie out of bed, but she refused to get up. She curled against Harvey and wrapped her arms around the girl in an awkward embrace. Had Tobias not known any better, they could've been mistaken for mother and daughter.

Tobias kept looking toward the stairwell in paranoia. How Vance hadn't managed to wake up from all the sobbing was beyond him. He reminded Maggie that they didn't have time to waste. Jason would be suspicious soon when Harvey didn't arrive back home, and they needed to plant the seeds of doubt in his mind and utilize every minute his fear provided. First, Tobias just had to figure out what to do with the body. As long as she was hidden well, it wouldn't matter what Vance tried saying to defend himself. He knew Jason well enough to know that once he saw red there would be no breaking through to him. It would be a case of reacting first, and thinking about the consequences later. But all this hinged on Vance still being at the farm for the altercation to take place. If he woke up from Maggie's crying fit all bets would be off. They might not have enough time to recover the money, and Tobias would be damned if they went through all this bullshit in vain. He was tired of living in filth with shattered expectations and having to come up with some creative new hustle just to tread water a little longer. For once, he'd love to walk the streets with his head held high and a sense of purpose, but first he just had to jump through this one last hoop, and soon he'd be relaxing on a white sandy beach with nary a care in the world. But what to do about Harvey? Where best to stash her body that no one would suspect? As Tobias looked at Maggie curled up against Harvey in a fetal crescent moon, inspiration struck as quickly and violently as lightning. He knew what he had to do, and he intended on acting before his resolve weakened to rust. After all, as his mother liked to say, why put off for tomorrow what could be taken care of at the moment?

Maggie didn't want to part with Harvey. She attempted to claw at Tobias as he pried her away. She inexplicably started to rant about her grandfather and how he killed all her dreams with his hands that liked to creep up beneath her silken nightgown when her mom wasn't around. She was always too busy with her boyfriend of the moment to be bothered with the little details like what her daughter might like for dinner or what might happen in her absence. It was only by a sheer miracle that Vance somehow managed to sleep through all the havoc.

Tobias dragged Harvey's lifeless body out of the farmhouse and did what had to be done.

45

When Tobia came back inside the farmhouse later after the handling of the disposal was completed, Maggie was still lying catatonic on the mattress. Tobias handed her the glass pipe and she took a hit in a lackluster way he'd never seen before. She exhaled a cloud of sweet poison and sat up in a daze. Her gaze was blank, but at least her hysterics had tapered off. By the time he talked her into going out to the truck she was almost back to her old self again, although her responses became almost deceptively chipper when they pulled onto the road leading to Jacob's place. Tobias warned her not to act too strangely when Jacob answered the door. Her unhinged laughter in response did little to alleviate his concerns. Sure enough, when the time came, she was a little off, but Jacob was too pale and shaken to notice. After hearing the supposed imminent threats from Vance, Jacob peeled out of the driveway so fast that he left a skid of rubber trailing halfway down the block.

Tobias did a quick circle around the property once he was gone, peeking through the windows to make sure there were no signs of activity within. After he was satisfied that the place appeared empty, he checked the front door. Jacob had left in such a hurry that it was unlocked, and it creakily opened up onto a mud room. There were an assortment of shoes and boots placed orderly in a row on a rubber floor mat beside the entryway. On a lark, he checked the pockets of a jacket with a fur-trimmed hood that hung from a coat hook in the corner, but found nothing noteworthy but a yellow Bic lighter that he pocketed for later. A rapid upheaval of the cupboards in the kitchen revealed nothing of interest as well. Maggie walked into the room as he was finishing with the last cupboard above the fridge. A mess of pots, pans, tupperware, and random plates, bowls, and cutlery were strewn across the room in complete disarray. Maggie inventoried the chaos, and then with a dismissive shrug, walked past Tobias to check out the dining room. It was bare aside for a long water-stained maple kitchen table and a couple of Sennheiser speakers, one of which had a vase upon it which was filled with roses and surrounded by a floral halo of dead petals. She briefly glanced out the sliding glass door as Tobias moved on to the living room, but nothing caught her eye. Tobias searched through the entertainment center, but the cubbies led to little in the way of revelation, aside from the fact that Jacob was apparently a fan of Tarantino and Gus Van Sant films. Maggie pulled the the lever on the side of the forest green La-Z-Boy, and felt within the nooks of the plush cushion, but came away with nothing but loose change and an old tattered receipt to Best Buy that was so faded she couldn't even make out what had been purchased.

    Tobias entered the hallway and dug through the claustrophobic confines of a linen closet, but as with every other attempt, he came away with nothing to show for the fruits of his labor but a dull sense of frustration.

    The bathroom was a complete shithole. The toilet and shower tiles were covered in a layer of mold that had been neglected for so long it had turned black and furry, like a peach gone to rot. The vanity beneath the mirror was filled with a basic garden-variety clutter of hygiene products and toiletry items, but, much to the chagrin of Tobias, there were no prescription meds to be found in the medicine cabinet.

    Tobias ran upstairs, glancing at the clock over the stairwell in paranoia as he went past. Meanwhile, Maggie moved on to the last room of the main floor. The first thing she noticed upon entering was the giant canopy bed that held dominion over the room. It had billowy silk netting that was tied tightly against the hand carved bed posts like the masts of a whimsical feminine pirate ship, and reminded Maggie of the same bed that she'd always wanted as a young girl. The walls of the room were painted a delicate shade of pink that she associated with the powdery American League baseball gum her first boyfriend used to alway chew before they started their tentative makeout sessions. On the walls were two posters. One was a hand drawn depiction of a girl dressed up in the chainmail of a knight approaching the tower of a castle that another girl was trapped in. A river of tears streamed down from the eyes of the maiden who was held captive above. The second poster featured a young man with long raven black hair that was in a band named Milkweed. He was sulking in the middle of a heavily graffitied alleyway with piercing brown eyes that spoke of angst and loss and the damage that comes from needs that can only be met by needles. He was dressed in a business suit that had been shredded with a razor blade and featured a tie that was covered in skulls and crossbones. The posters reminded Maggie of the sharp contrast between the fledgling years of her childhood and the early awkward stage of entering womanhood with a fractured sense of self and an endless tirade of doubts. The room undoubtedly belonged to the girl that had just been disposed of. The realization took Maggie's breath away and made her feel dizzy. She sat down on the bed before her legs could go out from under her. She tightly closed her eyes and took a trembling breath, and silently willed her vertigo to wash away. She could hear Tobias stumble in the room above, and the familiar sound of his mumbled curse snapped her back to reality. There was no time to waste. The last thing they needed was a confrontation with Jacob. She had Lily to think of. It was a shame that Harvey had to die; that her young life with so much potential had to be snuffed out and tragically cut short before having a chance to make a meaningful mark on the world, but it was equally unsettling to imagine her daughter having to grow up in a place of perversion under the tutelage of an immoral thug lacking any sense of morality or warmth. She had to keep the big picture in mind and find the strength to face and conquer the horrors of her past. The only way out was through, after all, and she intended to kick down any fucking barrier that stood in the path between her and the future she had with the daughter she'd never been given the chance to know.

 Maggie checked under the canopy bed but found nothing but an old pair of ballerina slippers. She went through the nightstand and dresser. In the nightstand she found a paperback edition of *The Perks of Being a Wallflower*. The dresser was filled with clothes and a hairbrush that likely doubled as a microphone for Harvey when she sang and danced to whatever contrived crap currently passed as music for tween millennials.

It was in Harvey's closet that Maggie finally struck paydirt. The zipper bags were buried at the bottom of a wooden antique toy box, beneath an avalanche of various plush stuffed animals that Harvey had outgrown. But the zipper bags weren't the only items of importance lurking in the shadows.

Maggie yelled for Tobias and he stormed down the stairs in a whirlwind. He released a blood curdling shriek of joy that sounded more pained than celebratory when he saw the bags cradled in Maggie's arms. He motioned for Maggie to follow him back to the truck, but failed to notice the look of gravity on her face. While they'd managed to find exactly what they were looking for in the toybox, an unexpected surprise had soured her happiness...

46

And now she sits in the motel room at the rickety kitchen nook with the object of her unease clutched firmly in her hands. It's a furry pink diary that belonged to Harvey, and she's found herself flipping through the pages listlessly over the past few weeks, relishing in the pain it provides like a masochist cherishing the sting of a whip. Like a tattoo, the diary is a constant visual reminder of the consequences of desire, and like something conjured from the void of a lucid nightmare, it grounds her to the reality of the sickness that exists and thrives in this world. Like a cut rimmed with a crust of dried blood, it's a scar she can bathe in and soak in until the stains of humanity can no longer be denied or avoided.

Sometimes Maggie flips the diary open and picks out a passage at random without looking. More often than not, the sentiment of the passage echoes with something she herself would've written as a child. In one paragraph, Harvey complains about not getting an allowance for all the chores she does, and Maggie used to always get into similar prolonged arguments with her mom over the same issue, and much like her mother, Jacob's explanation about a lack of allowance is that the electricity keeping the lights going was more than a worthy substitute, not to mention the water that flowed through the tap and provided her with showers. While some of the parallels in the passages are subtle, others are downright eerie. Harvey took ballet lessons and wanted to be a ballerina when she grew up. Harvey also talked about wanting to have a baby when she was older, and damned if one of the possible baby names she picked out as an option wasn't Lily. It was enough to make Maggie's arms break out in goosebumps, and she couldn't quite shake the feeling that somehow Harvey was the light to her darkness. That somehow maybe Harvey would've been able to achieve everything that she herself had failed at if given the right opportunities. If only her path of lightness hadn't been eclipsed prematurely.

Maggie sets the diary down and glances out the window over the kitchenette. The desert sand is kicking up in a brisk dance, and the sun is peeking through a patch of clouds like an electrified mango, casting everything below in a ghastly glow that brings to mind thoughts of nuclear radiation and terminal cancer.

"You know, I once dated a guy who was in love with New Mexico," she says. "He fancied himself a poet and an artist. He was obsessed with Georgia O'Keefe and her vaginal flowers, and the habit she had of replicating the same paintings to capture a new perspective in an object and bring life to something that's supposed to remain stagnant and passive. He told me the ultimate objective of art is to take the ordinary and bland aspects of life that we've taken for granted after years of growing old and cynically complacent, and to reinvent and transform them into something extraordinary and new. To give life and a heartbeat to the dull moments, so that we can re-experience them through the eyes of a newborn. I never quite understood what he found so fascinating and appealing about the repetition. It always seemed so boring and pointless to me, but now I think I finally understand."

Tobias looks up from the pile of money he's been hovering over like a fly on shit. "This better not be some more of that self loathing bullshit," he says. "I'm getting sick of all your pity. What's done is done and can't be undone. How many times do I have to say that? Pining over something that can't be changed is a complete and utter waste of time. It's indulgent."

"It doesn't matter what you say," Maggie explains. "Just like O'Keefe's paintings, I may look the same from the outside, but I've changed, and I'm never gonna be the same."

"Enough with the theatrics!" Tobias yells. "It's wearing me down! We've been blessed, and all you can do is sit around and mope!"

"It was my idea to give her the pills," Maggie says. "Her death is on me. You can live in fantasyland if you'd like, but I can't trick myself into thinking that everything is alright when clearly it's not."

"Well, you'd better learn to improvise and fake it til you make it then, because we're never going to get Lily back if you keep staying distracted like this. I'm not heading out to Las Vegas until I know you're fully onboard and have your head straight. We can stay in this motel until we both rot for all I care, which would be a shame considering how close we are and how far we've come."

Tobias starts grabbing the stacks of money from the coffee table and throwing them back in the bag. He pockets a couple crisp hundreds from the final bundle, and proceeds to take the bag and shove it inside the heating vent, which he secures back into place with screws.

Maggie joins Tobias on the couch, and it's still clear from the expression on her face that she's not nearly ready to end this argument. She reaches inside her purse and pulls out a glass pipe. There is still a small skim of meth left within. She puts the pipe to her lips and holds the lighter beneath the bulb of glass. The silken spiral of smoke that invades her lungs brings with it the minimal amount of relief she seeks.

"Let me have a hit," Tobias implores. Maggie stops him when he reaches for the pipe and holds up her pointer finger.

"On one condition," she says. "And don't try bullshitting me, either. Where did you hide Harvey's body? I need to know."

"And how is knowing going to make any difference?" Tobias asks. "Do you think it's going to somehow make you feel any better?"

"It's not about feeling better," Maggie insists. "There's nothing you're capable of doing that's going to make me feel any better at this point. My feelings are irrelevant. I just want to know the truth. Is that too much to ask?"

Tobias pauses before responding. He's not quite sure of the best way to proceed. "Let's just say she's somewhere safe and probably won't be discovered for a long time to come. Let's leave it at that."

Maggie isn't satisfied with his vague explanation. "Did you drag her out into the woods? Is she a feast for the wolves?"

"No," Tobias says.

"Did you bury her out in the silo under the hay where we fucked?"

"No," he says again. "Like I said, I put her in a safe place. She has the moon watching over her, whether it's day or night."

"Can you be any more fucking cryptic?" Maggie asks sarcastically. "I want a real fucking answer, and I want it now. I'm not kidding around."

"It's a place we've both visited many times. Now quit worrying your pretty little head over it. We've got to keep looking forward. It's unhealthy to fixate over this."

Maggie punches Tobias in the chest. She's had enough of his games. "Don't patronize me."

Tobias raises his hands defensively. "Don't make me out to be the bad guy. Everything I've done has been for you. I mean, let's face it. I didn't have to tell you I discovered the money. I could've taken off in the middle of the night and you would've been none the wiser. But I didn't. Hell, I could have left you back at the casino after swapping out the stained bills at the Icarus Redeemed slot machine. If you don't think I've done this all for you than I don't know what to say. I mean, Christ, just take a look around. I'm in the middle of the godforsaken desert. What the fuck more proof do you need from me?"

Maggie laughs sarcastically. "Give me a break. Your days were numbered in Minnesota no matter how you look at it, regardless of me. After you chose to take the money you willingly gave up everything. It's not like you had much to lose. Squatting on a farm isn't exactly living a life of luxury. It's not like you have any friends or family to care about. You couldn't be any more distant from your sister Kristi if you were on a different continent. Your dad is no longer around. Neither is your mom, but even if she were, she wouldn't recognize you from Brad Pitt anyway. Your friends are all deadbeats. Of course you have no regrets. You've been living in hell. The only way you could get any lower is by finding a trap door."

"Fuck off, Maggie," Tobias rasps. "Quit trying to demonize me. It's not like you're any better. Who the fuck do you think you're kidding!? You wanna shit talk me about how my dad was an abusive asshole and my mom lost her mind? Well, two can play at that game, sugarpie. Your mom was a money grubbing fame whore. Is it fair if I throw that in your face? How about if I talk about how your grandpa was a dirty old child diddling pervert, and blame it on you? Would that be fair? What if I suggested that you led him on and encouraged it? Hell, what if I suggested that you probably even *liked* it? How would that make you feel?"

"Ohhh, fuck *yooouuu*…" Maggie growls, her voice dropping to a dangerous octave Tobias never knew she was capable of. She grabs him by his leather jacket and pulls him toward her, slapping him in the face as he nears. The surprise of the sudden attack catches him off guard, and as he pulls away, he accidentally backs into the coffee table and loses his footing. The glass coffee table shatters as his elbow crashes through it.

"Jesus Christ, you crazy bitch!" he yells, as Maggie drops down on top of him amid the scattering of shattered glass and starts pummeling him with her fists.

Tobias grabs her by her arm as she reaches in to swing at him, and shoves her backward with all his might. She falls sideways and he twists around trying to gain leverage by grabbing her leg. Unfortunately for him, as he's reaching in to clasp her by the ankle, she takes the opportunity to cock it back and kick him square in the face. He hears a sharp crack like a stick being snapped as his nose breaks, and pauses in shock and disbelief as blood sprays from his nose in an arc. While physical altercations are nothing new to their relationship, she's never caused him to bleed before.

"Fuck you, you fucking asshole!" she screams as she shrinks away from him. Her hair is a shaggy blonde mess, and her body is a live wire. She stumbles to her feet and hobbles over to the door, leaning against it for support like a boxer in the final round.

Tobias remains on the ground, sopping up the blood from his mangled nose with his balled up shirt. He knows he's pushed Maggie too far with his sharp comments, but he's in too much pain to give much of a fuck, and anyway, it isn't his fault all this started. She was the one who pushed him into a corner and wouldn't relent. What the fuck did she expect?

"Have fun frollicking out in the desert!" he yells, as she staggers her way through the door. "Your pale ass can use all the sun it can get!"

The parking lot outside the motel is practically deserted. There are only two other cars parked beneath the flickering neon sign of *Norma's Oasis*. A young girl in a Hello Kitty shirt is standing in front of a Coca-Cola vending machine with her little brother. They look over at Maggie with concern as she approaches them. It's obvious they've heard everything that transpired in the motel room.

"Are you okay?" the little girl asks Maggie, looking up at her with big brown imploring puppy dog eyes.

"I'm just fine," Magie responds, although the quaver in her voice indicates that her words couldn't be any further from the truth. "No need to worry about me, honey. But you really shouldn't talk to strangers. You never know what the consequences might be. Believe me."

The children stare at Maggie in bewilderment as she walks past them with her head held high, a shifting look of resolve strengthening itself in her eyes. The little girl's brother starts bickering once Maggie is out of his line of sight. He complains that he wanted a can of Orange Crush instead of Mountain Dew. The little girl isn't fazed in the slightest. "Beggars can't be choosers," she says in the well-versed exasperation of a school teacher trying to keep control of a classroom that's perpetually on the verge of spiralling out of control.

"I don't wanna drink Crush," the boy whines, with tears welling in his eyes. "It's not fair!"

"Well, life's not fair!" the girl shouts back, obviously mimicking something she's been told many times before. "Deal with it!"

"You're a bully," the boy cries back, his lips trembling. "I'm telling mom!"

The rest of their argument fades into obscurity as Maggie walks away, but she can't shake the feeling that it brings. Whether young or old, petty arguments all sound the same. She feels shame realizing that her conflicts with Tobias must be just as trivial to outsiders. It's permissible to be overly emotional and reactionary as a child, but she's a full grown woman. There's no excuse for being so dysfunctional and out of control anymore. She should already have all her emotional baggage sorted through and filed.

Maggie walks toward the car parked in front of room 187. It's the same car Tobias has been fixating on all morning. As she walks, conflicting emotions war for jurisdiction on her face. It doesn't have any noticeable sirens, but she knows an undercover cop car when she sees one.

No one is in the vehicle, but the silhouette of a figure standing in the window of the motel room is unmistakable.

Still feeling indecisive, Maggie stops in front of the door to the room. Two potential futures stretch before her, shimmering like a mirage in the heart of a desert.

One future is plagued by doubts and insecurities. After all, she's made it a bad habit of jumping from one shit scenario to another. Just because she's come into some money doesn't change the fact that she is ill-equipped to handle the realities of the world around her. If she can't handle her own problems, what good will she be raising a child? The more she delves into her own inadequacies and temperamental setbacks, the more she realizes that she probably doesn't deserve to have Lily back in her life. Maybe if she was in control of her drug use she could handle her emotions better. But she can't keep fooling herself. She's no longer doing drugs, nor is Tobias. The drugs have clearly taken over the reins, and all the work they've done to keep the veil of illusions over their eyes has come unravelled. While Tobias might feel fine using drugs as an endless coping mechanism, and rehashing the same old arguments over and over again like an actor practicing a script, Maggie is finally sick to death of it all. She no longer experiences any thrill or rush. The excitement has flared out. To pretend otherwise is simply foolish.

But, there's another part of her, delusional as it may seem, that dreams that things can still work out for the best. If she can talk Tobias into joining treatment maybe they could hit the reset button. They have plenty of money to live off for the near future, and they could use this down period to maybe find some legitimate source of getting more income. Maybe she could serve at a restaurant. She used to wait tables at Applebee's when she was younger. She has more than enough experience. Not only that, Tobias is mechanically inclined. He could always find work through craigslist, or get a job at an auto body shop. Worst case scenario, a gas station was always hiring. It wasn't completely beyond reason that they could pick up the pieces of their shattered past and rebuild a brighter future. Stranger things have happened. Besides, could she really live with herself knowing that she brought a life into this world just to be mistreated and neglected when she could've done something to prevent it? Shouldn't she at least attempt to get her shit together for Lily's sake? After all, it isn't Lily's fault that her parents have been such colossal fuck ups, and Maggie is well aware of the consequences that neglect and abuse can bring. The hatred and self-loathing can spread like ripples on a pond. It can consume and transform much in the same way that the tentative flickerings of a flame can flare into a full fledged forest fire, leaving nothing but ashes and ruin in its wake.

. In one regard, she feels a sense of sweet relief. After all, this lifestyle has taken a toll, and an expiration date was inevitable. But does she have what it takes to bring everything to an end?

As she's still busy debating the best outcome for her future, the door of the motel opens before her hand, which is still hanging in midair preparing itself for the courage to knock.

A dark skinned man with concern in his eyes greets her. He only says three words, but his words are loaded with a weight that bears down on her soul like the burdens of a child swallowed and forgotten by time:

"Can I help you?"

-February 16th, 2018

About The Author

Michael Loeffler is a University of Minnesota alumnus that lives in the Twin Cities with his black cats who bring him great luck. He loves Minnesota and his friends and family dearly. This is his first novel, and as such, he would appreciate any feedback he can get. You can reach him at buildingruin@gmail.com and he would be happy to start a conversation, despite any indication in the photo below that would suggest otherwise.

Made in the USA
Middletown, DE
26 March 2019